COLLATERAL
DAMAGE

Sunny Aleshire Kaiser

ISBN 979-8-88540-867-7 (paperback)
ISBN 979-8-88540-989-6 (hardcover)
ISBN 979-8-88540-868-4 (digital)

Copyright © 2022 by Sunny Aleshire Kaiser

All rights reserved. No part of this publication may be reproduced, distributed, or transmitted in any form or by any means, including photocopying, recording, or other electronic or mechanical methods without the prior written permission of the publisher. For permission requests, solicit the publisher via the address below.

Christian Faith Publishing
832 Park Avenue
Meadville, PA 16335
www.christianfaithpublishing.com

Printed in the United States of America

Prologue

October 2004

He sat alone, out of place among the derelicts and degenerates. They wore the penance of their pasts on their faces. The disturbed man with tufts of gray sprouting around his barren sphere stood in the corner mumbling incoherently. The sleazy fellow with shades of purple and blue surrounding his swollen eye sat in the chair near the door. His shabby T-shirt expressed his lewd opinion on life, revealing his soft belly hanging in folds over the top of his pants. Next to him sat a gaunt young woman, scantily clad in a tight tank top with a black bra peering from underneath. The top of her left bicep displayed colorful ink drawn in a picture of a rose pierced by a dagger. George Patterson didn't know what they had done to get here, nor did he care.

The clock on the wall taunted him as it counted off each passing second with a loud tick, tick, tick. He waited and watched the rigid steel door at the far end of the narrow room, tightly guarding what lie just beyond its entrance. The fading light passed through a bank of windows behind him, casting an orange hue on the rigid gray steel door. He stared intently at the door, willing it to open. At any moment, his son would emerge through that door. How long had he been waiting? He glanced at the clock. Three hours had passed since he handed over the funds securing his son's freedom from this dreadful place.

George never imagined he would be in this position, posting bail for a son accused of murder. Even his worst nightmares couldn't have prepared him for the torturous doubts or the not so subtle insinuations by so-called friends. His once peaceful little town buzzed with gossip and mistrust. Friends and neighbors scurried past with whispers and skeptical glances. People he'd known for years actually believed his son was guilty.

"Patterson!" A raspy voice beckoned, stirring him from his thoughts. "Patterson!" The voice repeated with fierce impatience.

Slowly, he rose and walked toward the window on the other side of the room. A rotund woman sat behind a layer of bulletproof glass. Her jet-black hair rose up an inch and a half from the top of her head in an overgrown crew cut. The severity of her uniform only added to her masculine appearance. If not for her ample bosom, George might have suspected she was a man. Her dark bushy eyebrows furrowed into a harsh line across her forehead as he approached.

"You forgot to sign this," she barked as she thrust a piece of paper and pen into the small opening at the bottom of the window.

He carefully picked up the paper and glanced at the "X" highlighted in yellow. He didn't even bother to read it. He had already signed his life away in the event that David decided to flee. What was one more? He quickly scribbled his signature and placed the paper back in the opening. George didn't care what it cost; he wanted David freed from this place.

The brusque woman snatched up the paper, gave it a cursory glance, and nodded for George to return to his seat. She offered him no assistance in determining how long he would continue to sit and wait.

The hands on the clock pointed downward. "Six thirty," George muttered under his breath as he returned to his seat.

George noticed a folded copy of *The Bend Bulletin* on the corner of the table next to him. He pulled it out from beneath the pile of magazines. As he caught the first glimpse of the headline, his heart sank. There on the front page in big bold letters, "Person of interest has prior relationship with victim" "Suspect in custody." The media had been relentless in their coverage on this story. Perhaps it was the nature of the crime or perhaps the location—Sisters, Oregon, population fourteen hundred. Whatever the reason, reporters felt as if it were their God-given right to scrutinize every aspect of his life, snooping, hoping to uncover some speck of dirt to make headline news. One reporter had already uncovered secrets that George wished hadn't been made public. The reports made it sound as if David was justified in killing Coach Fisher and gave the impression that David was guilty. As he read the article, he allowed himself to think about what he had been pushing from his mind, what he had been trying to avoid: the possibility that David was guilty.

At that moment, the door finally opened, and David emerged, a mere shadow of the boy who had left years ago. His two-day-old beard only added to the rough edges of David's haggard appearance. George leapt from his chair and ran toward his son, throwing his arms around him. Innocent or guilty. It didn't matter. David was home at last.

Book 1

Kate

Chapter 1

March 2004

George hurried out the door, fumbling with his keys. Construction season had officially started, which meant his hardware store would be busy for the next six months. That morning, he had written orders for at least thirty thousand board feet of lumber and sold four DeWalt saws, three nail guns, and various other tools. Now he was running late as usual. He promised Kate he wouldn't be late for her appointment, but then Ned started telling fish stories, and once he started, he didn't stop.

George hopped up into the cab of his Ford pickup truck. Days like today, he cursed his decision to buy a black truck. The unseasonably hot weather turned the inside of the cab into a sauna. By ten o'clock, the thermometer on the bank already read seventy degrees, quite a feat for the middle of March. The weatherman had forecast mid-eighties by the end of the day. By the time George left at two, the temperature was very close to that mark. The heat merely added to the frenzy of the day.

As he pulled out onto the street and started the twenty-minute drive to Kate's doctor's office, George felt a knot developing in the pit of his stomach. He couldn't shake the feeling of impending doom. When the doctor asked for him to be there today, he knew instantly that the news couldn't be good. If the doctor had good news, he would have told them over the phone and certainly wouldn't have requested that George accompany Kate to her appointment.

During recent months, George had noticed that Kate had lost some of her exuberance. On more than one occasion, he'd found her lying down early in the evening, complaining of stomach discomfort or simply being worn out. She often grumbled about feeling bloated and constantly bombarded him with the ever-dreaded question, "Do I look fat?" He simply wrote it off to menopause. They were at that age. Their kids were grown, and they had three beautiful grandchildren. For some time now, he had been bracing himself for the change—expecting it, the way you expect to pay taxes. The guys that came into his hardware store often told horror stories of their wives' moodiness and hot flashes. Maybe that was all that the doctor wanted to talk to him about. Still, he couldn't shake the uneasiness gnawing at the back of his mind.

Normally, the drive from Sisters to Bend had a calming influence. The snowcapped mountain peaks hovered over the high-desert plains, creating a serene backdrop along the two-lane highway. Today, even the beauty of this place he loved couldn't allay his fears. On weekdays like today, the number of cars traveling on this stretch of highway in either direction could be counted on one hand. He enjoyed the solitude of the road. Here, away from the demands of his store, the quiet lullaby of rubber meeting the road cleared his head. It gave him the chance to think. But today, he didn't want to think about the reasons he'd been summoned to Kate's doctor's appointment. Even the beauty of this place he loved just could not allay his fears. The same road he had driven for years seemed to go on endlessly.

As he approached his turn, he gave a lingering glance at all the new urban growth that had appeared in the past few weeks. Since he only ventured to Bend every couple of weeks, he noticed changes more readily than Kate did on her daily commute. The entire landscape of the north end of Bend had been forever altered as developers had come in from California and, over the past ten years, had built big box stores, chain hotels, and shopping centers. Each month, new houses cropped up on Aubrey Butte, most of them touting price tags upward of a million dollars. George didn't understand where all the people were coming from. Bend wasn't exactly a thriving metropolis, so where did this influx of people work? Just ten years ago, the butte had been covered in juniper and lodge pole pines. Now it seemed that no place was safe from urban sprawl. The small town he called home was gradually transforming into a creeping, yuppie suburbia. With all the houses came cars, and now traffic jams were an everyday occurrence. It took fifteen minutes to go the two miles he needed to get onto Neff Road. Once he hit the side streets, it was just a matter of minutes before he crested the butte and drove down toward the hospital. He pulled into the parking lot ten minutes late and parked among a sea of SUVs.

He found Kate sitting patiently in the waiting room, casually flipping through a magazine.

"Hi, hon. Sorry I'm late," he said, looking at his watch.

"It's okay. Dr. Richards is running a bit behind anyway." She flashed him a smile, like the smiles he'd seen for the past thirty-five years, one that said "I love you in spite of your inability to be on time."

He sat down in the chair next to her and held her hand. He didn't want to think about the possibilities of what Dr. Richards might say. "Ned Magee came in today." He started a usual banter to avoid the tension of this moment. "I guess Bev was offered a job in Portland, so they're going to move over there this summer."

"Wow, I never thought they'd move back to the valley." Kate smiled. Her casual response was her attempt to put up a good front, but her foot shook like a jack rabbit.

He wondered why doctors did this to people, why they made them sit and wait for bad news. Was it some sort of torture method they all learned in medical school? George opened his mouth to continue their conversation when a voice beckoned them from the waiting room door.

"Mrs. Patterson?" The young girl in blue scrubs beckoned from the doorway.

They both stood and clasped hands as they walked through the door and followed the girl down a narrow corridor. George slid his arm around Kate as they were ushered into a small office at the end of the hallway. The room was tastefully decorated with deep mahogany bookcases, a paneled desk, and plush leather chairs. Behind the desk, a floor-to-ceiling window framed a picturesque view of Mt. Bachelor. George wondered if the prestige of doctors was measured by the view from their office. If so, then this doctor had made it. He waited until Kate was seated, then he collapsed into the chair next to her. They sat quietly for a few minutes.

He finally broke the silence, venting his frustration. "This is ridiculous. We waited all weekend for this appointment, and now we've been waiting almost twenty minutes. Where is this illustrious doctor of yours?"

"Shhh." Kate motioned for George to keep quiet. "Will you keep your voice down? Dr. Richards is a very busy doctor," she said, her voice soft and low.

"Maybe you need a doctor who is less busy. Maybe then they could figure out why you've been so tired all the time," George ranted but was cut off as the doctor entered the room.

"Sorry to keep you waiting." A tall distinguished-looking man in his midforties moved from behind them, walked around, and stood behind the desk. "I'm Dr. Richards," he said, holding out his hand. George shook his hand without getting up.

"So what's the news, Doc?" George blurted out impatiently. He didn't want to wait another second for the doctor to give them the news, whatever it was.

The man sat down, opening a manila file on his desk. "I wanted both of you here to discuss some of Kate's test results." He addressed them both but then turned and looked directly at Kate. "After your annual, we had the additional workups done, as we discussed."

George hung on his words—"as we discussed." He looked to Kate, who looked directly at the doctor and nodded her head in agreement. The doctor was still talking when George snapped back to the conversation.

"The pelvic ultrasound shows a mass above your right ovary. That explains the lump I felt during your annual examination. The mass coupled with the elevated levels found in your CA125 is enough to warrant a laparotomy."

"A lap-o-who?" George questioned. He got the distinct impression that Kate knew exactly what was going on, but he felt as lost as if he had been dropped off at a Mary Kay cosmetics party.

"A laparotomy is a procedure in which we can take a look inside Kate's abdomen and biopsy this mass to get an understanding of what it is and if it is malignant." He spoke directly to George this time. Kate glanced at him apologetically. George felt as if he'd just had the wind knocked out of him, but Kate appeared completely undisturbed, as if she had anticipated what the doctor was saying. Unlike George, Kate analyzed everything before talking about it. She wanted to have all the questions answered, to know exactly what the problem was and the most probable course of action before worrying anyone else. He preferred to share his burdens, to get alternative points of view, and deal with things as they arose. Sometimes he felt excluded by Kate's need to keep things harmonious.

George grabbed Kate's hand. "So what's next?" George summoned the courage to ask, though the answer scared him to death. The word malignant had jumped out like a deer on a deserted road. He knew enough about medicine to know that wasn't good.

"First, I'd like to schedule the laparotomy for this Thursday." The doctor began.

"So soon? Is that risky?" George jumped in, his heart racing. Thursday was only three days away, and the doctor was already talking surgery. He wondered just how bad this really was.

"No, not at all. A laparotomy is a day surgery. It's very noninvasive. I'll give you a booklet that you can take home with you which details the entire procedure, and you can call me or my nurse with any questions. In the meantime, I'd also like to get you scheduled for an MRI, just to be safe," he said, looking directly at Kate. "I'd like to see if this is the only mass we need to deal with. It will also give us a much clearer picture of the mass above your ovary."

The doctor's tone didn't sit well. George sensed he was purposefully withholding something—something horrible. His mind began to run through all the possibilities, but only one word kept creeping to the forefront—*cancer*. No matter how hard he tried to consider other alternatives, he kept returning to it. Cancer.

"George. George." Kate's voice brought him back to reality.

"Yes. Can you repeat that?" George responded.

"Dr. Richards wants to know if we should schedule the surgery for morning or afternoon." Kate looked to him for a decision.

"Thursday?" George tried to shake free of the cloud of disbelief surrounding him. He tried to recall what he had scheduled for the week. But if this nagging fear turned out to be true, what did it matter. He forced an answer. "I guess in the morning. We have a shipment that comes in late Thursday afternoon. I really should be there for that."

"All right. Then I'll have my nurse make all the necessary arrangements." Dr. Richards stood and motioned for them to follow him out into the hall. George helped Kate out of her chair as if she were some frail old woman. He knew she was the same woman he had walked in with, but somehow, now he felt an uncontrollable urge to take care of her, protect her. In the hallway, Dr. Richards handed his nurse a piece of paper, then disappeared down the hall. A raised counter with built-in cupboards and shelves served as the main nurses' station. Forms and charts were piled all around the desktop. George pulled Kate in for a squeeze while the nurse busily talked on the phone. He placed a soft kiss on top of her head while they waited.

When the nurse hung up the receiver, she handed them a stack of papers and said, "Your laparotomy is scheduled for nine on Thursday morning. It will be performed across the road over at the hospital. Here is the preadmission form you'll need to have filled out when you arrive. Try to get there around eight so they can get you in on time." She paused briefly, grabbing some more papers and handing them to Kate. "Now for prep, you will need to fast the night before. So nothing by mouth after seven o'clock in the evening until after your surgery. Here is the booklet that Dr. Richards told you about. It describes the entire procedure. And as always, if you have any questions between now and then, just give us a call. Lastly, I scheduled your MRI for Wednesday morning. It's a quick procedure. Just don't wear anything metallic. Dr. Richards will notify you when we get the lab results from the biopsy."

Her entire spiel sounded rehearsed, as if she had said it a thousand times. George was still trying to absorb what the doctor had just told them, and now the nurse dispelled even more information in sixty seconds flat.

"Thanks. Krissy." Kate smiled taking the forms. She led George out the door and down the hall.

George needed time to absorb the shock before facing the drive home, and Kate would be in no mood to cook. They decided to go out to dinner before heading home. Dining out was a rare treat for both of them but, primarily, for Kate. It was usually reserved for celebrations. Kate worked in Bend and George at the store in Sisters; they seldom had the opportunity to go out, but tonight they both needed it.

They went downtown to the Pine Tavern. Every major life event had been celebrated with a dinner inside its walls—anniversaries, birthdays, promotions, and weddings. They'd held the rehearsal dinner for their wedding in the main dining room, the one with the old growth ponderosa pine growing right up through the center. Then when it came time for Rachel to get married, they held her rehearsal dinner at the exact same table in hopes that it would bring Steve and her the same good fortune that Kate and George had shared. They did the same when Michael married.

As they were seated, George noticed that Kate appeared surprisingly unaffected by the news that the doctor had just thrown at them. Kate was keeping something from him. George knew it. He set down his menu. "Okay, Kate. What aren't you telling me?"

Kate set her menu down and looked at him from across the table. She didn't even attempt to be coy. Instead, she looked him directly in the eye. When her eyes met his, they were quiet and strong, but for the first time, George noticed the fear hidden behind her smile. Kate swallowed hard and forced a half smile as she began. "The test that Dr. Richards mentioned, the CA125. It tests for a protein in the blood that is produced by cancer—typically ovarian cancer." Kate said the words as if it were no big deal, just any other health affliction. "My test came back over five thousand units per milliliter."

George shook his head. "So what does that mean?"

Kate shrugged slightly and gave a half smile. "It means that I probably have cancer. I told Dr. Richards to be as vague as he could while we were meeting today. I didn't want you to be overwhelmed by the information."

"Overwhelmed?" George nearly shouted as he said it. "Overwhelmed!"

"Shhh. George. Please, I need for you to stay calm. I need for you to be my rock if I'm going to face this." Kate looked at him, imploring him to agree.

"All right, Kate," he said, his voice calmer. He took her hand in his. "But you should have told me. Aren't you scared?"

"A little." She let out a nervous laugh as she said it. "But my mom always said that which does not kill you makes you stronger." She let go of his hand and picked up her menu again.

But what if this does kill you? George thought to himself. He couldn't say it aloud; fear prevented him. Instead, he turned the conversation to the inevitable. "What do we tell the kids?"

"I don't want to worry them, so let's not tell them just yet." She spoke softly and calmly as she set her menu down once again.

"You're having surgery on Thursday." George looked at her incredulously. "What are we supposed to tell them?"

"We'll tell them that I'm having a test because essentially, that's what this is. We'll simply tell them that the doctor is going to sedate me, and you need to drive me." At that moment, he couldn't tell if she was trying to convince him or convince herself.

"Kate," he said, exasperated. He understood her desire to not worry the kids, *but what if…* He couldn't bear to finish the thought.

She held up her hand to quiet him. "Look, until we know exactly what we are dealing with, I'd just as soon not tell the kids. They have enough to worry about without worrying about their mother. All right?" Her eyes were soft as she pled with him.

"Okay," he conceded, reluctantly. He picked up the menu and began to scan it again. When the waiter arrived, George ordered a nice wine and appetizer, something he never did, but Kate always requested. Normally, he saved such extravagance for celebrations. The news today was anything but celebratory, but he wanted Kate to enjoy tonight and tomorrow and the rest of her tomorrows. But how many tomorrows did she have left?

Chapter 2

The next two days, George felt distracted and edgy. He misplaced the paperwork for two crucial orders and snapped at one of the stock boys for no apparent reason. In keeping Kate's wishes, he even went so far as to avoid his kids at the store, something he never did but felt was necessary so that he didn't slip up and tell them. He blamed his obvious grumpiness on the rumors circulating about one of the big home improvement warehouse stores moving into Bend. No one bought his excuse, yet no one questioned him about his strange behavior.

Wednesday night, George lay awake. He tried to pray but fumbled over the words. He wasn't sure what he should pray for, other than to make Kate well again. Kate was the religious one. He accompanied her to church on Sunday, but he never joined any of the church small groups like Kate. It wasn't that he didn't believe. He did, and he read his Bible regularly. He simply didn't feel comfortable discussing his spirituality with anyone else. He'd gone to a Bible study once before and found a bunch of old men dissecting a verse and counting down their days. That was enough for him. He went to church to appease Kate, but he'd always believed that his faith was between him and God and no one else. He'd grown up attending a church with a long list of dos and don'ts. If he did the dos and abstained from the don'ts, he had a chance at getting into heaven. Kate opened his eyes to the truth found in the Word. She showed him what love truly meant.

As he lay there, he thought about God and wondered if Kate's cancer was some form of punishment. He'd never quite understood why believers were still afflicted. Why Kate? She embodied every Christian virtue—love, kindness, charity, patience, faith. It seemed tragic to make her suffer when others who lied, cheated, and stole lived healthy, happy long lives. Why did God allow such disproportionate injustice?

He would gladly trade places with her, if he could, to take the cancer on himself. Watching helplessly while she withered away would be far more excruciating than enduring the disease. There was absolutely nothing he could do to alleviate her pain or add days back to her life. All that he could do was stand by and pray that the doctors were skilled enough to cure her.

Several times, he tried to doze off, but his mind kept mulling over the fears he'd never thought he'd have to face. He'd always assumed he'd be the one to die first—with his high cholesterol and on-the-job stress. He'd always figured she'd have to be looking out for him, not the other way around. Kate was a nurse. Granted, she worked with children, but still she knew medicine. She knew how to take care of herself. Surely she could recognize all the warning signs. So how did she wind up with cancer? It didn't make any sense.

At exactly four-thirty, the alarm reverberated in the darkness. George heard Kate stirring softly, her hand slapping against the little black box on the nightstand until the noise stopped. George felt the soft mattress sink as Kate got out of bed. George never got out of bed at this hour of the morning unless fishing was involved. The store opened at seven o'clock, and he rarely got up before six thirty. Normally, he could sleep through anything. He was known for it. The kids used to tease him about falling asleep in a chair watching a game or outside on the patio, but he hadn't been able to sleep a wink all night. The *what ifs* plagued him incessantly. As soon as he heard the water start running, he pulled himself out of bed. He sat on the edge of the bed, feeling every one of his fifty-nine years encroaching upon him. Every ounce of energy had been depleted, agonizing over the outcome of today's procedure.

A long strained silence filled the cab of his truck as they drove to the hospital. It was odd that after thirty-five years of marriage, they found it difficult to talk about this. Kate appeared lost in thought.

He wondered if she was as scared as he was, but he couldn't find the words to ask. Neither of them wanted to speak first, letting the silence grow more and more strained with each passing minute. George tried to think of something witty or clever to say to put them both at ease, but he feared that ill-timed humor might increase rather than decrease the tension.

A soft palette of red hues peered over the horizon ahead of them as he drove east. It reminded him of the old sailor's credo—red sky at night is a sailor's delight; red sky in the morning is a sailor's warning. He knew it was a silly superstition; still he couldn't shake the fears that had kept him up all night.

East of the Cascades, the land turns from vibrant green valleys to rough high-desert plains. The area is wild and largely unpopulated, with the exception of the town's buildup around the rivers, like Bend. St. Charles Medical Center served as the main hospital for all Central Oregon. The original hospital had been built in downtown Bend when the logging boom began in the 1920s. As Bend grew, the hospital grew with it. Now with the population explosion in Bend, St. Charles seemed to be constantly under construction. As George drove across the tattered parking lot, he could see the effect of the population boom firsthand. He tried to avoid the construction fencing that girded the current hospital expansion underway. He managed to find a parking spot near the new entrance.

Kate led the way through the hospital doors. Instinctively, she knew where to go and what to do. If George had been left to his own devices, he would have been lost, fumbling around the corridors, but she took them directly to admitting. After twenty minutes of paperwork, they finally sat down in the waiting room. A few minutes later, a young nurse came out to get Kate. George stood with Kate and walked her toward the door. He pulled her in for a lingering embrace before letting her go.

"The procedure should only take about an hour. After that, she'll be in recovery," the nurse told George as she led Kate back through a large metal door that swung shut behind them. He stood frozen, staring blankly at the cold steel door. Somewhere deep in his gut, he knew that nothing would ever be the same.

"Excuse me," a surly woman spat, her tone in direct opposition to the meaning of her words. She gave George a forceful nudge as she squeezed passed him. Suddenly, he realized that he was still standing in front of the door, staring at it. He stepped back, embarrassed. As he crossed the room again, he caught a glimpse of them rolling Kate down the hall on a gurney. Kate blew him a kiss as she was wheeled down the hall to her operating room. George paced the halls for about fifteen minutes but finally sank into one of the chairs in the waiting area. He picked up a magazine, not even really seeing what it was, and began unconsciously flipping through the pages.

"Mr. Patterson." He heard the voice beckoning. "Mr. Patterson." The voice repeated, and he felt a hand on his shoulder. Slowly, he opened his eyes. At first, it took a moment to orient himself. He sat upright as soon as he realized where he was.

"Kate," He rasped out. His voice crackled from his small nap. He cleared his throat quickly, then continued. "Is everything all right?"

"Everything is fine," the young nurse reassured. "Your wife is awake in recovery. I thought you might want to go see her, but I was afraid to wake you. You looked so peaceful sleeping there."

George practically leapt from his chair. "Where is she? Can you take me to her?"

"Certainly." The young nurse smiled. "Just follow me." She led him down the corridor and through a set of double doors. They entered a private room at the end of the corridor. Kate sat on the bed flipping through a magazine, fully clothed. "Mrs. Patterson, you were right. He was sleeping." The young woman smiled and left them alone.

George could hardly believe it. Kate looked perfectly fine; just as she had when he brought her in this morning, maybe a little more tired, but certainly not sickly. "Is everything okay?" George questioned.

"It went smoothly." Kate smiled.

"So what is it? Did they tell you what they found?" He couldn't wait any longer. She looked perfectly healthy, and he wanted some assurances that everything would be all right.

Kate chuckled softly. "They only took a biopsy. The doctor won't know anything for at least a day or two." She patted his shoulder as she swung herself down off the bed. "We'll probably hear something on Monday or Tuesday. Until then, let's just enjoy our weekend."

She appeared so calm and collected. Was she still under the influence of sedatives from her procedure, or was she really unbothered by it all? He was climbing the walls. He wanted to know how soon this nightmare would be over.

Chapter 3

Originally, Kate's MRI had been scheduled for nine o'clock Wednesday morning, but Kate switched it to Friday. Uncertain of how she'd feel after the laparoscopy on Thursday, she had arranged to take Friday morning off. She didn't want to arouse any suspicions or gossip at work by taking off too much time, so it seemed easier to schedule the MRI during time she already planned to take off. As it turned out, the decision to take off Friday morning had been a good one. Even though she'd convinced George she felt fine, her body complained loudly with tightness and aches from the procedure the day before.

That morning, she informed George he wouldn't need to come with her. She told him he was off the hook and could just go to the store; she'd be fine. She'd explained that an MRI was basically a fancy X-Ray, and all she would have to do is lie there. That was true, but what she hadn't told him was she didn't want George to come with her for this test. With the uncertainty of what they might find, she didn't want George there to see it. He didn't understand all this. She had been a nurse for thirty-five years and took for granted the fact that she understood the mechanics of medicine. While she was familiar with all the tests and procedures, she had to remind herself that for George, this was all foreign and confusing. She wanted to know all the facts before worrying him too much. She could tell that he was already concerned. The word *cancer* had scared him enough. There was so much they didn't know yet. They didn't know what stage of cancer she had. For all they knew, she could merely have stage two cancer, and surgery and chemo could eradicate it. At least that's what she kept trying to tell herself; but something inside her told her it was much worse than that.

Kate sat quietly in the waiting room and flipped through a magazine without even looking at the pages. The MRI procedure didn't worry her, but the results did. She hadn't felt right for some time now. It started with a small pinch in her side. She'd told herself it was simply part of growing old, but she knew better. Each time it happened, the pain worsened a little, but she couldn't bring herself to get it checked out. The prospect of what the doctor might find and the treatment that would follow kept Kate snuggly in denial. She ignored it, hoping and praying the pains and fatigue were just part of menopause. After two years of little things not feeling right, she went in for her exam. That was in February, and now after two months of tests, she would know conclusively if her fear had been warranted. She had no one to blame but herself.

The technician came out and took Kate back. As instructed, she changed into the robe that resembled a blue burlap sack. She wore no jewelry. She had even removed her wedding ring and placed it in a zipped pocket inside her purse. The technician led her down a long hallway into a room that seemed dwarfed by the enormous machine inside. Kate lay on the cold metal table and tried relaxing as the technician had instructed. *Relax.* Maybe they should paint it to look like the beach instead of a plain gray room with an enormous white machine sitting in the center like something out of a sci-fi movie. Kate closed her eyes and meditated on one of her favorite worship songs. *And when the darkness closes in, still I will say blessed be Your name.* She sang it over and over in her mind and even caught herself humming the tune. In no time, the technician announced they had gotten all the images they needed.

"How long before Dr. Richards will have these?" Kate sat upright, swinging her legs off the side of the table.

"Oh, he should have them in about an hour. Everything is digital now and we simply upload to a secure server and he can log in to look at them," the technician answered as he pressed buttons on a digital screen to move the machine back out of the way.

"Thanks," Kate said and jumped off the table. It was simply amazing the advances in technology. When she started as a nurse in the 1970s, the only images they could get were of bone by X-ray. Then in the 1980s, they developed CT scans and ultrasound which could view soft tissues, but you had to drive to Portland to get one, and it took at least a week to get the results. In the 1990s, MRI entered the picture, which gave much more detailed pictures but again were only available in Portland. Now MRI was virtually everywhere, and apparently, they could just download the images like a picture off the internet.

Kate dressed slowly, debating what to do next. It wasn't quite ten, and she had taken off the entire morning. She exited the MRI office still undecided on what to do. She could go straight to work, but that wouldn't help her get answers any sooner. She read the directory sign on the wall and turned left and headed toward the elevators.

On the first floor just outside the lobby in the new foyer addition, St. Charles had an extensive library and medical supply store. Inside were books on every topic of medicine. Nurses came by and checked them out regularly when studying for their continuing education credit exams. Kate walked in and headed directly for the section on cancer. She found two books and checked them out. With the books in hand, she walked up the long staircase in the main lobby to the cafeteria. She bought a Tzao tea and a blueberry scone and found a table. After thirty minutes, she had read enough to understand what might lie ahead for her. *Jesus, please give me strength.*

She got up with new resolve and headed for Dr. Richards' office. She stood in his waiting room ten minutes later.

"Excuse me." Kate caught the attention of the young receptionist sitting behind the desk.

"Can I help you?" she asked politely.

"Yes. Um. I don't have an appointment, but I was wondering if I could talk with Dr. Richards?" Kate stammered. She hated when patients would just drop by and hope to get squeezed in at the clinic, so she fully understood what an inconvenience this would be.

"Your name?" the receptionist asked.

"Katherine Patterson."

"Let me check." The receptionist picked up the phone and pressed a button. She said something in soft tones. A second later, she placed the phone on the base and looked up at Kate. "You can go back now."

Kate walked back through the reception door to Dr. Richards' office. She found him sitting behind his desk looking at the computer screen.

"Please come in. Have a seat." He typed something quickly on the keyboard and clicked the mouse a couple of times before giving her his undivided attention.

"Thank you for seeing me. I know I didn't have an appointment, but I—" Kate started as she sat in one of the chairs.

"Don't worry about it. It happens more often than you would think, especially in my line of work." He sat down in the chair across from Kate. "I just got your MRI results, and I'm guessing that's what prompted today's impromptu visit."

"Yes, and I wanted to talk with you before bringing my husband in. He's a bit more reactionary than I am." Kate wasn't sure how to voice her concerns with him.

"I see. So what would you like to know?" He folded his hands on his lap.

"What's the prognosis?" She didn't want to chat. She wanted to know precisely what she was dealing with so she could prepare herself before letting her family know.

"Kate, are you sure you wouldn't rather wait for George?"

"No. I want to know what I'm up against, and I think it's better I hear the news without him here, without having to worry about how he feels about it."

"Are you certain?" He looked at her with concern.

Kate knew by the grim expression that the conversation to come wouldn't be pleasant. But she needed to do this. She needed to know and to fully understand what lay ahead without the worry of how George might react. "Yes. I need to know what I'm dealing with so I can prepare my family."

"All right." He paused briefly and adjusted the screen on his computer to face her. He punched a few keys and brought up the images from her MRI. "The MRI shows multiple metastases throughout the abdominal cavity, which we saw in the laparoscopy. Those can be removed through surgery—"

"But?" Kate interrupted, sensing that he was holding back the worst of it.

"Yes. But there are two tumors in the brain—one about the size of a quarter, the other the size of a golf ball. They can't be removed with surgery. You'll need to undergo some form of cancer-reducing treatment. I'll be referring you to an oncologist here in town that can follow your case."

"Is it terminal?" She tried to detach from it, to use medical terms so that it would seem as if it wasn't really happening to her.

"I hate to use that word. The cancer does seem to be of an extremely aggressive nature."

"So my chances are what—fifty-fifty?"

Dr. Richards removed his glasses and rubbed his temples. He looked Kate straight in the eye. "Look, Kate, I've known you a long time. I delivered two of your grandchildren." He paused as if bracing himself. "I'm sorry. I honestly don't know, but from what I have in front of me, it doesn't look good. Dr. Gibson, the oncologist I'll send you to, will be able to give you a better estimation of overall prognosis, given what approach in therapy he deems best."

"Do you think I can beat it?"

"I'm sorry, Kate. I just don't know." He shrugged and shook his head. There was nothing more to be said. But the message had been conveyed, the seriousness of her condition underlined by his demeanor.

"Thank you, doctor." Kate stood and shook his hand.

As Kate left the doctor's office, she found it hard to breathe. Her heart felt weighted down. The worry and fear had been replaced by an overwhelming sense of dread. She had studied scriptures that taught her to feel joy in times of trouble. Right now, she found it hard enough not to curl into a ball and cry, let alone be joyful. *Jesus, why? Why this now? I have beautiful grandchildren. I want to see them grow.*

Without thinking, Kate drove across town. By rote, she found herself parked in the lot above Drake Park. The park had been a part of Bend practically forever and named for one of the pioneering men that brought industry and prosperity to the booming young town. The lush green park provided an oasis in the sea of dingy yellow and brown of the high desert. Days like this, the Deschutes River crept slowly past through Mirror Pond in a hue of deep blue reflected from the endless sky. The pond was as smooth as glass and reflected the mountain peaks like a mirror. Ducks and geese had returned to nest after their long journeys from the south. A pair of trumpeter swans had been imported and made the park their home. In the fall and spring, geese swam in the tranquil waters. They sought refuge in the tall reeds along the banks of the river, under the shadows of the towering ponderosa pines, just as Kate sought refuge from the news she'd just received.

Drake Park reminded Kate of her childhood. As a girl, she had been fortunate enough to live in one of the houses across from Drake Park. Whenever she was upset, she would find a park bench and watch the birds on the water. They provided solace for Kate. She needed to be alone to let the news sink in, and the only place she could do that was in Drake Park.

Nothing could have prepared her for the harsh reality that cancer had invaded her body. Like a silent enemy, it crept through her, destroying her body. Death itself didn't scare Kate. She knew she had a place secured for her in heaven, but the getting there petrified her beyond comprehension. Kate considered herself a strong woman and perhaps a brave woman. She had borne three children and lived in a region where men were still men. The harsh winters, the coyotes, the bears, the rattlesnakes, none of them frightened her, but the thought of withering away while cancer slowly killed her was enough to give her the willies. And the thought of everyone fussing over her for what little time she had left, it was more than she could bear. She didn't want to be remembered as a frail woman unable to care for herself. She wanted her family, especially her grandchildren, to remember her as a vibrant woman, full of life.

Kate sat on the park bench and watched a mother duck with her three babies in tow. The mother duck navigated the water to a marshy area on the other side of the river to the safety of her nest. Kate knew the motherly instinct to protect her children. But how could she protect them or even prepare them for this? Rachel would take the news gracefully. Publicly, Rachel would appear stoic, the great pillar of strength. But behind closed doors, she would fall apart. They were so much alike that way. Michael, on the other hand, would show everyone exactly how he felt. He wore his heart on his sleeve and didn't care who saw it. She feared he wouldn't take the news well at all. He was her youngest and still sought her guidance for most of life's concerns. This would devastate him. Then Kate's thoughts turned to David. She had been unsuccessful in bringing him back anywhere near the nest. David had an intensely independent streak which had put him at odds with his father more than once. During David's high school years, she acted as the peacemaker as often as she could, but David and George ultimately wound up in a battle of wills. David had won the war by refusing to return home. It had been fifteen years. She wondered if she would see him again before she died.

She never fully grasped why David stayed away. Sure, he and George had their differences, but no more than any other father and son. They weren't bad parents; David had never been abused or even ignored. If they had been at fault, wouldn't Rachel and Michael have fled too?

No, David's efforts to distance himself were deliberate. In college, he'd done everything he could to purposefully hurt both of them. He joined Greenpeace during his sophomore year and told George that by selling lumber, he was raping mother earth for profit. His junior year, he went to Washington, DC, to join in pro-choice demonstrations and campaign for the Democratic candidate for president. His final act of unadulterated defiance, just before his college graduation, he announced he had converted to Buddhism.

For years, she had tried and failed to comprehend why. Every time she reached out to David, he firmly slammed the door shut with another insult. She didn't know who was wounded more by David, her or George. They never talked about it. The mere mention of his name could fill the room with tension. It started bitter disputes which did nothing to bring David home. She suffered silently, never mentioning his name. George refused to talk about his absence.

Kate closed her eyes. *Lord, I know You have a purpose for this. I know that no matter the outcome of this dreadful disease, that You will use it for good. I just pray that somehow this can unite my family once again.*

After an hour of crying and praying, Kate picked herself up and returned to her car. Using the rearview mirror, she replaced the makeup washed away by tears. She now knew what she had to do. If she was dying, her family, especially George, wouldn't know just how sick she actually was. They would see her fighting and living. She had no intention of being convalesced. If she was in fact fighting a losing battle, she would do so on her terms.

Kate checked herself once more in the rearview mirror before starting the car and heading back toward St. Charles Hospital. She parked in the lot at quarter to one. It was still the lunch hour. She hoped she might get lucky. Inside the office, the receptionist opened the glass window. "May I help you?"

"Yes. My name is Katherine Patterson. I was wondering if I could talk with Dr. Gibson for just a moment."

Chapter 4

The call came into the store at one o'clock Friday afternoon. When Kate called George from work and told him that Dr. Richards wanted to see both of them in his office, he nearly dropped the phone. Kate had said they wouldn't have results until Monday. If they had them now, the news couldn't be good. George quickly hung up the phone. He grabbed his keys, made up some excuse, and darted out the door. Outside, the sky turned dark and gray. George couldn't help but feel that it was an omen of things to come. He climbed into the cab of his truck. *Dear God, please let it be a mistake, some slipup at the lab. Please let Kate be okay.*

They sat in the same chairs they had been in four days before. Dr. Richards came in and shut the door behind him. This time, Kate reached for George's hand. The grave expression on the doctor's face told it all.

"I'm sorry, Kate," Dr. Richards began. "The biopsy confirmed our suspicions. The mass is malignant." He paused before continuing with the torrent of bad news. "The MRI isn't any more encouraging. There are multiple metastases throughout the abdominal cavity. And there are two tumors in your brain."

George felt as if he'd just been sucker punched by a heavyweight champion. His head went numb. No, not Kate. No. Not cancer. The doctor continued talking, but George couldn't hear him. A loud humming sound rang in his ears as memories flashed through his mind—Kate in her wedding dress walking toward him, Kate holding their first baby boy, cradled in her arms. Stunned didn't even come close—he was petrified. This was Kate, his wife, the center of his world. Life without her was unimaginable. He looked over to see Kate sitting stoically, her hands folded neatly in her lap as the doctor explained the horrific findings. As the doctor described where the tumors were located, all George could imagine was a dark menacing force with its fatal fingers wrapping around her, choking the life from his beautiful wife. He couldn't believe she sat there so calmly.

Slowly, George dragged himself back to hear the doctor saying, "I'd like for you to see Dr. Walter Gibson. He's an oncologist in the cancer program at the hospital. He is one of the best in the field." He paused a moment and pulled a card off his desk and handed it to George. "I've made an appointment for you this afternoon."

They found Dr. Gibson's office across the street on the west side of the hospital. George kept his arm around Kate's shoulder as they walked in through the plate glass doors. He wanted her as close to him as possible.

For such a grim venue, surprisingly, the waiting room emitted a nurturing atmosphere. A huge aquarium with brightly colored fish swimming about adorned the far wall. The adjoining wall was covered in a floor-to-ceiling mural of children and adults flying a kite. George suspected they decorated so cheerfully to mask the dismal prognosis shared on the other side of the waiting-room door.

No sooner had they checked in when a cheerful nurse escorted them through the door to Dr. Gibson's office. Unlike all the other doctors' offices George had visited before, this office had an open and welcoming design. The furnishings were arranged more like a living room than a formal office. A middle-aged man stood behind his desk and came over to greet them.

"Hello. I'm Dr. Gibson." He had a warm, friendly smile that George felt he could trust. He wore round wire-rimmed glasses that matched a round face which blended into a slightly receding hairline. He led them to a seating area. "Please sit down." He gestured in front of him to a group of chairs set in a circle. Once they were seated, the doctor chose a seat close to them. "Dr. Richards sent over your films and pathology report, but I'd like to start with what you already know."

"Not much." Kate began. The doctor held his hands clasped together and nodded along as Kate explained what they had been told. "All Dr. Richards told us is that it's carcinoma and that it has metastasized beyond the abdominal cavity."

"Kate, George, let me be honest with you. This is going to be difficult at best. I know today that you have had a lot of information thrown at you. It's probably a bit overwhelming and, more than likely, a little disconcerting." He looked from Kate to George and back to Kate again as he spoke. "I'm not going to lie to you. The spread into the soft tissues surrounding the liver and the tumors in the brain are consistent with stage four spread of ovarian cancer." He kept his tone as light as possible with the news he had the burden of dispensing. "Now my job is to discuss treatment options and recommend the best course of action for your particular circumstances that will not only treat the cancer, but it will preserve your quality of life." He looked directly at George. "Kate will need a substantial amount of physical, emotional, and spiritual support during this process."

George grabbed Kate's hand. With their fingers intertwined, he brought her hand to his mouth for a small kiss. "She'll have it." The words caught in his throat on the way out. It was all he could do to keep from breaking down, but he knew that wouldn't help Kate right now.

"That's what I wanted to hear." Dr. Gibson continued, "Today, I'm going to discuss some options. Then I'd like to get together again on Monday to discuss our timeline." He paused for a moment as Kate and George nodded in agreement. "Unfortunately, this type of cancer is fairly chemo resistant. That, coupled with the rapid spread of the tumors, complicates any treatment strategy. For starters, we cannot remove all the tumors surgically. I would, however, recommend a hysterectomy and debulking procedure."

George hung on to the words as the doctor spoke them. Most of the medical terms flew over his head, but hysterectomy he understood. From the moment they walked into Dr. Richards' office four long days ago, he wondered how long it would be until he heard that word. Now that he'd heard it, he wished he hadn't. One of his fishing buddies, Wayne, nearly wound up in divorce after his wife's hysterectomy. It took nearly a year to even out her hormones and bring her personality back to the woman she was before the surgery. But if it could save Kate's life, he would support it. George nodded along as the doctor talked more about the condition, most of which George didn't understand.

"Once Kate has recovered from the surgery, our secondary treatment protocol would be a radiotherapy or radiation therapy. Now there are still some significant risks and side effects with this therapy." The doctor rattled on.

"Will I lose my hair?" The words seemed to jump from her mouth. George could hardly believe that Kate was worried about her hair. Here the doctor was talking about cancer and life hanging in the balance, and Kate wanted to know if she was going to lose her hair. True, she had beautiful shoulder-length auburn hair, but George could grow accustomed to anything, so long as she was still alive with him.

"Probably." The doctor smiled at her question. George caught the look of dejection on Kate's face as the doctor stood and walked over to a shelf near his desk. He returned with a stack of pamphlets. "Here are some reading material. I've included materials on ovarian cancer, the hysterectomy procedure, typical side effects of radiation treatment, and also a booklet on coping. It will explain all the side effects typically associated with this type of treatment." He handed them to George. "Please read them over the weekend. We can discuss any questions or concerns you have on Monday."

George accepted the booklets. He stood and helped Kate from her chair. All those years she had spent taking care of him and the kids, now it was his turn. He took her arm and led her out, nodding to Dr. Gibson on the way out.

*****

The illusion was complete. Both doctors had reluctantly agreed to keep the severity of her condition from George. If her time had come, there was virtually nothing the doctors or she could do about it. God alone controlled that. In the meantime, she would not squander what precious little time she had left being treated like some delicate flower too brittle to touch. If George knew the truth, he would hover over her every second of every day. She wanted her final days to be spent living as if nothing had changed. The only way to ensure that was to make certain that George didn't know the real prognosis.

Dr. Gibson's words echoed in her mind. "With this rate of progression, I can only estimate that you'll have a few months, but there is a slim chance that radiation therapy might work." A chance. A chance was all she could ask for, all she could pray for.

"Are you all right?" George looked at her with those soft puppy dog eyes that reminded her why she loved him.

"I will be," she lied and nodded bravely.

"Do you want me to drive you home?" he offered.

"No. I think I could use the quiet time to absorb this." The day had passed in a blur. She needed to reflect, to pray. If she was going to hide the fact that she was dying from George, she needed time to plan.

"Are you ready to tell the kids?"

"I suppose we have to," she answered reluctantly. She didn't want to burden them with the news, but she realized it too was inevitable. She couldn't hide this from them.

"When do you want to do it?" he pressed.

"Let's wait until tomorrow. I'll be ready tomorrow."

"Do you want me to try and find David?" He hesitated as he asked it, and Kate knew why.

"No!" Kate snapped back. "When David comes home, I want it to be because he wants to, not because I'm sick." Honestly, she was afraid David wouldn't come even if he knew just how sick she was. And the thought of her son rejecting her that way tore her heart to pieces.

Chapter 5

Saturday afternoon turned out to be a beautiful spring day. The dark clouds from the day before dissipated, leaving a clear blue sky in their wake. The only evidence of their existence was the lightly moistened ground and the stabbing ache deep in his heart. George looked out the sliding glass door at the bounty of spring. Daffodils and crocus bloomed against a frame of vibrant green grass as they had year after year. This year, spring came early. Usually, spring in Central Oregon came late and ended early. The long winters thawed into spring around late April or early May. June often brought the summers they were famous for, but the arid climate would dull the vibrancy of the grass, and the deer would devour the flowers long before their beauty could be fully enjoyed. He found it ironic how closely life mimicked the seasons, how loved ones could be snatched away in the prime of life.

The night before, George and Kate had agonized over how to tell the kids. Should they tell them right off, or should they let them relax before pouncing with the news. George enticed the kids to come over under the guise of a barbeque so as not to alarm them. Rachel and Steve arrived promptly at three with Braden and Jenna in tow. The little cherubs bounded through the house enthusiastically.

"Grandpa," they sang out in unison.

He couldn't help but melt when Jenna clung to his leg, looking up at him with her soft angelic face. She would turn three in June, and Braden just turned five the month before. At the sight of his grandchildren, his face brimmed with joy despite the nagging ache in his heart. Rachel caught up with her children on her way to the kitchen. She balanced a bowl of her famous potato salad in one hand and carried a canvas bag in the other. Steve followed with a grocery bag filled with juice boxes and crackers for the kids.

"Where's Mom?" Rachel asked casually as she opened the refrigerator and began moving items to make room for the bowl.

"She's laying down for bit." George tried to keep his tone as nonchalant as possible. He didn't want to give away the gravity of Kate's illness before their "talk."

"Is she all right?" Rachel peeked up over the fridge door, a note of genuine concern in her voice.

"She's just a little tired," he lied.

"Well, it's no wonder," Rachel bantered on, as she shuffled items in the fridge. "I don't know why she insists on working in Bend. That commute every day, it's got to wear on her."

"You know your mom." George assuaged her need to vent. From the time she was a little girl, Rachel never held back her opinion. There was never any question about how Rachel felt about something because she happily expressed her opinion whether asked for or not. She came by it honestly. George too voiced his opinions whenever something was on his mind. Kate, on the other hand, remained a mystery. She rarely shared what was on her mind, even if asked point-blank. When she did speak up, it meant she was passionate about the topic.

"Yes, I do. She's just plain stubborn. There's just no talking to her sometimes." Rachel closed the fridge door with her hip.

"You're right," George agreed, trying hard not to laugh. *If that wasn't the pot calling the kettle black.* Rachel was just as obstinate as her mother. Both women were equally hardheaded, but neither of them would ever admit it. When the two butted heads, it was a long drawn-out battle, but Kate usually won.

The very first time he met Kate, George knew she was a force to reckon with. If she had her mind set to get something, nothing could stand in her way. Lucky for George, he was what she wanted.

In the summer of 1967, Bend was still a small logging community. George worked for the forest service, fighting wildfires and replanting areas consumed by fire. On the weekends, he and his forest service pals would pile into his candy-apple-red Ford Galaxy. With the top down, he could squeeze five of his buddies in the car with him. The night he met Kate, he had three guys with him and some girl his aunt Mildred had set him up with. They drove up Highway 97 to the new hamburger drive-in with roller skating waitresses that brought the food right to the car. As fate would have it, Kate was their waitress. She rolled up to the car with her fire-red hair pulled back in a ponytail and smile that could light up the night's sky. She took every opportunity to flirt with George despite the girl in the passenger seat. When she brought out their food, Kate slipped him a small piece of paper with her phone number on it. When she skated, off, she turned and gave George a wink.

George felt somewhat intimidated by her directness and shoved the paper in his pocket without a second thought. All week, the guys ribbed him over the run-in with the red-hot redhead. George would simply blush and keep working. But that was not the end of Kate. On Friday night after work, George walked into the house to find Kate sitting in a chair, chatting pleasantly with his aunt. When he walked in, Kate smiled coyly as if it were a mere coincidence that she was there. George couldn't refuse. After he took her out once, there was no turning back. He was hooked, which was precisely what Kate had wanted.

Later, he found out that she had followed him until she figured out where he lived. A red Ford Galaxy wasn't hard to spot in a town like Bend. The rest was, as they said, history. When he told his aunt and uncle about it, his uncle had told him, "The girl's got moxie. Don't let her go."

That was thirty-seven years ago. He prayed that Kate had enough moxie left inside her to fight the cancer. Slowly, he turned back toward the window and watched Jenna chasing Braden around the yard.

"So when is Michael going to get here?" Rachel asked snidely. Unlike Rachel, who always arrived on time for everything, Michael showed up whenever he felt like. He always said nothing started until he got there, so why hurry.

"When he gets here, I suppose." George shrugged. "Michael has his own timetable. I told him to be here at three, so he'll probably be here around four."

Rachel carried bags of vegetables over to the counter. "Dad, when are you going to learn? When it comes to Michael, if you want him to show up on time, you tell him the event starts an hour before it actually does."

"It's just a barbecue."

Rachel shook her head and began puttering around, slicing vegetables and readying everything for the barbeque.

"Come on, George," Steve said, placing a hand on his shoulder. "Let's go outside and see what kind of trouble Braden and Jenna have found."

George led the way through the sliding glass door to the patio outside. Steve went out to the yard and chased the children, while George sat on the porch swing. It had been a gift for their thirtieth wedding anniversary. He watched Braden and Jenna scurrying around, blowing bubbles and chasing them. Even the innocence of childhood couldn't take his mind off Kate. He hated to even think the word—*cancer*. How could something so malicious invade their happy life? Cancer was something that happened to other people, older people—not them. They were still in the prime of life. Jenna jumped up on the swing and tucked her head under his arm, bringing George's dark thoughts to an abrupt end.

"Hi, Papa." She sang, leaning up against him. A few minutes later, Kate appeared through the screen door. Jenna jumped out of the swing and ran to her, throwing her arms around Kate's leg. "Nana!" she exclaimed.

"There's my favorite little girl," Kate said sweetly and pulled Jenna up into her arms. George noticed that Kate winced as she lifted Jenna. He wondered if Kate was in pain. If she was, she'd never tell him.

Michael emerged from the patio door right behind Kate, sipping from a big soda cup from the local corner store. George wondered if he would ever grow up. Even though Michael was technically grown and gone, he still acted very much like an irresponsible adolescent. He was habitually late for everything, including work. He never had more than two or three dollars in his pocket. If he did, he would go out and blow it on new snowboarding gear or CDs. George had hoped that fatherhood would compel him to grow up, but after eighteen months, Michael hadn't changed a bit.

"Where are Nikki and Conner?" Kate looked behind Michael as if expecting someone else to appear.

"They're not coming. I guess Conner is teething again," Michael said, plopping down into one of the chairs. "I thought that was all over and done."

"Show's how much you know," Rachel spat in a condescending tone as she emerged with platters of food. She set them on the table in front of Michael. "Conner is eighteen months. He's probably getting his first molars."

"Is that the last of them?" he asked with a hint of desperation in his voice.

"For a while." Rachel smiled smugly at her little brother.

"Good!" He sighed. "He's driving me crazy. He won't eat. He won't sleep. He's cranky and throws his binkie at us in protest. I'm exhausted," Michael ranted.

"You could've brought him," Kate said sweetly, holding Jenna in her lap. "Sometimes a dose of Grandma is just what the doctor ordered."

"I needed a break from all that crying." Michael held his hands over his ears as if to dramatize the effects of a crying child.

"What about Nikki?" Rachel shot back.

Michael simply shrugged in response. He picked up a pickle slice off the platter and popped it into his mouth, just as Rachel playfully slapped him on the back of the head. He made some feigned sputtering sounds. "What 'cha doing? Trying to kill me?"

"Naw. Just maim ya," Rachel teased. She disappeared into the house to get more platters and bowls. George took his cue to light the barbeque. As soon as he lit the barbeque, everyone started milling around the table, getting their plates ready for George's famous German sausages.

After they finished eating, the kids ran inside to watch a *Wiggles* video. Rachel began puttering around, picking up the plates and napkins.

"Leave it for it a minute." Kate smiled up at her daughter. "Please sit."

Rachel did as her mother asked, with a perplexed look on her face. George knew the time had come. They could no longer hide behind the comfort of a family barbecue. The time had come to face reality, and the reality was Kate had cancer. He picked up on Kate's suggestion and stood behind her for support.

"What's up?" Rachel questioned.

Kate reached her hand up to find George's. He heard her gulp and draw in a deep breath before she began. "I have cancer." The words came out more abruptly than he'd anticipated.

Rachel stared at her incredulously. "Are you serious?" she burst out with a half-laugh, half cry in her voice. She grew quiet in response to the stoic look on Kate's face. "You are. Where? I mean…how…" Rachel stammered, shaking her head. She reached for Steve's hand for support.

"It's ovarian cancer," Kate started. "I'll need surgery. Probably this week, and then I'll start radiation therapy."

"How serious is it? What are your chances?" Rachel blinked back tears that started to pool in her eyes.

"As good as anyone else's, I guess." Kate shrugged. "It's a roll of the dice, but it's in God's hands. He has a purpose for this. We'll just pray for healing." She smiled sweetly at her children.

"Hah. Some God," Michael burst out, his lips pursed. He tossed his cup still half full of soda down on the table, sending sprays into the air. "He let you get it in the first place. If He really cared, He wouldn't make you go through it at all." He spouted, forcing his chair back. He stood without another word and walked off.

"Michael!" George scolded. Michael waved him off as he crossed the backyard.

"Let him go," Kate soothed. "He needs to go blow off steam."

"All he ever does is blow off steam," Rachel complained. "When will he ever grow up?" She began sopping up the spilled soda when

Kate placed her hand gently on hers. Rachel looked up at Kate with tears brimming in her eyes. "You're going to beat this." She nodded. "You have to, Mom. I need you." Tears streamed down her face.

Kate was already crying. She simply mouthed the words, "I know."

Rachel sniffed back her tears. "What about David? Are you going to tell him?"

"No," Kate protested. George waved his hands above Kate's head trying to ward Rachel off from the subject, but it was no use.

"Why not?" Rachel said indignantly. "Maybe a good dose of guilt might be what he needs to pull his head out—"

"Rachel!" Kate interrupted. "Please, just let me fight the cancer, not my family."

Rachel nodded; the tears returned. A small voice diffused the moment.

"Mommy, why are you crying?" Jenna asked, climbing up onto Rachel's lap.

"Because Nana told me some bad news." Rachel said, smiling down at her little girl.

"What did she tell you?" Jenna asked.

"Nana is sick." Rachel tried to explain without making it sound too grim.

"Did she throw up?" Jenna scrunched her nose at the thought.

"No." Rachel let out a little laugh.

"Well then, she'll be fine. Can we color?" Jenna asked. Rachel looked to Kate who nodded, and the subject was officially dropped.

Rachel disappeared into the house led by Jenna. Steve followed close behind. George waited until the door slid shut before he sat in the chair next to Kate. "We'll beat this thing," he said encouragingly.

Kate nodded, patting his hand on the table.

"I'll go get Michael. He should have cooled off by now." George stood and pulled the chair out for Kate, something she never let him do, but now she permitted him. He realized this disease would change everything, even the little things.

George walked out the back gate and down the winding path to the creek in the canyon below. For as long as he could remember,

Michael ran off to the creek whenever he needed time alone. The day David left for college, Michael spent hours throwing rocks into the creek rather than face the emotional goodbye. Michael had idolized his older brother and took it especially hard when David left. Today delivered a blow worse than anything they'd ever experienced before.

George carefully stepped down the rocky slope, climbing across fallen trees and boulders. He found Michael sitting on his favorite rock under a towering ponderosa pine. The creek surged with late spring runoff, and Michael sat throwing rocks into the water.

"I thought I might find you here," George began. He stood on a rocky ledge five feet above Michael's favorite spot.

"Does she really have cancer?" Michael didn't bother to look up.

"I'm afraid so."

"What's going to happen if…" Michael's voice trailed off. Neither of them wanted to say it.

"Let's just hope and pray that the doctors can get rid of the cancer." George tried to sound optimistic. He hopped down from the ledge and sat next to Michael, placing his arm around his son's shoulder. He could see that Michael had been crying and was trying to hide it. George picked up a rock and tried to skip it across the deep pool in the bend. Michael picked up a rock and did the same. Father and son sat quietly, trying to forget the battle that lie ahead.

*****

Rachel unlocked the door and set her keys and purse on the table just inside the door. Steve took the kids upstairs. He always seemed to know when she needed a break. This was definitely one of those times. She kicked off her shoes and slowly walked into the den. She sank into a large leather chair and rubbed her temples. Her head hurt from the crying and the worrying.

She turned on the computer and waited as it booted up. She typed the email, choosing her words carefully. Her mother had said she didn't want to tell David, but he needed to know. It might change things. Besides, he had a right to know. She paused at the end, rereading what she had typed and hesitated a moment before clicking on send.

Steve came up behind her and stood above her with his hand on her shoulder. "Your mom's a tough old bird. If anyone can beat it, she can."

"Thanks." She needed those reassurances right now.

"Emailing David?"

"Yeah." Rachel nodded and waited for the send confirmation window to pop up, before closing out of the email program. "I know Mom said she didn't want us to tell him, but he needs to know."

"I know," he agreed as he rubbed her shoulders softly and bent over to kiss her cheek. "Are you going to be long?"

She clicked another icon on the desktop. "I just want to look up a couple of things." She glanced back at him and placed her hand on his briefly before turning back toward the computer.

"All right. Then it's time for a movie and popcorn," he said as he turned to leave the room.

Rachel googled "Ovarian Cancer." She scanned the resulting web links and clicked on the top result. If she were going to help her mom, she needed to find out as much about the enemy as she could.

*****

Across town, Michael turned on the light to his workshop, a tool shed that he'd added a workbench and an overhead light to. He pressed play on the boom box, and the smooth Texas blues of Stevie Ray Vaughn poured from the speakers. Michael ran his hand over the long piece of alder on the bench. He already sketched the outline and had started chiseling around the rough edges. He loved creating things from wood. He used old-school tools, hand tools, something few people did anymore. He loved tools. He grew up surrounded by them, and he enjoyed the solitude of working with his hands. It was the only time he felt in control of his life. Things had just started to settle down again after Connor's birth. Now everything was out of control again. His mom had cancer. She tried her best to make it sound like it was nothing to worry about, but it was cancer.

He wondered if Rachel would call David or, better yet, if David would actually show up. The last time he'd seen his so-called brother, he had ridden in the back seat of the family car five hours only to stay in some roadside hotel, then have breakfast at a pancake house before being shuffled into an auditorium to watch David cross a stage with a thousand other people and pick up a piece of paper. An hour after David's graduation, they were back in the car for the five-hour return trip. David met with them briefly afterward for a photo and to collect his gifts. David didn't want to see them anymore than Michael had wanted to see him. Eleven years had passed without so much as a phone call or post card. David hadn't so much as acknowledged Michael's graduation, his wedding, or even the birth of his son. Still he hoped for their mother's sake that David had the *cojones* to show up.

*****

Sunday morning, George got up early. He made waffles and bacon for breakfast and was dressed and ready for church by the time Kate stumbled into the kitchen. He wanted to show Kate he was behind her. Since she constantly nagged for him to attend Sunday morning service with her, he figured that taking the initiative to go would show his support. Besides, maybe if he was more willing to go, God would be more willing to answer his prayers and heal his wife.

Kate poured herself a cup of coffee and helped herself to the waffles. She sat at the kitchen table across from George. Normally, he would be fishing or still be in his robe and slippers and have the Sunday *Oregonian* spread all over the table. This morning, he read the brochures that Dr. Gibson had given them. He knew Kate had probably read numerous articles and done some research on this. He didn't want to be kept in the dark about what was going on, not when it was this serious.

"What got into you?" Kate inquired, sipping from her coffee cup.

"I have no idea what you're talking about," George commented lightly. He caught a skeptical glance from across the table.

"Well, if I knew that you'd respond like this, I'd have gotten cancer years ago," she teased.

George shot back a half smile in her direction. He knew that she was still coming to terms with her diagnosis, but he wished she wouldn't make light of it. He continued to read, while Kate ate quietly. When Kate went to finish getting ready, he loaded the dishwasher. After reading the booklets, he felt he needed to help her as much as possible. Kate never wanted to appear weak, so she rarely asked for help of any kind. George would simply have to do things for her without her asking for them.

Mountainview Church sat next to the middle school and faced south with a full view of the majestic snowcapped mountains the town was named for. The mountain range Three Sisters with the peaks of *Faith*, *Hope*, and *Charity* defined the character of the small community built under their shadow. Unlike some other small towns in Oregon that could be defined by two taverns and a post office, Sisters was a community rich in character. All throughout the year, various festivals and events drew the community together with purpose. In June, Rodeo fever filled the air. The town threw open the welcome mat and turned back the clock to a page out of the Old West. It seemed as if the entire town was involved in at least some aspect of the rodeo. In July, the quilt show came to town, followed by the antique fair and the jazz festival.

Whenever a fellow citizen had a need, the town would rally together to help. During the forest fire season, men showed up with shovels and chain saws ready to help. Women showed up with sandwiches and lemonade. Over the years, the population had grown, but the spirit of community remained.

For such a small community, Mountainview boasted a fairly large congregation. They had outgrown the capacity of their meager building. They had already built a new addition to house a larger sanctuary, and now they held two services every Sunday. This time of year, everyone eagerly attended to catch up on what their neighbors had done during the long winter months. George followed Kate to their normal spot, a row halfway up the sanctuary on the left side.

George tried to listen to Pastor Mike O'Connell's sermon, but thoughts of what lay ahead distracted him. Kate would need to quit her job. If she quit, what would they do for insurance to cover her treatment? Radiation therapy didn't sound like a cheap therapy. How would he react if she lost her hair? He knew it seemed trivial, but could he look at her without staring…without making her self-conscious? What about housework and taking care of her? Would he need to hire someone? Would they be able to afford it? Ironically, the sermon's topic was keeping faith in times of uncertainty. Pastor O'Connell spoke about God's purpose for all things. George recalled Kate's comment the day before about there being a purpose for this. He just couldn't make any sense of why God would allow Kate to get cancer in the first place. He shook his head just as he heard Pastor O'Connell recite from Proverbs, "Trust in the Lord with all your heart and lean not on your own understanding." George wondered if it was that easy. He trusted God with his life, but could he trust God with Kate's?

Chapter 6

Monday morning, George sat alone at the kitchen table, waiting for Kate. He stirred his coffee unconsciously, staring at the newspaper, deep in thought about the day ahead of him. Being the first of the month, there would be an increased volume in orders from local contractors. It would be an extremely hectic Monday, and to add to the pressure, he would spend most of the morning at Kate's follow-up appointment.

He heard Kate on the phone in the other room, making some excuse to have the morning off. Kate worked for one of those large medical clinics that sprung up next to hospitals with doctors from pediatrics to geriatrics and everything in between. Gone were the days of one doctor in one office. Now, to reduce overhead and malpractice insurance costs, doctors banded together in groups, sharing office staff and nurses. Dr. Richards's office was directly upstairs from the office where Kate worked. George wondered how Kate kept her personal issues under wraps with all the doctors in one building.

"Here you are," Kate said as she entered the room. There was a hint of surprise in her voice as if she hadn't expected to find him sitting there.

"Yep. You found me. I was hiding right here in plain sight," George replied. He looked up in time to catch a censuring glance. Kate feigned disgust over his punning humor, but he surmised that deep down, she loved it. He watched her mill around the kitchen, shuffling dishes and gathering her purse and keys. As she moved, George noticed that her normal exuberance had diminished. Normally, Kate had a tangible enthusiasm apparent in her everyday demeanor. Whether she was washing dishes or taking out the trash, she always had a smile on her face and a bounce in her step. But today, he noticed the smile was less radiant, and the bounce was all but gone. He didn't know if things had changed that quickly or if he simply noticed them now that he was paying closer attention.

"Ready to go?" She stood above him tapping her wrist.

"Sure." He forced a smile. He picked up his paper and set it in the recycling bin. Then he followed her through the kitchen, setting his coffee cup in the sink on the way out. A week ago, he would have left the paper and the coffee cup on the table, not giving it a second thought. But now, things were different.

As he pulled his truck out onto Camp Polk Road, George wondered if this was how it was going to be, doctor appointments and hospital visits consuming the vast majority of their time. The drive to the hospital took half an hour without traffic. Add to that another hour or so at the doctor's office, only to turn around and spend yet another half hour on the road. Part of him resented all the time that would be lost traveling to and from the hospital, but he'd endure anything so long as in the end, Kate got better.

Kate didn't want to miss any more work than she had to, and he was anxious to get back to the store, so they decided to drive in separately. As he drove, his mind wandered in a thousand different directions. The questions that plagued him during the church service echoed once again. How long it would be before Kate would lose her hair? What would they do if Kate had to quit her job? Would Kate be too sick to take care of the house? If so, who would cook? George could barbeque and make pancakes, but that was the extent of his culinary talents. He was still lost deep in thought when he pulled into the parking lot and took the spot next to Kate's Explorer. He jumped out, and they walked in together.

The waiting room was empty this early in the morning. Dr. Gibson walked in a few seconds behind them and gestured for them to follow him back. George and Kate sat down, while Dr. Gibson set down his briefcase and shuffled some papers on his desk. "Well, how are you guys this morning?" Dr. Gibson opened in a tone entirely too chipper for what they were about to discuss.

"Good. Considering." Kate shrugged, looking from George to the doctor.

"Good to hear." Dr. Gibson nodded. "Did you get a chance to look over the material I sent home with you?"

"Yes," George replied simply. He had read the pamphlets Sunday after church. He read them and reread them until he understood the best way he could what was happening to his wife. The pamphlets on the surgical procedures gave a general overview as well as listing very specific areas of concern accompanied by what to do in case they occur. On the other hand, the coping guide merely listed broad categories but nothing concrete on how to deal with it all. It didn't say "if your wife has been diagnosed with cancer do this…"

"Any questions?" Dr. Gibson asked.

George shook his head quietly. He doubted that Dr. Gibson had any magic elixir to help him deal with all this.

"Okay, then let's cut to the chase. Friday after you left, I spoke with Dr. Richards again, and we mapped out a proposed treatment plan for you." He directed his comments to Kate. "For starters, I'd like to schedule a hysterectomy and debulking procedure the first part of next week. That will give you the rest of the week to make arrangements with your employer and to find someone to assist you around the house. Due to the size and extent of the tumors, we will need to do an abdominal procedure. You won't be able to bend or lift anything for two weeks following the procedure. You'll need to be off work for eight weeks following the surgery to allow proper healing," Dr. Gibson explained. "And during those eight weeks, we will schedule your radiation treatment."

"Won't the surgery make her weak for the other treatment?" George questioned. Everything he had read on the radiation therapy suggested that it would wear her out, and he feared that surgery would just do her in.

Dr. Gibson nodded as he spoke. "Yes, the surgery will compromise her immune system."

"Then why do surgery at all?" George asked naively.

"That question comes up a lot. If we're going to be treating the cancer, then why the surgery too?" Dr. Gibson began. "Clinical studies have shown that treatment is more effective following surgery. Surgery reduces the number of cancer cells that ultimately need to be eradicated. Radiation or chemotherapies are far more effective with fewer cancer cells to treat. So we remove the bulk of the cancer, which not only increases Kate's chances for survival but also decreases her chances of recurrence."

George grew silent. The doctor had explained the rationale but still had not alleviated his fears. Kate was strong, but he feared this beast she faced was stronger.

"So if we proceed with the surgery next week. How long are we looking at before we begin the radiation therapy?" Kate asked.

"Once Dr. Richards clears you. Generally, about two weeks after surgery," Dr. Gibson explained.

"What will the treatment involve?" Kate inquired. George suspected she already knew most of the ins and outs of the therapy. Kate had probably checked it all out on the internet. Her question was more than likely for his benefit.

"The radiation therapy will be five doses a week for six weeks. Each week we will monitor your white blood cell and platelet counts to ensure the radiation isn't too much for you."

Kate nodded again and sighed heavily. "Okay. Let's get the ball the rolling."

"All right. I'll get the surgery scheduled, and my nurse will give you a call with the details," Dr. Gibson replied.

George offered his hand to help her stand. The hospital loomed on the horizon through the window. This was their life now, doctor visits and treatment sessions, at least eight weeks' worth. When he got back to the store, he would talk with Rachel. They would find someone to clean, maybe even cook. He didn't want Kate to worry about anything other than getting well again.

"Do you want me to go with you to talk to Greg?" George offered as they walked out together. Kate had been Dr. Greg Lund's nurse for eighteen years, even before he joined the clinic. He and his wife, Julie, had been over to their house innumerable times over the years. They had a friendship that transcended the employee-employer relationship. It would be difficult for Kate to tell him about this.

"Thanks for the offer, but I think I can handle it." Kate forced a half smile. He was curious if she was being her usual 'I can handle anything Kate" or if she was simply in denial about her condition. She gave him a quick kiss before climbing into her SUV.

*****

The drive back to the store went by more quickly as he mentally checked off lists of things to do. He'd need to find someone to help Kate, someone she trusted and someone who could tolerate Kate's obstinacy. And with all the time he'd spend driving back and forth to hospital visits, he'd need to hire some help at the store. He was already shorthanded. With the early heat wave they'd been having, contractors were getting a jump on the construction season.

George got back to the store at ten o'clock. As he had anticipated, there were four contractors standing at the counter, and only two able bodies helping them. He walked around the counter and jumped right in to tend to his customers.

By three, the morning appointment had become a distant memory, until Ned came in. "Sorry to hear about Kate," Ned said, a note of genuine concern in his voice.

George stood there dazed for a moment. He hadn't expected news to travel quite so fast, but Ned's daughter-in-law, Vicki, worked in the business office at the clinic. Now that word was out, he didn't know how to respond.

"Tell Kate we'll be praying for you guys." Ned smiled and took his packages and left.

It took a few seconds for George to shake off Ned's comment before helping another customer. How was he supposed to focus on work after a comment like that?

Once the store finally emptied, and the rush of customers had subsided, he was left alone to ponder Ned's comments. "We'll be praying for you" echoed in his mind. George had never been the type of man that anyone prayed for. He had been blessed most of his life, and he prayed for others. He'd never been on the receiving end as far as he knew. The whole idea of it made him feel weak, like he wasn't man enough to handle this on his own. He wasn't sure he could handle this.\

Chapter 7

Kate went directly to work after her appointment with Dr. Gibson. She had already taken off three days in the last two weeks. She didn't want to arouse suspicions any more than she had to. People would know soon enough. The clinic was its own self-contained community, and news traveled fast. When Dr. Richards had decided to join the clinic, Kate had thought of changing doctors. But she'd gone to him for years, and she figured she didn't have any health issues noteworthy for people to talk about, so why worry about it. And honestly, it didn't bother her if people knew about the cancer; she just didn't want to be on the receiving end of their pity. As she walked in the pediatric office, she plastered a smile across her face. Impatient children and weary mothers filled the waiting room. For some unknown reason, their office got busier in the spring than during the winter when everyone was expected to catch colds or the flu. She passed by the snot-covered kids and their nervous mothers and knew it would take all the self-control she had to focus on them instead of her own concerns. *Please, Lord, give me strength.*

Kate hustled all day shuffling patients, taking vital statistics, and administering shots. She enjoyed the hectic pace. It offered a diversion from dwelling on her prognosis. Instead, she focused on the incidental sufferings of children—some scrapes, a few shots, a kid with allergies.

By the end of the day, Kate was exhausted. She sat in her chair, filling out charts, waiting for all the other staff to leave. She wanted to address Dr. Lund in private. The whole idea of telling Greg felt like telling her parents she'd failed a math exam. Greg depended on her to do a job. She felt as though she were disappointing him by not being able to fulfill that obligation. Certainly, he could find another nurse. But they spent years developing a rapport, an intrinsic trust. He knew beyond a doubt, that her instincts were right about patients. It saved him time and allowed him to see more patients. Now he'd have to start over again with someone new. He'd have less time with his patients. Maybe it was silly to think of illness as failure, but she had let him down. Being a nurse was her job, and now she had failed.

"Hey, Greg. You got a minute?" She stood at the door to his private office.

"Sure." He set aside the medical journal he'd been reading and pointed to the chair on the other side of the desk.

Kate drew in a deep breath as she sat in the chair across from him, still unsure how best to tell him. "I'm going to need to take a leave of absence."

"I guessed something was up. It's not like you to have time off more than once in one week." A look of concern crossed his face. "So what's up?"

"There's really no easy way to say it…" She paused. Why was it so hard to tell him? Why was she afraid of telling people? It wasn't as if she'd committed a crime, and yet she felt ashamed by her weakness. Somehow, she should be stronger, immune. "I have stage four ovarian cancer." She blurted it out before chickening out.

"Kate. No." He shook his head. "I don't know what to say. I'm so sorry." He sank back into his chair. "Do they have a plan yet, or are you still sorting it out?"

She was grateful he focused on the disease and treatment. It made it easier for her to talk about it. "We're going to start with surgery and follow up with radiation therapy."

"Who are you seeing, if you don't mind my asking?"

"Walter Gibson."

"Good. He's the best you can get." An awkward silence followed. Neither of them knew quite what to say. "Do you want anyone to know why you're out? I know you're an extremely private person. I wouldn't want there to be any intrusion."

"I'm sure everyone will find out eventually. But I'd rather it wait until I'm on leave."

"So how soon before you'll need to be out."

"Next week. My surgery is Tuesday." Even as she said it, it was hard to believe. Just one week ago, she had seen Dr. Richards for her follow-up appointment to go over her test results, and now… It was all happening so fast.

"I'll get the paperwork down to HR. Are you sure you don't want the rest of the week off?"

"I'm sure. But I might take off Friday to do some shopping with Rachel."

"That sounds like a good idea."

"Thanks." Kate forced a half smile.

"You'll let me know if there's anything Julie and I can do for you."

"Sure." Kate nodded although she had no intention of asking for help. She was just relieved that he had made it easy for her. "I should be getting home. George will be waiting for me." She stood and turned to leave.

"Yeah, it's about that time." He stood and shuffled some papers on his desk. "Julie and I will keep you in our prayers."

"Thanks." She slipped out of the office quietly. Once around the corner, she let out a sigh of relief. She could handle people praying for her. She'd seen the power of prayer firsthand. She would welcome all the prayer she could get; she just didn't want the pity that accompanied it.

*****

The week passed by in a blur. Kate put in extra hours, making sure that everything was ready for her to go on leave. She'd stocked all the rooms, ordered extra supplies; she'd even notified one of the drug reps that they were running low on his brand. She took extra time to write down and update procedure documents. It was the least she could do.

Every once in a while, she'd catch some glances in the hallway and sensed that people knew, yet no one mentioned it. She supposed that polite conversation didn't allow for coworkers to come right out and say, "So I hear you have cancer." At least she had that in her favor.

Thursday night, Kate waited until all the other staff and even Greg had gone to ensure she was alone. Then she cleaned out her desk, leaving only small impersonal items, like pens and paperclips. It must have looked as if she were quitting or retiring, but if she didn't come back, she didn't want to burden someone else with the responsibility of cleaning out her desk and figuring out what to keep and what to throw away.

Kate stood in the doorway and took one last lingering glance around. She hated to think it, but she had to face the grim but very real possibility that she might never return to work again.

Friday morning, Rachel met her at her house around seven. Every year, they drove over to Portland or Salem to go shopping for Christmas and Easter. Just a few weeks earlier, they had gone over to Salem for a day, but Kate wanted the extra time with her daughter. It wasn't about shopping. Their outings were the only real time they spent together without kids and husbands and all the other daily demands. During their shopping trips, they talked and laughed and simply enjoyed each other's company. If they didn't go now, it would be at least eight weeks before they had another chance. And perhaps this would be their last getaway.

With that in mind, Kate chose the destination, downtown Portland. Portland held so many fond memories, and she wanted Rachel to share that with her. As a young girl, Kate's mother took her there as their special time, usually around Christmas. The Rose City carried an air of sophistication and culture, at least the closest they could find in their corner of the world. They saw the Nutcracker ballet and dined in fine restaurants, and of course, they shopped. In the 1950s, Meier & Frank was the epitome of style and sophistication, at least in the northwest. But for Kate, the store had a magical atmosphere, in part due to all the elegant clothes and furnishings throughout the store, in part due to the modern conveniences in elevators and escalators that she never saw in Bend, but mainly because Santa Claus lived on the tenth floor, not merely a department store Santa with a chair and some elves but an entire village with all things St. Nick.

Kate hoped that one day Rachel would feel the same affection about their trips. Perhaps she would remember their trips as magical, special times as well, and pass that on to Jenna. To ensure they got everything in their day trip, she planned their excursion down to the minutest detail. Her goal was to ensure they experienced as much as they could in what little time they were afforded. Kate strictly enforced one rule throughout the day. No talking about her illness or the upcoming treatment.

They lunched at Rose's Deli, a Portland landmark. Both of them had sensible salads but splurged on the decedent chocolate cakes they were famous for. Afterward, they walked up Fifth Avenue toward Pioneer Square. Kate took them into the historic Meier & Frank building. Upstairs, Kate found an adorable lavender-and-white dress for Jenna. The ensemble came complete with a sun hat and jacket. On the next rack over, she found a purse and little white gloves. Rachel protested, but Kate insisted that Jenna have the perfect Easter dress, even though they'd bought her a cute pink-and-white dress just weeks before. Then they shopped for Braden, and Kate found a navy suit. After Rachel's insistence that Braden would never wear a suit, and Steve wouldn't care much for it either, Kate placed it back on the rack. Later, Kate found him and Conner nearly matching outfits, khaki chinos with long-sleeved button-down shirts made of twill and denim and sweater vests and ties. The outfits were so adorable Rachel finally agreed.

Afterward, they strolled through the luxurious Pioneer Place to see how the other half lived. They wandered through Saks Fifth Avenue, stopping and admiring some silk scarves that cost more than they had spent all day. They marveled at the displays at Tiffany & Company. Rachel ogled the sapphires and diamonds. Then they each bought an iced mocha and headed toward the Mecca of shopping in the Northwest—Nordstrom's.

Twice during their day out, Kate had needed to sit because of pain in her side. She had told Rachel it was because of new shoes causing blisters on her feet. She could tell that Rachel didn't believe her for a second but humored her all the same. All in all, the day had lived up to her expectations. She only hoped Rachel would remember their last shopping trip together with fondness.

Chapter 8

Sunday morning, George woke at 4:30 a.m. He slipped out of bed carefully, trying not to disturb Kate. Using only the light from the closet, he dressed quickly and headed downstairs. Freshly brewed coffee waited for him along with some snacks he'd set out the night before. Over the past decade, George developed a custom of going fly-fishing on Easter morning before church services. It allowed Kate time to prepare for dinner, and it gave him a chance to unwind before the activities of the day began. George poured a cup of coffee in his travel mug, grabbed the bag of snacks, and walked out to his truck. His waders, fly rod, and tackle were all tucked away carefully in the storage box mounted on the bed of his truck. He quietly backed out of the driveway, turned, and headed west.

Half an hour later, he pulled his truck to the side of the road. He killed the motor and walked around to the rear of the truck. He dropped the tail gate, slid on his waders, and grabbed his fly rod. With one free hand, he closed the tailgate before heading down the dimly lit trail. Soft whispers of golden light edged over the top of green ridge behind him, slowly scouring out the darkness as he made his way down the path to the banks of the Metolius.

At a quarter to six, light began pouring over the ridge in hues of pink and orange. The river murmured its familiar song as it rippled across the rocky ravine. George stood at the bank surveying the area. The manzanita bushes were still wrapped in slumber, their dead leaves hanging as part of their long winter's nap. The lush green grass sprouted near the water's edge, showing the first signs of spring. The scent of pine and juniper lingered like French perfume. This was his sanctuary. Later, he would return home to get all spit and polished. He would go to church with Kate, and afterward, the kids and grandkids would come over for the big dinner and Easter egg hunts. But here, this is where he knew God, away from the busyness of life—out in the untamed wilderness. This is where he could witness God's glory and majesty and feel Him ever present. There was no more fitting time than Easter to come and draw near, and this was the only way he knew how. Kate read books on how to experience God, but George found that out here in stillness, he didn't need to find God. God found him. From the time he was young, whenever he needed to talk to God, he headed for the hills. After his mom died, and he was forced to live with his aunt and her self-absorbed brood, George took a job with the Forest Service. He spent his days hiking through these very woods and marking trees. That's when he discovered God lurking in the treetops, speaking through the wind and water.

As he waded into the ice-cold waters, George began a simple dialogue with his Creator. "Another beautiful day You've given us. The bite should be good today. But I suppose You already knew that." He navigated the river bottom and the current like a pro, slowly and steadily moving toward the sweet spot—the place where his line and the fish would most surely meet. "I keep telling myself that You have a plan, a reason for all this. You always do. But can You help me understand? Maybe I would understand better if it were happening to me and not Kate." George lifted his rod skyward, and with a smooth, controlled motion, he cast his line across the water, whipping the line just above the top of the water. He took a few steps further into the water, all the while conversing with God. "Today is the day of redemption, the day You sent Your Son to show us the depth of Your grace and love. It's a day of life and second chances. Please let Kate have another chance. Please don't take her from me. Not yet."

Just as the words escaped his lips, he felt a familiar tug at the end of his line. The tip of the rod bent forward slightly, and he snapped back with a sharp pull. The line sang out melodiously, "Zing," as the fish stripped the line from the reel, and George worked quickly to coerce the fish to the bank. He gently lifted his prize, a beautiful brown trout. Gingerly, he removed the hook before releasing the fish back into the water. George took the early catch as a sign of good things to come. He drew in a deep breath and nodded his head. "I can only hope," he said softly.

George fished for a couple hours before heading back to the house. He entered the house through the garage door into the kitchen. The scent of bacon and onion greeted him at the door. He found Kate puttering around the kitchen, making all her dinner preparations. Every year, she baked a ham with scalloped potatoes—her grandmother's recipe—and green beans with bacon, onions, and crushed peppercorns. Kate preferred to have everything ready to bake when they returned from church so the kitchen could stay clean until after dinner. So every year, Kate prepared all the food and even set the table before they left for church.

"Oh, there you are. I was starting to wonder," she said cheerfully, looking up from the pan she stirred. She resembled a giant bobblehead doll with curlers stacked high on her head.

"What were you wondering?" George teased. He grabbed a piece of bacon and chomped off a big bite.

"That's for the green bean casserole," Kate scolded. She slapped at his hands coming nowhere near them. "I wondered if you had forgotten what day it was."

"Nope. It's Sunday. How could I forget? It's the only day I get to go fishing."

Kate rolled her eyes and shook her head. "I swear if you could, you would go fishing twenty-four seven."

"Naw." He shook his head playfully. "I'd have to take some time off to watch football." He backed away from her as if expecting to get hit.

"Ugh. Why don't you go wash up so that we're not late to church on Easter?" She shooed him away with a gesture of her hand.

"It's Easter? Hmm." He stroked his chin as if pondering some great philosophical work. "I suppose if we were late, God would understand."

"Why's that?" She arched her brow curiously.

"Jesus was a fisherman." He darted from the room as he said it. He knew he was pressing his luck.

He climbed the stairs two at a time and walked the short hallway to their bedroom. He kicked his shoes off at the end of the bed before he noticed that Kate had already tidied up their bedroom. The bed looked as if it hadn't been slept in, with the quilt perfectly smooth and all the pillows lined up just so. It even appeared as if Kate had already vacuumed, and it wasn't even nine o'clock yet. He picked up his shoes and set them in the corner.

Kate had laid out his brown pinstripe suit on the bed, complete with socks and a tie. George hated ties. He hated suits. He only owned two and only wore them twice a year. It appeased Kate and beat the alternative, weeks of snide mutterings and not-so-subtle sulking. He'd learned early on to give a little or suffer a lot.

George pulled his socks off and placed them in the hamper—a new habit he had developed in the past two weeks. For thirty-five years, she had asked him to put his clothes in the hamper. For thirty-five years, he didn't do it, until a doctor told him she had cancer.

As he headed toward the shower, he noticed Kate's dress hanging on her closet door. Something about it caught his eye. Maybe it was the cut or the shimmering green fabric. Something. Normally, Kate bought a more practical dress from the sales rack or a suit that could be worn for work. But this one was different—whimsical, romantic, elegant. Why the sudden change? Why would practical-minded Kate buy something like this? Perhaps he read too much into it; after all, it was just a dress.

He let go of the paranoia and set a towel on the counter. After his shower, George took some extra time trimming his beard. Kate liked it kept short. He honestly didn't care. He could go months without shaving without a care in the world. Although the shorter cut did disguise the gray that crept across his face a little more every day, but it did nothing to hide the deepening creases around his eyes.

*****

The parking lot at Mountainview Church overflowed into the middle school parking lot. People poured into the sanctuary which doubled as a gym for the youth groups on Wednesday night. Some churches added extra services for Easter and Christmas, but Mountainview Church merely added more chairs. George had tried to get there early enough to sit in their normal seats but found that they were occupied by some visitors from out of town. They settled for chairs closer to the front.

Easter services were always the same. Some dramatic skit depicting the torment of the cross, followed by an austere sermon about the price paid on the cross. Then the choir sang familiar hymns. George did his best not to nod off during the service. Easter service always made him feel as if he needed to take a bath. Why couldn't they talk about the power and might of redemption rather than focusing on the price and sacrifice? After the final prayer, Kate dried tears from her eyes while George stretched.

As they headed down the steps, Pastor O'Connell shook George's hand. "Glad you could come today. Do you want me to come and sit with you on Tuesday?" he asked.

"T-Tuesday?" George stuttered, caught off guard.

"For Kate's surgery," the pastor added with an eager look.

George ran his hand over his head and rubbed the back of his neck nervously. He knew Kate's surgery was on Tuesday. What he didn't know is how the pastor knew and why he thought he needed to be there. "I, I think I'll be okay. Unless…" He turned and looked at Kate, searching for some clue about the pastor's knowledge. "Unless Kate wants you there."

Kate wore a wide patient smile and said, "That's all right. Everything is going to be fine. George knows how to get ahold of you if we need you."

"Well, all right then." Pastor O'Connell smiled and dropped George's hand. "I'll keep you in my prayers, and you two have a glorious afternoon."

Once in the safety of his truck, he questioned Kate, "So how did Pastor O'Connell know about your surgery? Isn't it sort of a private thing—being a female-type operation?" He felt his inner guard dog barking. The whole thought of Kate's impending surgery was tough enough without other men trampling on that territory.

"Calm down. I asked to be put on the prayer chain at church," Kate responded matter-of-factly.

"So what? Now the entire town is going to know you're having a hys…a hyster—?" George couldn't even bring himself to say it aloud.

"A hysterectomy, dear," Kate said calmly. "And I don't see why it should bother you. It's my body that they're going to cut on."

"I just don't like the thought of everyone in town knowing." George knew that in a small town like Sisters, eventually, everyone would find out anyways, but he didn't like Kate blatantly telling everyone. It was too intimate a detail to share with just anyone.

*****

When they pulled into the driveway, Rachel, Steve, and the kids were waiting for them. Braden and Jenna looked as if they were waiting for Disneyland to open, the way they had their little faces pressed against the windows of Rachel's Expedition. No sooner had George put his truck in park when the grandkids came bounding out of their mother's SUV toward him.

"Grandpa," they sang out in unison.

"My, don't you two look spiffy?" George commented.

"You like my dress, Grandpa?" Jenna sang out, holding her lavender-and-white ruffled sensation out at the sides. Her brown ringlets bounced beneath her matching bonnet. All George could think of was Shirley Temple singing the "Good Ship Lollipop."

"I sure do," he said, kneeling down to receive a hug.

"Did the Easter Bunny stop here?" Braden asked, getting directly to the heart of the matter.

"You know, come to think of it, I did see some baskets in there this morning. You think they might be for you?"

"Yes," Braden cheered, hopping up and down.

George walked over to the front door with Jenna and Braden close behind him. He barely got the door unlocked and opened before the two kids ran in. The honey ham, scalloped potatoes, and green bean casserole blended into one delectable scent that filled the air and surrounded them as they entered through the front door. The table was set with linens and fine china, Kate's grandmother's china, as it had been every Easter before. A huge arrangement of Easter lilies and fresh-cut spring flowers—tulips, daffodils and irises—set in the center of the table is a firm reminder that it was spring.

On the coffee table in the great room, three enormous baskets were arranged in a semicircle. Each basket looked as if it had been made by a professional candymaker, but in truth, Kate had spent hours selecting and decorating each item in each basket. She always took special care with the gifts she gave. Each child and their particular likes and dislikes were considered in every item in their baskets. Jenna and Braden wasted no time in identifying which baskets were theirs.

Rachel retrieved a few items from the car and set them in the kitchen as they waited for Michael.

"Mmm, Mom, that's the best smell in the whole world," Michael bellowed as he came in the front door. Nikki and Connor followed close behind. Nikki led Connor over to show him his basket, but he seemed more interested in the brightly colored glass Easter egg decorations than the mounds of candy hidden behind cellophane. Michael headed straight to the kitchen and picked at the food before it could be presented on the table.

"Just wait a minute and the food will be on the table and we can sit down to eat." Kate slapped at her son's hands.

Minutes later, they all settled around the table, each in a spot they had claimed by either birthright or marriage. Once they were all seated, Kate gave George a small nudge, and they all held hands and bowed their heads. George usually deferred the mealtime prayer to Kate. She was more articulate and more experienced in these things. But at her urging, today, he would take lead over the family in prayer.

"Dear heavenly Father," he began just as she had so many times before, "we come together today to celebrate Your victory over the grave and Your gift of life. We thank You, Lord, for our many blessings and the family here to share them with us. We ask that You bless this wonderfully delicious food to the needs of our bodies and the hands"—he gave Kate's hand a quick squeeze—"that prepared it. Keep us mindful of the true meaning of today and what it means for each of us. In Your name."

"Amen," everyone said in unison.

George surveyed the scene around him, taking in the sights and sounds of his family. Only for a moment did his thoughts turn to David and his absence. He wondered if there would ever be a family gathering where everyone would join together. His gazed stopped at Kate, and his stomach fell. *Would there ever be another holiday that Kate and David would sit at this table together?*

After dinner, the kids could barely contain themselves. They headed outside to the backyard before the table had even been cleared. George presided over the customary Easter egg hunt, and this year, Kate left the dishes to watch too. He noticed small changes in the past two weeks, changes in him and changes in her. He had become more attentive, more protective. She took time to savor the moments, the small details of life. She left the dishes to sit and watch the sunset. Or she'd stop vacuuming to watch the deer in the yard.

He walked over, put his arm around her shoulder, and watched the grandchildren search for eggs in the backyard. Rachel and Michael guided their children around trees and peeking under bushes until every last egg was found. The grandkids came over and showed off their eggs as if they were made of pure gold. Kate fawned over her grandchildren as if they'd discovered ancient treasures. They sat on the swing and enjoyed the spoils of the hunt.

Chapter 9

Tuesday morning, George woke with the alarm at five o'clock to find Kate already dressed and reading a book. "Couldn't sleep?" he asked with a yawn.

"Nope. Anticipation." Kate set her book down and rubbed her eyes. She looked as if she was ready to go.

"Anticipation over a surgery? You're some kind of nuts," he muttered as he headed for the shower. He let the steamy water run over him, loosening his tired joints. He never had trouble getting out of bed to go fishing, but for work and for something like this, he simply did not want to wake up.

The hot shower cleared the cobwebs. George dressed and went downstairs. Kate puttered around cleaning the counters and putting things away.

"What are you doing?" George asked as he poured a cup of coffee into a travel mug.

"Cleaning," she said flatly as she scrubbed a spot on the tile.

"I can see that, but why?" George reached around her for the sugar bowl and stirred two heaping spoonfuls into his coffee.

"I'm not going to be able to for a while, and I know you won't scrub the counters and things." She moved the coffee maker and some canisters back into place.

"You're right, I won't. That's why I asked Rosita to come clean the house twice a week while you're recuperating," he said with a grin. He hadn't even asked Kate when he'd made the arrangements with Rosita. Kate wouldn't trust her home to just anyone, but Rosita had been cleaning the store for seven years. She was like family.

"You didn't." Kate shot him a skeptical glance.

"I did." He smiled.

"I thought you said that we wouldn't need anyone, that you could take care of things." She placed her hands on her hips taunting him.

"I'm going to be taking care of you." He placed an arm around her waist and pulled her in for a kiss. "Come on. Your bag is already in the car."

The doctor had given Kate a list of items to pack since she'd be in the hospital for four or five days. She'd had the bag packed since Saturday. George followed her lead and placed the bag in the car on Monday night.

Kate didn't say much on the drive in, and George was afraid to ask any questions. He was lost in his own thoughts. He still hadn't quite figured out how he would handle commuting in to see Kate while running things at the store. Rachel had offered to help out, but she already had enough work to do. She had suggested George try out their yard manager, Don, to deal with the store. At first, George dismissed the idea, but now as he drove to the hospital again, he knew he needed to do something, and Don might just be the answer.

George pulled into the main parking lot at six fifteen. In the past few weeks, he'd learned how to maneuver around the construction areas. He found a spot near the front entrance. George held Kate's hand as they walked through the revolving front doors. A lone clerk sat at the admitting desk at the far end of the deserted lobby. A woman in a blue jacket pushed a cleaning cart and maneuvered a duster around the sculptures in the foyer. Kate walked directly to the admitting window and checked in. After the seemingly reams of paperwork, they took a seat in the empty waiting room.

"So this is it," Kate said.

"Yep. Are you sure you're ready for this?" George gave her hand a gentle squeeze.

"What choice do I have?"

"Good point."

"Will you do something for me?" Kate turned to face him.

"Anything."

"Will you pray with me?"

"Of course." Under normal circumstances, he might feel uncomfortable praying aloud in public. But circumstances had changed, and besides, there really wasn't anyone around.

They bowed their heads, and Kate clasped George's hand in hers. "Father, I just ask that You would give the surgeons the skills and wisdom they need today, Lord. Please keep me in Your loving hands while I lay at the mercy of this disease. And Lord, please help George. Guard his heart from fear." She gave his hand a gentle squeeze. "In Your Son's name. Amen."

"Kate Patterson." The nurse came out of nowhere.

They both stood. George toted her bag as he followed Kate and the nurse into a small room.

"You can change into this gown." The nurse set a blue hospital gown on the bed. "You will need to remove all jewelry. Leave it with your husband." Then she turned to address George briefly. "We will take her bag and anything left in this room to her room upstairs once she is in recovery. When she is settled into her room, we will page you to the main lobby." The nurse talked fast and flitted around the room, gathering items from the cupboards behind the bed. "Once you're changed, you'll need to lie on the bed so we can get your IV started. I'll be back in a few minutes." The nurse left and Kate began changing.

"Did you want me to hold your ring?" George sat in a chair in the corner trying to stay out of her way.

"I left it at home in my jewelry box." She slid the gown over her shoulders and motioned for George to help her tie the strings in back. He jumped up and fumbled over the cotton ties. "I knew they would ask me to remove it before surgery, so I just left it at home. My purse is there too." He hadn't even noticed that she wasn't carrying it.

Once Kate had the gown secured, she finished removing her clothes and turned down the blankets on the bed. George helped her get situated and pulled the blanket back over her. The nurse came back with another woman in a white lab coat. George sat back in the chair as they scurried around hooking things on Kate. The woman in the lab coat inserted a needle with a tubelike object on it into Kate's arm and taped it firmly into place. Then she left, and the nurse asked Kate a series of questions, like when she last ate and various other personal questions. George felt like leaving for a while but didn't want to abandon Kate.

"All right. An orderly will be by to pick you up in a few minutes." The nurse took a chart with her and left.

"It'll be all right." Kate smiled at him and reached for him with the hand not wired to the bed. George walked over and held her hand up and kissed it.

"I love you," he murmured softly. It went without saying, but he needed to say it before she went into surgery.

"I love you too." She smiled, gently rubbing his hand with her thumb.

A young man in blue scrubs knocked on the door lightly as he opened it. "Ready?" He half asked, half ordered. He pushed the door all the way open and locked it into place. George stood back as he moved the bed around and then pushed it forward. It was then that George realized it sat on four large wheels. The orderly wheeled Kate down the hallway, and they disappeared through the large white double doors.

George looked around wondering what to do next. He wasn't accustomed to waiting around for anything. At the store, he managed to keep busy from the time he arrived until the time he left. He rarely had an idle moment. Now he wasn't sure what to do. The clock at the end of the hall read seven thirty. He had no idea how long he would have to wait. He decided to get a bite in the cafeteria.

"Hey, George," a familiar voice beckoned. Fred Bricker approached wearing his uniform. Fred had gone to high school with George but then joined the military. He served with the Special Forces and fought tours of duty in Korea and Vietnam. When he returned to Bend, he joined the police force and had been elected sheriff during the last election.

"Hey, Fred," George said as he recognized his friend. "What are you doing here?"

"Some wino wrapped a car around a semitruck just north of LaPine this morning. I was down in the ER taking some statements,"

Fred said, all business. "Just came up here for a cup of real coffee, not that foo-foo stuff they serve downstairs. What about you?"

"Me. Oh." George grabbed a tray and set it on the counter. "Um. Kate's having her surgery today."

"What for? If you don't mind me asking?"

"Um," George stammered. He felt strange talking about it. That's why he hadn't told anyone. How did you go about telling your friends that your wife has cancer? "We found out a couple weeks ago that ah… Kate has…" George paused, shaking his head from side to side. "She has cancer."

"Kate? Ah that's too bad." There it was, that sympathetic tone George had heard all too often in the past few weeks, friends and customers alike, sharing their concern over Kate's health. Every time he heard that tone, he cringed. And somehow, hearing it from a friend was worse. Fred put a hand on George's shoulder. "But, hey I've known Kate a long time, and she's one hell of a fighter. She'll beat this."

"I know. I keep telling myself that." He tried to sound a little more upbeat.

"Midge and I will keep you guys in our prayers," Fred said solemnly.

"Thanks." George swallowed. He still didn't know how to respond when people said they were praying for him. George wondered if his discomfort showed on his face.

"After Kate gets through this, we'll all have to go up to Odell and catch a boatload of fish." Fred changed the subject.

"Yeah. Sure." George felt a little more comfortable talking about the possibility of fishing trips. When people dwelled on the cancer and asked all sorts of questions, it made him uncomfortable.

"And then later on, we can sneak away for a weekend and hit the summer steelhead run over on the coast." Fred smiled.

"Now you're talking." George could actually feel his mood alter as the conversation turned to fishing rather than Kate's illness.

"Next weekend, I'm going over to the valley to go fishing with my son." Fred smiled.

"Really?" George tried not to sound too jealous.

"Yeah. Last Saturday, he took a couple of his buddies up on the Columbia. He found the sweet spot between Knappa and Rainier. They limited out on spring Chinook before noon. He landed a beautiful sixteen pounder. Emailed me pictures of it," Fred elaborated. "He bought one of those new Alumaweld Intruders. Looks real nice and invited me over to see if I can catch a springer myself."

"Hope you catch one." George tried not to sound too jealous. He longed for the opportunity not only to fish for spring Chinook but to fish with his son.

"With any luck, I will, and I'll bring some smoked salmon over for you and Kate."

"Thanks. We'd like that."

"Well, duty calls." Fred held up his coffee in a waving-like gesture and walked around the corner and out of sight. George actually felt relieved to be alone again. At least with Fred, he could talk about fishing, something the both of them could talk about for hours. It filled the awkward silence that inevitably followed the news about Kate.

George took his coffee, a blueberry muffin, and a copy of the *Oregonian* and found a table. A few nurses sat at a table in the corner. Other than that, the place was completely empty. Through the large panes of glass along the wall, George could see the sunrise reflecting off the snowcapped mountains. The day was just beginning, yet he felt as if he'd been there for hours. And this was just the beginning of Kate's battle. Kate would sleep here tonight and then stay for at least three more days. Then there would be treatment and who knew what else. For the next six weeks or so, he would spend more time here than he did at home. With three more hours to kill, George decided to explore his new home away from home.

Down the hall, a curved stained-glassed wall beckoned him into a chapel. Inside, a Zenlike rock altar more closely resembled an Eastern temple than a chapel. George dismissed the idea of spending any time there, but through the chapel, he discovered a doorway which led to a rooftop garden. Outside, the crisp morning air nipped at his face. A soft wind blew out of the south, making the already cool thirty degrees feel like a bone-chilling nineteen. The garden, albeit small, provided a nice escape from the endless corridors and waiting rooms inside. Miniature trees and shrubs adorned a short gravel path which led back to a rock waterfall and pond. Atop the rock ledge sat a life-size bronze statuette of a young girl gazing into the tranquil pool of water. The slow movement of water across the rocks put his mind at ease. There was something peaceful about the movement of water, just like his beloved Metolius. Every spring, Kate asked George to build a pond in their backyard. Every year, he came up with some excuse why not to. This year, he would have no excuse, and she wouldn't need to ask.

In the main lobby, George flipped through a dozen home-and-garden magazines. At noon, a nurse informed him they had moved Kate to a private room, and he could see her. He followed the nurse up to the fourth floor.

Kate's room had a large window with a view of the northern cascades. With the clear blue sky, he could see the tip of Mt. Hood in the distance. The room came complete with a private bath, despite the fact that Kate would be bedridden for two days. In the corner, a large wood-paneled cupboard concealed her bag and had a counter for any personal items. The room was nicer than some hotels.

"Nice room. Maybe I should break my leg or something so I can get a room here," he teased.

Kate shook her head at her husband's attempt at wit.

"So everything went smoothly," he reported as if it were news. "How are you feeling?"

"Tired," Kate answered groggily.

George settled into a chair in the corner and watched as nurses busily set up IV bags and hooked up monitors to his wife. They attached a clip to her finger and put a cuff around her arm. They plugged in wires and punched buttons. Once they left, it was quiet again. Kate lay on the bed, her eyelids heavy.

"George. You don't have to stay here with me."

"But you'll be alone."

"I'll be fine. I'm going to sleep most of the afternoon. The drugs they gave me will ensure that. Why don't you go back home?"

"Are you sure?" He felt powerless. All he could do for her was sit and watch her. He did not want to leave her alone. What if she woke up? The only other time Kate had stayed overnight in the hospital had been when each of the kids were born. This was much more serious; surely, she needed him around for moral support.

"Yes, George. Please. I love you. But I know you'll go crazy if you hang out here all day. The nurses will take good care of me." Kate looked drowsy as she pled with him.

He didn't need any more convincing. Kate wanted him to leave. He would go. "All right, but I'll be back after dinner." He dodged the IV cords and kissed her forehead.

He paused at the doorway and watched as she drifted off to sleep. She was right. He would go crazy watching her lying there hooked to all the monitors. He didn't sit still well, especially in hospitals. Still he felt as if he had to do something, and now he knew what he was going to do.

Chapter 10

On Saturday morning, he arrived at the hospital promptly at eight just as he had all week. He had finally taken Rachel's advice and let Don Carter manage things at the store. Don had worked for George for nearly ten years. Faithfully, he attended to the lumberyard, never missing a delivery even during winter with a foot of snow on the ground. Don always came through for the customer and for George. Cautiously, he handed over the reins to the store, just in the mornings. It allowed George time to come in and visit Kate each morning and would allow him the freedom to care for her as she recuperated.

George pulled up to the covered drive at the main entrance. To accommodate Kate's fragile state, he drove Kate's Explorer which sat lower to the ground than his truck, making it easier for Kate to get in and out of. He arranged with the nurses to meet him at the entrance at eight. Kate couldn't wait to get home. She had healed so quickly from her surgery, Dr. Richards almost let her go Friday afternoon, but he felt it best to monitor her one more night.

Saturday morning, the nurses brought Kate down to the front entrance at five minutes to eight. An orderly met George at the door with Kate's belongings, her bag and two boxes with the flowers she had received while there. Moments later, a nurse pushed Kate out in a wheelchair.

"Take it easy," the nurse chastised as Kate tried to stand on her own.

George took Kate's hand and helped her lean against him as she stood and then slid into the passenger seat.

"Do I need to get one of these for the house?" George pointed to the empty wheelchair.

"I can walk," Kate said indignantly. "I'll just need help standing up and sitting down."

"Remember no stairs for at least a week," the nurse reminded.

"No stairs?" George looked to Kate questioningly as he helped her swing her legs inside.

"No stairs." Kate smiled with a half-raised brow. George knew that Kate had no intention of complying with the nurse's orders.

George thanked the nurses as he shut the passenger side door.

On the drive home, George caught her up on the events of the past week. The five days that she spent in the hospital seemed more like a month. There had not been an opportunity to be alone during the few times that George had come to visit. They hadn't spent any time just the two of them since the morning of her surgery. Now he had her all to himself once again. They talked about everything from the news to all the ads for the upcoming elections.

George pulled all the way into the garage to make it easier for Kate to get into the house. He cut the motor, jumped out quickly, and ran around to the passenger side door before she had a chance to open it. He knew she would try to be brave, but he was equally determined to help her heal.

She swung her legs out the door and tried to brace herself on the door when George stepped in. He forced her to use him for balance.

"Now, don't try to be brave," he scolded. "You just had surgery. Rachel helped me set up a bed for you on the couch."

Rachel had spent most of the evening before helping him move furniture to clear paths and set up everything she would need within arms' reach of the couch.

"I don't need to camp out on the couch. I'm perfectly capable of walking. I'm just a little slower than usual." She retracted her arms from him once she had her feet firmly on the ground.

"All right. No camping. But you still need to take it easy." George opened the door for her and then retrieved her bag. He rushed in front of her and opened the door between the mudroom and the kitchen.

"George. Don't fuss over me." He could hear the frustration in her voice.

"I wasn't." He felt like tying her to the couch for the next six days, but she would need to get up occasionally. He wanted her to heal, to reserve her strength for fighting the cancer, but he knew his wife, and she would not be a good patient.

"You are."

George set her bag by the door and allowed her to walk around. Rosita had come out the night before with Rachel and cleaned everything, and the ladies from her Bible study had arranged to bring a meal a day for the next week—all so she would follow doctor's orders and rest. But Kate found something to keep her busy. She rearranged the pillows that George and Rachel had laid out for her. Then she straightened the magazines and books on the table next to the couch. George watched for a moment, then went to the garage to retrieve her boxes of flowers and things. He knew that arranging them would give her something extra to do.

"Once you get settled. I have something to show you," he said when he returned to find her alphabetizing the books that Rachel had set out for her.

"What did you do?" Her tone sounded accusatory.

"You'll see." He motioned for her to follow him through the sliding door onto the deck. He took her hand and helped her down the back steps, taking each step one at a time. "Keep your eyes shut."

"I feel silly."

He waited until she stood firmly on the level grass before flipping the switch. "Okay. Open your eyes."

"Oh, George," she gasped.

Under the large ponderosa pine in the center of their yard, he had cut in a pond and built rock terraces up from it. The beautiful stone terraces stepped down gradually into a bubbling pond. Water cascaded down softly from one level to the next. George had gotten one of the regulars from the store to help him. In less than a week, he had created a tranquil getaway in their backyard. At one of the artsy shops in town, he'd been able to find two bronze statuettes similar to the ones he saw at the hospital. One was a child running with a net of some sort and the other a boy sitting with a branch as a fishing pole. That one he set over the edge of the pond. He also found a ceramic angel bending to touch the water.

"What do you think?" He grinned, proud of the work but more proud of the reaction in his wife.

"What do I think?" she repeated, wiping tears from her eyes. "I think it's the most beautiful thing I've ever seen. What got into you?"

"I saw the one at the hospital, and you always said you wanted one." He led her to the new log bench which was placed directly across the lawn from it. "See, from here we can watch the sunset together."

She rested her head on his shoulder. That was all the thanks he needed. He only hoped that they could watch sunsets together for a long, long time.

Chapter 11

By Friday, both of them suffered from cabin fever. Kate didn't handle the inactivity well. She was accustomed to a hectic pace, and when forced to rest, she became irritable and took her hostilities out on George. Whenever he tried to do something for her, she snapped at him. Whenever she wasn't able to do something herself because she couldn't reach or drive, she'd become moody. After six days of card games and rented movies, George was more than ready to take her to her follow-up appointment with Dr. Richards. He hoped the doctor would release her from her bed rest and let her get out a bit more. He wasn't sure who had it worse, him or Kate.

The appointment with Dr. Richards didn't take long. He examined her incision, took her blood pressure, and sent her on her way. He told her once more to take it easy and get lots of rest, but she had officially been released from bed rest and could even drive, if she felt the need; however, he preferred if she kept it to short distances for the time being.

From Dr. Richards's office, it was a short drive to the cancer center. But with all the construction around the hospital, it took a few passes in the parking lot to figure out where they needed to go. St. Charles was constructing a new neurological center where the main parking lot once was. Dust covered every square inch of remaining parking lot, making it difficult to distinguish the edges of the parking lot. A temporary chain-link fence marked the perimeter of the building site. Inside the fence, pallets of bricks and other building materials were left scattered around utility trailers advertising the contractors of choice for electrical, plumbing, and building construction. A narrow drive skirted the edge of the temporary fence and bordered a pond on the other side. George's full-size truck barely squeezed down the single-car-width drive which led to a small parking area for five or six cars. George gauged the size of the lot and the size of his truck.

"Hold on," he told Kate as he put the truck in reverse and looked over his shoulder. He backed up the entire length of the drive, running over at least one curb in the process. He spun the truck around 180 degrees in one fluid motion and quickly found a spot that had recently been abandoned.

"Was that really necessary?" Kate glanced at him disapprovingly.

"I could've parked down there, but we'd have been stuck until everyone left, so I turned around." George nodded toward the small lot below. He opened the door and got out, jogging around to the passenger side. "Now wait for me to help," George scolded.

"I'm not an invalid," Kate snapped back, trying to lower herself down. George got there in time to help her down.

"Yes, but Dr. Richards just said to take it easy."

"Yes. Easy, not helpless." She nudged him away and walked on her own.

They walked down the drive they had just attempted to drive down. All the construction going on around had pulverized the pavement. A black chain-link fence and cement retaining walls guarded the only area left unscathed by the construction, a small marsh and duck pond. Two geese nestled under the aspens which surrounded the pond. A third honked loudly, making its presence known.

George opened the door and helped Kate inside. He found her a chair in the small waiting room. A large fishbowl-like bay window made up a large portion of the waiting area with chairs arranged inside its angled windowed walls. George notified the receptionist of their arrival and was given the customary set of forms to fill out.

"You'd think they could just get a copy of the ones we filled out at the last doctor's office." George muttered, handing the clipboard to Kate. He wished he could help her, but he had no idea what insurance company they were with or what a subscriber was.

"They can't because of something called HIPPA." Kate smiled, filling in the blanks on the form like a pro.

"Do I want to know what a Hippo is?" George asked.

"Not really," Kate chuckled. She finished the forms quickly and handed them back to George who took them back to the receptionist.

A short time later, a nurse appeared to lead them back. George allowed Kate to hold on to him as she pulled herself up. He could see she was still in a lot of pain, whether or not she ever admitted it to him.

"Right this way." The nurse seemed extremely cheerful for such a dreary occupation. She led them down a small corridor the same blue-gray color as the waiting area. There were only a few exam rooms and two large doors with bright-yellow radioactive stickers on them. They were ushered into a small office with barely enough room to sit down. "Dr. Mayer will be with you in just a minute."

A short woman soon appeared in the doorway. "Hello, I'm Dr. Julie Mayer. I'm the radiation oncologist here at the cancer center." She had a slight accent. George could not tell if it was French or Canadian but didn't want to ask. She squeezed past George and Kate and found a way to her desk. "Dr. Gibson sent over your post-op MRI scans. It appears they got all the cancer out of the abdomen with surgery. Our primary concern is the tumors in your brain. As Dr. Gibson probably told you, they are inoperable where they are located. However, with our technology, we should be able to reduce the size of the tumors—"

"So when would we start?" Kate interrupted.

"As soon as Dr. Gibson releases you from post-op care," Dr. Mayer said.

"That should be a week from now. Then what's next."

"Um. We'll start with a simulation. We use that to mark where the treatment rays are to be directed. We used to tattoo people. Now we use plastic molds placed over them that are marked."

"And after that?"

"After that, you will start treatment. Come. I'll show you around. And afterward, if you still have questions, I can answer them at that time." Dr. Mayer led them down the hallway toward one of the doors with a large yellow radiation warning sticker.

In the simulation room, the doctor explained that the machine was actually a CT scanner that they used to align the patient and take scans to directly pinpoint where the beams of radiation would be directed during treatment. She demonstrated how they used boards and plastic objects to secure the patient to the table while trying to keep them as comfortable as possible. The doctor pulled out a plastic mesh mold that looked like a shell of a human body made from white plastic netting. "This is placed over the patient during the simulation and treatment to ensure that they don't move during treatment. Precision allows us to treat the tumor without causing any damage to the surrounding tissue. Even a slight shift can send the radiation beams to the wrong spot," the doctor explained.

A shiver crept up his spine at the thought of them placing it over Kate's head. It looked like something out of a horror film.

The doctor and technician went on to explain more about the procedure. "Then the CT scans are uploaded to our computers, and our dosologist creates a treatment program for you."

The doctor continued walking and led them to the other door with the radioactive sticker on it. "This is the treatment room. Treatment sessions only take a few minutes, but before the treatment can be administered, Kate will be secured to this table." She pushed a button, and the table rose up off the floor and moved diagonally toward a large machine that looked like something out of Star Trek. "These beams"—she went on and held a piece of plastic in a certain spot revealing a series of red laser beams.—"allow us to align the patient perfectly with the machine."

"What are those?" George nodded toward an open closet filled with what looked like miniature blue sleeping bags.

"Those are leg immobilizers," she answered without any detectable change in the inflection of her voice. She sounded like a tour guide for a theme park, ready with the answer to any obscure question. "They're used to secure a patient's legs to the table if they are having any kind of abdominal treatments." The doctor pushed another button, and the machine growled and clicked and beeped as it turned around to create a half tunnel around the table. "Each session only takes about fifteen minutes."

"Fifteen minutes? That's it?" George expected lengthy visits. Ned Peters had told him about his brother's treatment for prostate cancer. He actually had to stay in the hospital overnight during some of his chemo treatments.

"With radiation therapy, we pinpoint where the radiation goes and for short durations. Much like chemo, the goal is to kill the cancer cells while preserving the healthy cells around it. Too much exposure to radiation defeats that purpose."

"Oh." George nodded as if he understood, but he didn't—not really. He understood the part about wanting to kill the cancer. He followed as the doctor showed them some of the other areas. There were some couches for patients to lie on and watch videos. There was a large bulletin board area for resources to help with diet, supplements, even wigs and makeup. George tuned out for most of it.

"So we'll set up the simulation for Monday and hopefully start treatment the following Monday."

And so it began, their life of cancer treatment. Someone at the helm of a computer controlling laser beams and gamma rays was in charge of saving her life. But would it be enough?

Chapter 12

George managed to get all of Kate's appointments scheduled for nine o'clock throughout the duration of her treatment. By chance, the coveted time slot became available when a patient transferred to Portland to be near his family. For George, it was an answer to prayer. The nine-o'clock appointment time gave him the opportunity to check on things at the store before driving into Bend. That way, he could still maintain a degree of control over the store while taking care of Kate.

Monday morning, he took her in to start their new routine. The simulation appointment took nearly two hours, but the nurse assured him that treatment visits rarely lasted more than twenty or thirty minutes from the time they walked in until the time they left.

Each day, Kate grew visibly weaker. Dr. Mayer explained that the weakness was normal; as her cells were killed off by the radiation, it took extra energy for Kate's body to repair itself. Another noticeable side effect, her hair had started to fall out in patches. She arranged for Rachel to come over and shave her head. Soon afterward, she began wearing hats, stocking hats, baseball caps, scarves—all the time.

"At least I don't have to waste time shampooing or drying my hair anymore," she had joked with one of the ladies from her Bible study.

"If it's good enough for Sampson…" she had commented to another. Kate hid her vulnerability masterfully, beneath a facade of strength and independence. But it bothered Kate more than she let on.

Mother's Day followed her second week of treatment. Normally, George, Steve, and Michael took their wives to brunch after church services, but the radiation treatment produced a constant headache that sometimes induced nausea. The idea of going out to a nice restaurant with Kate in her current condition seemed pointless. Besides, George suspected, she would feel self-conscious with the scarves and hats. So instead of going to brunch, the kids and grandchildren all came over to the house after church. George brought brunch to them. One of the new carpenters in town, Paul, an older gentleman from back east somewhere, had mentioned that he was a classically trained chef. George arranged to let Paul in before church, and when they returned, he had prepared culinary marvels George could not believe. At least, by having the brunch at home, Kate could retreat to her room if she needed to.

"Do I look all right?" She adjusted her hat slightly.

"You look fine," George answered without even giving so much as a cursory glance. "They're not coming over to see how you look."

"It's the first time the grandchildren would see me since I lost my hair, George.'

His first response was to say "so what," but he knew better. "They love their Nana no matter what." He kissed her on the cheek and disappeared into the kitchen.

Rachel and Steve were first to arrive bearing gifts and flowers. "Happy Mother's Day!" Braden and Jenna brought a basket of flowers and gifts over to her.

"Where are my hugs?" Braden and Jenna had stopped five feet away from her and held the baskets out at arms' length.

"Mom said we couldn't. We might hurt you," Braden announced, looking to his mother for confirmation.

Kate shot her daughter a searing glance. "It's all right. Just hug me gently." She reached her arms out to them.

Rachel nodded, and the kids snuggled up for a hug and handed Kate the baskets. Inside, Kate found handmade cards from Braden and Jenna and two scarves that she had eyed at Saks during their shopping spree.

"You shouldn't have." Kate sniffed back tears as she held up one of the brightly colored silk scarves.

George whistled as he entered the room. "Where'd you get those?"

Rachel looked nervously at Steve before answering. "Um. I bought them from Saks."

"As in Saks Fifth Avenue? The Saks Fifth Avenue?" George mock choked.

"Yes, Dad. Mom and I saw them when we went shopping just before Easter."

"You went to Saks?" George looked questioningly at his wife.

"Yes. They have one in Portland," Kate stated matter-of-factly.

"Oh." George walked over and sat next to her. "So are you going to give Rachel her present?"

"I want to wait and give Rachel and Nikki their presents at the same time," Kate said quietly.

A few minutes later Michael, Nikki, and Connor walked in the back door.

"Hey! Happy Mom's Day!" Michael exclaimed.

"Michael," Kate sang out.

"These are for you." He held up a hanging basket filled with dangling annuals in pinks and purples.

"Thank you," Kate said adoringly.

"And"—he grinned mischievously—"if you'll follow me, just for a second."

George offered her help, but Kate grabbed ahold of Michael's hand and pulled up off the couch. Michael led them to the garage. In the middle of the floor sat a large cedar chest with intricate carvings adorning the outside.

"Oh, Michael." Kate shook her head as her face grew red with tears. "How did you… This must have cost a fortune."

"I made it myself." He beamed, rocking back and forth on his heels.

"No," Kate gasped in disbelief. She ran her hand over the top of the chest. Each grandchild's name had been carved into a block with pictures identifying each of them—trees and deer for Braden, butterflies and flowers for Jenna, and trucks and tractors for Connor. The three snowcapped peaks had been chiseled into the front of the chest inlayed with different woods and stains to enhance the intricate lines of the mountains.

"You made this?" George questioned, inspecting the box's workmanship.

"Don't act too surprised, Dad. I work in a lumberyard. I've used a few tools in my lifetime," Michael shot back with heavy sarcasm.

"I just never knew." George was stunned. His aging adolescent son, Michael, was a master woodworker.

"Yeah. Well, there's a lot you don't know about me." Michael's tone was biting. He turned toward his mother. "So you like it, Mom?"

"Like it? I love it." She sniffed back tears. "I love you, son."

"I love you too." He leaned down and gently hugged her. "But enough of this gushy stuff. Let's go eat."

Michael led the way back inside. George waited for Kate who lingered by her newly prized possession. George still had a hard time believing that his son had made the box. Kate slowly turned to go inside, and George followed.

The breakfast bar in the kitchen had been cleared and converted into a buffet line. George's carpenter friend had treated them as if they had gone to a five-star restaurant. Pastries, eggs, crepes, salads, roast beef, and decadent desserts lined the countertop.

After they finished eating, Kate excused herself and returned with two matching boxes for Rachel and Nikki. She had purchased matching necklaces, gold, with heart-shaped lockets with the word *Mom* engraved and precious stones on the outside.

The festivities of the day quickly caught up with Kate. The kids, sensing Kate's need for rest, packed up soon after brunch ended. Kate waited only moments after they left before she went upstairs to lie down. George sent his friend on his way and started cleaning up the mess.

*****

Later that evening, Kate and George sat and watched the sunset. He was growing accustomed to their quiet times in the evening. Instead of watching television or reading a book, Kate would go sit on her bench, and he would come out and sit beside her. She never wanted to talk, just sit and watch the sky. He was amazed that each night, a different palette adorned the heavens. He'd never taken the time to notice before.

"I want to go to the lake house for Memorial Day," Kate announced abruptly, breaking the silence.

"Are you sure? Maybe we should check with Dr. Mayer or Dr. Gibson or something.'

"No! We don't need to check. By then, my treatment will nearly be complete. I want to go," Kate argued.

"Just the two of us?"

"Actually, I was thinking we should take the kids too.'

"But Kate—" he began.

"No buts, George. I really want to do this. We have every year before. This year should be no different."

She had clearly decided, and there would be no changing her mind. It was far easier to pass new legislation than change Kate's mind once her mind was made up about something. So they were going to the lake house for Memorial Day weekend.

Chapter 13

Kate's family introduced George to Odell Lake while they were still dating. Her father, Dr. Andrew Woodard, discovered Odell Lake when it was largely an untouched wilderness area. One of his patients, a cross-country ski instructor, had told him about it. One look was all it took for him to fall in love.

The Cascade mountain range housed dozens of lakes. Each of them shared some similar qualities such as water temperature, types of vegetation, and fish. But each lake also retained some features that made it distinctive from the rest. Odell Lake was no exception—five miles of sapphire-blue water surrounded by deep-green forests with Diamond Peak standing sentinel in the background.

The scenic views and superb fishing inspired Dr. Woodard to buy a house on the lake back in the mid-1960s. The house, more of a rustic cabin, had been built in the 1940s and added on to here and there. Every year, Kate's family spent holidays and at least two weeks every summer at their house at the lake. Each year, Dr. Woodard tried to take on one area of the house with help from local carpenters. Eventually, he took it from rustic to cozy. Kate told endless stories of when her father taught her to fish for the ever-elusive Mackinaw and the scrumptious Kokanee. Kate's mother had taught her every possible method to cook kokanee, including Kate's signature dish, Stuffed Kokanee.

When Kate's mother died, her father spent most of his time at the house on Odell Lake. He closed down his medical practice and stayed even during the winter months. He claimed that he fished nearly every day, but George suspected he merely wallowed in his misery alone. Kate's father followed his wife to the grave only two years after her passing. Kate had said he died of a broken heart. It wasn't until recently that George could fully understand that sentiment. George shunned her attempts to talk about what he would do when or if she loses her battle with cancer. "It wouldn't be fair to the kids and grandkids to lose both of us," she had said. *Fair?* What was fair about any of this?

George shook free of his downward spiral. He promised Kate he wouldn't focus on the disease or the treatment this weekend. It would be a cancer-free weekend. As they pulled up to the house, he made mental note of repairs that were needed. The front porch sagged at one end and needed to be jacked up and properly set. The shutter on the bedroom window hung cockeyed off its hinge. It would probably need new hinges. And the roof was missing a few shingles that would need to be replaced. He knew the list would continue to grow once they went inside.

He cut wide as he came up to the house to give enough room to back the boat in. Later, he would drive down to Shelter Cove and launch the boat. He backed the truck and boat into its spot effortlessly. Years ago, he had cleared the underbrush and made a parking area wide enough that all the kids could park without blocking any of the cars. Steve pulled up beside him. George used his foot to push aside debris on the path to the door. He unlocked the storm screen and front door, propping them open. Stale musty air hung in the house like fog. George walked directly to the sliding glass door and opened it to allow air to move freely through the house. Then they began the process of unloading the weekend's provisions.

"Are there really bears around here, Grandpa?" Jenna asked fearfully as they began unloading the contents of the truck.

"Yep. There sure are."

"Are they big scary bears like on Brother Bear?"

"No. Those bears live in Alaska. The bears around here are littler." He tried to remember how to explain things to a three-year-old.

"Oh. So they won't try to eat us?" Jenna asked wide-eyed.

"Naw. They like huckleberries, so they won't be around here until later this summer," he lied. He knew some bears came down to the lake for fish and grasses from early spring until late fall. But if they were lucky, the bears would stay away all weekend and not frighten poor little Jenna.

"Whew," Jenna said dramatically and wiped her hand across her brow for emphasis. "Braden had me worried there for a minute."

George just smiled. Maybe Kate was right. A weekend at the lake would be good for all of them. He grabbed the last two boxes of sodas and took them in the house. Inside, Rachel was busily putting groceries away and getting after the kids to either stay inside or outside, not continue opening the sliding door to the deck. George found the last remaining clear space on the counter and set the boxes down.

"Think you brought enough?" George remarked sarcastically.

"You did say that Michael is coming too. Didn't you?" Rachel replied.

"Yeah. He has to wait for Nikki to get off work, and then they'll head down."

"Well, then you may just have to go to the store for more," Rachel teased.

"We'll send Michael if it comes to that." George played along. He looked around the kitchen and living room area as if missing something. "Where's your mother?"

"She went to lie down for a bit. She had a headache. Probably from the drive," Rachel said, seemingly unconcerned.

"Okay. While she naps, I'm going to run down to Shelter Cove and see how the fishing has been." George wanted to check on Kate, but at the same time, he didn't want to disturb her. Besides, Kate was the one who wanted to come down here and go fishing. So it was his duty to go find out how the catch had been.

"Okay, Dad. See you in a few hours," Rachel said snidely.

*****

George drove down West Odell Lake Road into the Shelter Cove parking lot. The Shelter Cove Resort had been part of Odell Lake as far back as the 1920s. Even after all the time he'd spent at the lake, George knew very little about its history. He knew some of the buildings dated back before the 1920s but heard conflicting stories about their origin, not that it mattered. Some people argued that it started as a logging camp, others talked about the ski lodge that had been there but burnt down years before. All George knew was that Odell was the best place for kokanee fishing in Oregon.

George bought tackle and ice at Shelter Cove for over thirty-five years now. Not much had changed. Over the years, the resort changed hands a couple of times. They built a lodge with condos a few years back, but the rest looked exactly as it had for years. The rustic log building known to all as the general store still looked in need of repair, with the old screen squeaking upon every entrance and exit.

"Hey, Mac," George said as he entered. The old screen door screeched loudly behind him.

"Hey, George. How's it going?"

"Can't complain." He really didn't want to explain Kate's health issues to Mac. Actually, he found it comforting to talk to someone who didn't know about Kate's condition, someone who would talk to him about normal things like fishing and sports.

"So did you bring the whole clan this time?"

"Yep." He almost said except for David but didn't. Mac knew. And it didn't need any attention. George looked around the small interior of the store. Everything looked exactly the same as the summer before and the summer before that. Tackle hung on the walls, three aisles were stocked with a myriad of dry goods, and refrigerated cases filled with beverages and ice lined the back wall. An espresso bar had been added in the 1990s when the coffee fad exploded in the northwest. Above the coffee counter hung trophies of record-sized fish caught in the lake. George scanned over them looking for any new ones. Intuitively, his gaze stopped at the large mackinaw caught July 4, 1984, weighing forty pounds eight ounces, caught by David Patterson. George remembered the day as if it were yesterday.

They had gone out just before sundown, trolling for kokanee. The kokes were deep that day due to the heat, down around ninety pulls or so. David had the lucky pole that day and had nearly limited out when he had a hard hit. George slowed the motor as David struggled to reel in the fish. It fought so fiercely that the tip of David's pole bent nearly to the waterline. George tried to help, but David had insisted on landing the fish on his own. It took all the strength David's scrawny twelve-year-old frame could muster, but he reeled that fish all the way up to the boat. And what a beauty it was. The biggest mackinaw George had ever seen. Word spread quickly when they pulled into the marina, and Ol' Mac came down and measured and weighed it for the official records. When they cut it open, they found a whole kokanee inside. George figured that David must have had that little kokanee on his line when the mackinaw ate the little fish. David held the record of the biggest mackinaw caught in the lake until 1996 when someone caught a forty-one pounder. Yet there it still hung on the wall.

"So how's the bite?" George asked, shaking free from the nostalgia.

"They've been catching kokes over by the slide at around forty pulls. And off the point, they've been nailing them jigging. Same over in West Bay."

"Kate's been chomping at the bit to go trolling," George commented.

"Then you need to get some small silver flashers and a pink wedding ring." Mac walked over to the wall of tackle and began picking out some packets.

"All right. I'll take two setups and might as well throw in some beer cans too," George commented, looking over the wall of gear.

"Lures or the real ones?" Mac laughed as he said it.

"Lures of course," George said flatly. He suspected Mac used that same tired pun on everyone. "And I'll need two bags of ice and some white corn."

Mac punched numbers into the register then said, "All right then, that'll be twenty-nine dollars and seventy-five cents."

George pulled the money from his pocket. Mac handed him a plain brown paper bag and the two bags of ice. "I need to unload the boat. Can I still park the trailer down there by the launch?"

"Sure, just keep it roadside from the new lodge." Mac pointed in the direction of the new lodge.

"Thanks." George grabbed his goods, pushed the screen door open with his hip, and carried them out to the truck. He set the paper bag on the passenger seat and the ice in a cooler in the back. He drove around the circular drive and down the road to the launch. In one deft motion, he pulled the truck up at an angle across the road and backed the boat trailer straight down into the water. He launched the boat and parked the trailer where Mac had told him. He untied the boat from the dock and pointed it toward West Bay. Once out in open water he tested the motor at different speeds. As he got closer to the house, he cut the main engine and dropped in the trolling motor, a small outboard motor that resembled a lawn mower engine. There was nothing worse than getting all set up to fish only to find mechanical issues, so he always checked things out thoroughly before they left the dock to go fishing. He puttered along at two different speeds for about five minutes and double-checked the neutral position. Then he pulled the motor up and started the main engine again.

Serenity Bay sat on the northwest corner of the lake above Trapper Creek. Several houses lined the shore beyond the marshy grass area. For decades, three of the houses, including the one owned by Kate's family, had shared a dock. But years of neglect and one good winter storm finally sank the main dock. Some of its remnants still littered the beach. A software developer from Seattle bought the house next door and had designs on building a new dock with a swimming platform. On more than one occasion, he mentioned his grand design which also included rebuilding the house there. But in order to do this, he hoped to buy their house. Kate refused to sell.

George made a sweeping loop and headed back toward Shelter Cove. He nosed the boat into the marina and cut the engine. He drifted the boat over to the shore side of the dock and tied it tightly. George would get Michael to help him with gear after dinner. While Michael hated fly fishing, he loved trolling for kokanee, just like Kate. Their trips to Odell were the only time he could connect with Michael on fishing. David had been more like George. He loved the sport so thoroughly that he would take any chance to go fishing. George could remember when David was around eight or so; he would come down to the docks with a rod and a bucket of worms and sit and fish for hours. Occasionally, he caught a small rainbow trout, but mainly he caught small-mouthed bass. He'd bring his catch back to the house brimming with pride. Then when he wasn't looking, Kate would tactfully discard the small fish. George had always thought that eventually, he and David would get past their differences and be able to fish together.

George double-checked the boat and took the keys. He got in his truck and maneuvered the trailer between two large conifer trees and unhitched the trailer before driving back up to the house.

*****

"Something smells good," George commented as he walked in through the slider. The stale and musty air had been replaced with the aroma of freshly baked cookies—chocolate chip if George's nose was working correctly.

"Over there." Rachel nodded with her head toward a plate of cookies on the counter.

George grabbed two from the plate. "Where's your mom?"

"She went for a walk," Rachel said as she pulled another sheet of cookies from the oven.

"By herself?" George dropped the cookies and started toward the door.

"Of course not," Rachel said quickly. "I convinced her that the grandkids needed to go with her, and Steve went to protect Jenna from *the bears*."

Just then, the kids came bursting through the front door. "Grandpa. Grandpa. Can we go for a ride in the boat?" Jenna jumped up and down excitedly.

"Grandpa. Grandpa. We saw a deer with horns," Braden shouted out over his sister.

"In a little while," George answered Jenna first before responding to Braden. "Was it a big one?"

"Yeah. And I talked to it. I said 'Wha wha.'" Braden talked really fast and really loud.

"Wow. Did it talk back?" George acted really interested in Braden's story. Having the kids there reminded him of times when his kids were young, and Kate's father had been the Grandpa listening to the stories.

"No, it just ate some leaves off some bushes." Braden continued, "Grandma said that the does would be having their babies soon, and if we're lucky, we might see one."

"That would be something." George was just about to ask him another question when Braden spotted the cookies.

"Cookies! Mom, can I have one?"

"After you wash your hands. I'm certain you played with more than leaves on your walk." Rachel nodded in the direction of the bathroom down the hall. Braden and Jenna scampered off obediently.

"So, Kate, did you enjoy your walk?" George walked over and kissed her on the cheek. He could feel the chill on her cheek from a hike in the fresh mountain air.

"Mmm, very much so," she said as she took off her gloves and fleece jacket. She left the matching fleece hat on as she hung her jacket on a wooden peg board by the front door. "It was absolutely breathtaking. We hiked up past the railroad tracks almost to Midnight Lake. All the trees are budding, the wildflowers are starting to pop out, and the huckleberry bushes are covered in pink and white flowers."

George wished he would have gone. He didn't take walks with her as often as he should. She loved to hike. She went with Rachel every chance they got, and he'd only gone with them a handful of times. There were so many things he'd never taken the time to do with her. He couldn't remember how many times she'd asked him to get away for the weekend, to the beach or just over to Portland for a night on the town. He'd always found excuses not to. Not anymore. Once the doctor gave him the all clear, he'd take her out for a night on the town that she'd never forget. He'd do the works—a night at the Hilton and dinner at Jake's or maybe even McCormick & Schmicks, and he'd even suffer through whatever opera they could get tickets to. He looked at her with bright pink spots on her cheeks from the chill outside.

"Sounds wonderful."

"Oh, it was. But now I'm ready for one of those cookies and a nice cup of tea." She headed toward the kitchen.

Once she'd retrieved her cookies and tea, Kate settled into her father's favorite chair, a soft brown leather chair right next to the window, looking out over the lake. A childlike glow adorned her face as she nestled into the chair. Now he understood why Kate had insisted on coming here.

Chapter 14

Moonlight trickled through the blinds, casting shadows on the wall and illuminating Kate's slumbering face. George lay awake and listened to Kate's gentle breathing, her body still and peaceful. He watched intently the soft curves of her face and her hairless head, a near perfect sphere. Only at night did she dare to remove the hats and the scarves that protected her from her insecurity. He felt honored that she shared her vulnerability with him alone. The past few weeks, anxiety and worry had plagued him at night, keeping him from sleep. He trusted the doctors were doing all they could; he just didn't trust the cancer. And he got the distinct feeling that Kate wasn't telling him all there was to know.

He rolled back to his side. The bright-red numbers on the clock glowed three thirty. In a couple of hours, he would take Michael and Steve out fishing. Neither of them were avid fishermen; in fact, their trips to Odell were the only time either of them actually put a line in the water. George's love of fishing was often overshadowed by the dread of having to teach these two the basics every time they went out. When Steve and Michael came along, he couldn't just sit back and enjoy fishing, he had to bait the hooks, check the gear, and net the fish all while trying to steer the boat. Two hours with them, and he would be exhausted.

When the alarm rang at five, he got out of bed eagerly. Not much could keep him from a chance to fish. Hurriedly, he dressed without turning on the lights and then snuck out to the kitchen. He brewed a pot of coffee and filled the thermoses before either of his two companions showed any signs of life.

He dragged the two younger men down to the docks as they wearily followed. With the gear in the boat, they shoved away from the dock at six o'clock on the dot. George navigated toward the slide on the far side of the lake. The slide was an area of about five hundred yards or so where the land had slid down into the lake leaving behind a shale gray trail into the water. Beneath it, the water dropped to a depth of about eighty feet, and a cold current flowed through. George caught some of his very best fish there.

Fishing went slowly. George had to monitor the motor and bait the hooks. Steve had only been out with them once or twice and had to be told when he actually had a bite at the end of his line. Michael acted as if he simply didn't care, and George caught him dozing off once with pole in hand. After only an hour on the water and only five fish in the boat, most of which were caught by Steve, Michael complained of being cold and wanted to go in. George felt slightly chilled himself, but true fishermen stuck out foul weather. But when the wind kicked up and the white caps formed on the lake, George turned the boat back for Shelter Cove.

*****

After the morning out on the lake with the boys, George tried to convince Kate that it was simply too cold out on the water. By noon, the temperature still hadn't risen above forty, and the wind kicked up off the point. He didn't want Kate catching a cold, not with everything else.

"What do you think? I'm some sort of invalid? Some eighty-year-old woman?" Kate said indignantly.

"No. But in your condition—" George started.

"In my condition." Kate's eyes narrowed.

"Kate." He elevated the tone in his voice slightly. "You know full well what I mean. The last thing you need right now is to catch a cold or something."

"I'm not going to catch cold," she stated matter-of-factly. "I've bundled myself up as if we were going snowshoeing above Bachelor. I will be plenty warm."

George just shrugged in agreement. Arguing with her was futile. She had made up her mind, and now he was merely delaying their fishing expedition. However, he did insist on driving down to the docks instead of walking. Kate conceded to that point. George pulled the truck back up to the house and helped Kate into the cab. He saw a grimace cross her face as she lifted herself up into the seat. She was still in pain, though she'd never admit it.

As George pulled the boat out away from the dock, Kate nestled in the rear seat all bundled up in layers of clothing. He putted slowly out from the marina and then turned to the right and headed for Breezy Point, aptly named for the wind that kicked up off the lake. He picked up speed, not too much to avoid the up and down jarring as they slammed against the water. After ten minutes of mid throttle, George slowed the boat to a trolling speed and removed the poles still set up from the morning outing. He baited the hook for Kate and handed her the pole.

"How far out?" She asked like an old pro.

George glanced at the screen on the fish finder and read the depth where the little black fish icons showed up. "Looks to be between forty and fifty pulls."

Kate loosened the drag on the reel and began pulling and counting. Once she hit forty-five, she tightened the drag on the reel and sat back, pole gripped tightly in her hands. George counted off his depth and set his pole in the pole holder so he could steer as they trolled. He watched Kate soaking the sun that had just peeked out from behind the clouds. She beamed, just as if she were expecting a new grandchild. The fact that Kate could find contentment in trolling for kokanee was just one of the many reasons he loved her.

They had trolled for five or ten minutes before Kate broke the silence. "George?"

"Yes, Kate." He sat upright and checked her line to see if she had a fish on.

"I don't want you to worry about me." There was a quiet sincerity in her voice.

"What's that supposed to mean?" George didn't like where this conversation was headed.

"I mean if I don't get better…if this thing beats me."

"That's a helluva thing to say. You're going to beat this Kate," he snapped back. He hadn't meant to sound so stern.

"I'm just saying if I don't. I want you to know that I'm at peace with it. I know that may seem strange, but it's true. If my time is up, then so be it. I know that I'll go on to a better place. But I want you to know that and to go on living. If I die, I want you—"

"Kate—" He didn't want her to finish.

"No. Listen, George." Tears glistened in her eyes. "I don't want you to be like my father and give up just because I've… It wouldn't be fair to Rachel or Michael or me. If my time has come, it's my time to go home." She grew quiet and turned her head as she fought off tears.

George didn't know how to respond. He stared off into the horizon, sensing that Kate was through discussing it. He hated talking about death and dying, particularly when she was so fragile. They didn't talk about it, not earnestly. They'd casually mention the *what ifs*, but now in the midst of her treatment, it was a very real possibility, and he didn't want to consider the *what ifs*. Her comments made him wonder though. Did she know something about her condition that she wasn't telling him?

"Fish on." Kate practically screamed with delight. Her excitement broke the tense silence. George stopped the motor and grabbed the net. She quickly jerked the pole to set the hook and feverishly reeled the line in. He checked his line to make sure Kate wouldn't get caught on it. Then he peered over the side of the boat, and as Kate continued to reel, he saw the flashes of silver coming to the surface.

"There he is." George pointed to the fish writhing on the line. George moved past Kate and deftly scooped the fish into the net. "Whew. Look at that beauty," he said as he laid the net on the floor and held the line to remove the hook.

"Let's see." Kate peered over George's shoulder.

He looked back and caught her grinning from ear to ear just like the old Kate. He loosed the fish from the net and held it, putting one finger through the gill. "Looks like about sixteen maybe seventeen inches. Nice fish."

"Did you expect anything less?" Kate gloated.

"Not from you, my dear." He dropped the fish into the cooler and sat back down. He baited her hook, threw the line off the side, and started the trolling once again.

They fished until two and caught six fish. Kate landed five to George's one. When the wind picked up again, and the water got choppy jarring the boat, George turned the boat back for shore. Kate appeared relieved as they headed in.

*****

When they got to the house, Kate looked paler than usual. "I think I'll lie down for a bit," she said and headed directly to the bedroom without taking time to tell her tall fishing tales.

George took the fish outside to clean them. He knew Kate would want to eat a couple of them for dinner. There was nothing in the world like Kate's stuffed kokanee, and the fresher the fish, the better the dinner. He proceeded down to the fish cleaning station below the deck.

"Hi, Grandpa." He heard a voice and looked up to see Jenna peering down between the pickets on the rail. "Did ya catch some fishies?"

"A couple." He smiled. "Where's your mama?"

"Over there." Jenna pointed to the corner of the deck.

"Okay. Tell her I'm cleaning supper," George said and returned to the station. He heard Jenna's pattering feet above him. Then he heard a bloodcurdling scream. He dropped the fish in the sink and ran out from beneath the deck as quickly as possible to see what had happened.

"Shoo." He heard Rachel say. "Shoo."

He ran around the side of the house and up the steps onto the deck. He was greeted by Steve and Michael who were also running to see what the screaming was all about.

"What's all the commotion?" George asked.

"Beats me," said Michael as they hurried around the corner. There they found Rachel holding her arms in front of Jenna and

Braden as a young osprey flapped its wings and walked across the deck.

"What the...?"

George looked at the bird, its talons sticking in the pitted wood on the deck. With its wings extended, George would estimate the bird to be three or four months old, just getting ready to fly and leave its mother's nest. He extended his arms to stop the other two. If they caught the bird, the mother wouldn't help it, and it would die. They would have to find a way to help it off the deck.

"Rachel, take the kids inside," he commanded. The bird was frightened, and George wasn't sure what it might do to the kids. He heard the sliding glass door close.

Slowly, he crept along the rail of the deck, trying not to startle the young bird too much. Obviously frightened, the young osprey flapped its large wings attempting to fly, without much success. If he could get close enough, perhaps he could inspect the bird's wing to see if it had injured itself. But if he left any human scent on the young bird, the mother would never accept it back in her nest. Cautiously, George watched as the bird hopped along the deck and flapped its large wings, knocking over small plants in its way. It hopped onto one of the deck chairs at the table. When it flapped its wings again, it knocked some playing cards from the top of the table. In the process, it lodged one card in the feathers at the tip of its wing.

Now he needed professional help. The card would need to be removed before the bird took off. He snuck back down the steps and ran around and went inside. Michael, Steve, Rachel, and all the kids were pressed up against the windows along the deck watching the bird.

"Rachel, can you call down to Shelter Cove and tell Mac what's going on up here. See if he can get someone to come and rescue the bird."

"Sure." Rachel picked up her cell phone from the kitchen counter and began dialing.

George glanced down the hall and thought of Kate. She had said she wanted to rest, but he knew she'd hate to miss seeing this.

He walked down the short hallway and tapped lightly on the door, hoping she hadn't fallen asleep yet.

"Kate," he said softly as he opened the door and peeked his head in. When he saw Kate, he nearly fell through the door. Her eyes had rolled up, and she was flopping on the bed like the fish they had caught earlier that day.

"Rachel," he yelled as loudly as he could. When Rachel didn't appear, he took a few steps out into the hall and yelled again. "Rachel, come here."

"Dad. I already called Mac and—" Rachel said lightly as she began to enter the door. When she saw Kate on the bed, she squealed. "Dad, what happened?"

"I don't know, but get me your phone. Quick."

"It's right here," Rachel said, pulling the phone from her jeans pocket.

George snatched the phone and frantically dialed 9-1-1. "Rachel, please sit here with her," he said as the phone rang.

After only two rings, a voice on the other end answered. "Emergency dispatch. How may I assist you?"

"My wife is shaking... She has cancer, and we're at a fishing cabin. She needs help immediately," George rambled.

"Sir. Sir." The voice remained calm. "I need you to answer some questions for me."

George took a breath, trying to calm down. "Yes, what do you need to know?"

"First, where exactly are you?"

"We're at a fishing cabin at Odell Lake a mile off Highway 58." George tried to answer calmly. He tried to remember the exact address in case she asked.

He heard the tapping of a keyboard in the background. "All right. Your wife, tell me what is going on."

"She's shaking, and every so often, she flops on the bed. Her eyes are rolled back." He trembled as he said the words.

"Okay, sir. Then she is on the bed?"

"Yes."

"Good. Is she wearing a scarf or anything tight near her neck?"

"No."

"Good. Approximately how long has she been shaking?"

"I don't know. I just came back to check on her and I saw her and I called you."

"Does she have a history of epilepsy?"

"No."

"Is this her first seizure?"

"Yes, as far as I know."

"How old is your wife, sir?"

"What's that got to do with anything? Are you sending someone to help her or not?" George snapped, frustrated. He looked down at Kate who had stopped flopping but was still shaking as if she had the chills.

"Sir, I have notified AirLife, and they are preparing to come meet you. I am getting the background information they will need when they get there. So could you please tell me how old your wife is?"

"She's fifty-seven," George answered, subdued. "And she has stopped flopping now, but she's still shaking like she's cold."

"All right. You said she had cancer. Has she received treatment?"

"Yes. Um, she just finished a round of radiation treatments in Bend."

"Then you are from Bend?"

"Sisters," he corrected.

"Okay. And her name."

"Kate—umm, Katherine Patterson."

"Okay, sir. I have Flight Captain Bill Conklin on the phone. Go ahead."

"Hello, sir. I'm Bill Conklin, and I'll be flying to meet you. I understand you are located at Odell Lake."

"Yes. We are."

"Has your wife stopped convulsing?"

George glanced over at Kate to make sure she hadn't started shaking again. "Yes, she has."

"Do you have a vehicle in which she could lay flat while you drive?"

"Yes, I could lay her in the backseat of my pickup."

"Good," Bill said flatly. "I'd like you to wait fifteen minutes after her last convulsion ended and then carefully move her to your truck. Due to the tree cover around the lake, there is no safe place for us to land. I would like you to meet us at Crescent Lake Junction. It's about ten minutes from your location. There is an old airstrip there where we can land safely."

"Okay. Where exactly is the airstrip?" George snapped his fingers to get Rachel's attention. He motioned for a pen and paper. She grabbed a note pad and pen from the bedside table and handed them to him.

"It's on the west side of the highway. You will see it as you drive by, and then there will be a turnoff. Meet us at the old fire department building. It looks like an old barn."

"Okay." George jotted down the directions in case he forgot during the pandemonium.

"Okay, Mr. Patterson, we will see you in about thirty minutes."

George hung up the phone and looked down at Kate. Her face looked pale as newly fallen snow, and she breathed heavy like after a long run. George let his fingers graze over her face as he sat on the bed next to her.

"Well, what did they say?" Rachel asked impatiently.

"I need to wait a few minutes and then take her to Crescent Lake Junction." He felt as if the entire world were moving in slow motion. "Can you and Steve clear out the back seat of my truck? I need to lay her down back there."

"Sure thing." Rachel nodded her head and left the room. It was evident that she was frightened. George couldn't blame her, but Rachel always managed to keep a level head, and he needed that more than ever right now.

After Rachel left the room, George tucked the blue-and-green quilt around Kate. Kate loved that quilt. Her mother had made it for her when she was ten years old. It stayed here at the cabin.

"Okay, Dad. Truck's all ready," Rachel said as she reentered the room.

"Thanks. Can I take your cell with me?" George still held the small phone in his hand. His phone didn't have service until thirty miles south of Bend.

"Sure. We have Steve's too, so go ahead. Just keep us informed." Rachel hugged her dad.

George wrapped the quilt around Kate and lifted her from the bed. The cancer had taken its toll on her. She weighed practically nothing. George carried her down the hall and out the front door. Steve helped him slide her onto the back seat.

"Is Grandma sick again?" Jenna asked her mother.

"Yes, she is. And we need to pray for her to get better." Rachel held her daughter tight against her as they stood in the doorway and watched.

George closed the rear door on his truck and climbed in the driver's seat. Without hesitation, he started the engine and pulled away.

*****

The drive to Crescent Junction took eleven minutes, but for George, it seemed like two hours. Every time he got behind a vehicle driving less than sixty miles per hour, he'd pound his fist on the steering wheel in frustration.

"Come on, slowpoke," he muttered. "The gas pedal is the long skinny one on the right." Still, he made it there before the AirLife helicopter arrived. He pulled up to the building just as he had agreed upon with the flight captain.

George watched Kate in the back seat. She slept peacefully. Her breathing had returned to normal, but she still looked very pale.

He turned off the engine and stepped out of the truck. The airfield was quiet. The tall lodge pole pines that lined either side muffled the sound of cars on the highway. George used his hand as a visor and searched the sky for any indication that the helicopter was on its way. What if this isn't the place? He began to panic, until he saw a small red dot descending from the sky and heard the distinctive chop-chop sound of the helicopter blades. A moment later, dust flew all around him as the helicopter started to land. George stood back with his arms over his eyes to protect them from the dust and debris scattered by the rotors. He watched as two people, a man and a woman in blue jumpsuits, emerged from the side of the helicopter. They sprinted over to him.

"Mr. Patterson?" One of them yelled over the noise of the chopper.

George nodded and led them to Kate. The woman unwrapped Kate and found her wrist. She began taking her pulse and checking Kate out. She nodded to the man with her, and he ran back to the helicopter and retrieved a gurney. While he was running, the woman took Kate's temperature and listened through a stethoscope.

Slowly, they moved Kate onto the gurney and then loaded her into the helicopter without wasting a single second.

"We'll meet you at St. Charles in Bend." The man yelled over the noise of the helicopter.

"Can I go with you?" George yelled back.

"Not enough room," the man yelled back. "We'll take good care of her." The man ran around to the other side of the helicopter and got in.

The force of the blades blew rocks around George as he watched it ascend slowly skyward and then fly quickly out of sight over the trees. He would have to trust that she would make it there safely. He wanted to fall to his knees right there in the abandoned airstrip, but he didn't have the time for that. Kate needed him, and he wouldn't let her down.

Chapter 15

After five minutes of fiddling with the buttons on Rachel's phone, George found Steve's number and pressed the green call button.

"Dad?" Rachel answered.

"It's me," he answered, trying to hold the phone and steer at the same time.

"How's Mom?" She sounded frantic.

"She's on her way to Bend. They loaded her up in the helicopter and flew off."

"Good." Rachel let out a sigh on the other end of the phone line. "Are you driving up now?"

"Yep. Just getting back on the road." George turned back onto the highway at that moment.

"Okay. We're packing up here. Steve and Michael went to go get the boat."

"Tell them not to worry about the boat. Call Mac." George hesitated. He hated to do it, but things were different now, and he needed a big favor. "Tell him what's going on. See if he can store it for me for a couple of weeks, until I can get back up here to get it."

"All right. Then we'll be on the road soon."

"Okay. I'm going straight to the hospital."

"See you there," Rachel said. Just as he was about to hang up, she added. "And Dad. She'll be okay."

George pushed the red button to end the call and set the phone down in the center console. As much as he hated cell phones, he was grateful he had one now. It was his only lifeline between him and Kate.

He turned left at the Cascade Lakes junction. Snow usually kept the road closed until June, but this year, with record low snowpack, it had melted early, and the road was open. It wasn't much of a shortcut. Still with little traffic, it shaved thirty minutes off the drive easily. He navigated through the dirt roads he'd traveled a hundred times before without thinking. He focused on getting to Kate. Trees and meadows passed in a blur. George began a dialogue with God. "You know me. I don't have the fancy words or the rehearsed prayers. But I need help. I need her. I'm not ready to let her go. I know I'm supposed to accept Your will and be glad about it. But she's my Kate. She is the better half of me. You know that. You brought her to me, just as You brought everything good in my life to me. I'm not strong enough. I can't lose her now. Please, Lord, don't take her now."

George felt the teardrop hit the back of his hand. It was the first indication he was crying. *It's a good thing Kate's not here to see this.* He wiped his eyes with the back of his hand. It still reeked of fish. Everything had happened so fast. The fish were probably still lying there in the sink, Kate's prized kokanee.

He approached the Wickiup junction. *Five minutes to Lapine. Forty-five minutes to St. Charles.* He drove like Dale Earnhardt, passing any car going under the speed limit. Even though he'd begged God to spare her life, he wanted to get there as fast as he could to make sure he could see her one last time. Just in case.

Traffic slowed as he approached Sunriver and again as he approached the new parkway. Still he made it to the hospital parking lot an hour after he called Rachel. He barely had the truck in park before he jumped out and sprinted across the parking lot.

The emergency room lobby was packed with people suffering various calamities. George stood and waited to talk to the clerk at the admitting desk. The man in front of him had a kitchen towel soaked with blood wrapped around his hand. George overheard the entire story as the guy's girlfriend explained rather loudly how he had tried to work on the motor of his pickup truck while it was running. Every time the nurse asked another question, George looked at the clock. Fifteen minutes after he arrived, he was able to talk to someone.

"My wife was brought in by AirLife. I'd like to see her." George blurted out once he reached the desk.

"Her name?" The woman behind the admitting desk didn't even bother looking up.

"Kate Patterson." George craned his neck around the desk to try and get a glimpse, some indication that Kate arrived safely. The woman pushed some buttons on the computer and looked over the computer screen.

"I don't have a Kate Patterson," she said flatly.

"Ah, maybe it's under Katherine." He stood taller, trying to get a better view and get a glimpse of the screen.

"Yeah. There she is. They took her down to MRI. They should have her back up here in about fifteen or twenty minutes. I'll tell the nurse you're here. If you could please take a seat." The woman nodded in the direction of the waiting room. People now stood next to chairs that were already filled with people who had been waiting long before he had arrived.

George nodded and backed away. Kate was down in MRI. That meant she was doing fine because that wasn't surgery or intensive care. He leaned up against a wall near the corridor. The Mariners were playing the Red Sox on a television mounted on the wall. He wasn't able to hear, but he could see the score flash on the screen every five minutes or so. He caught it in glimpses as his eyes searched every face that passed by.

Every time a nurse walked by, he tried to get their attention, to no avail. Finally, he spotted Dr. Gibson with a nurse headed toward the main hospital. George jumped to his feet and ran to catch up to him.

"Dr. Gibson," George blurted.

"George," the doctor said with a smile of recognition.

"Have you seen Kate? Is she okay? Where is she?" George shot off questions in rapid succession. "No one is telling me anything."

"I just came from her exam room." Dr. Gibson lost the smile on his face. "If you can give me a minute, we can go over there and talk." He pointed to a series of small conference rooms along the far wall.

George nodded and stood back while Dr. Gibson talked with a nurse and jotted something down on a clipboard and handed it to her. George couldn't help but wonder if they were discussing Kate. He felt his heart pounding in his chest. Why hadn't the doctor just told him she was fine? Why did the doctor need to take him to a room to talk? He'd seen that sort of thing on shows like ER when they took the families aside to tell them they needed to decide whether or not to pull the plug. It seemed an eternity waiting, but then the nurse left, and Dr. Gibson walked toward George and led him across the hall.

"Please have a seat." Dr. Gibson gestured to the chairs around a small table.

"What's going on? Is she okay? Can I see her?"

"Hold on, George. I'm having her transferred to critical care so we can monitor her. She's resting right now."

George let out a sigh of relief. Critical care wasn't intensive care.

"She had a seizure, well, several small seizures to be exact. These seizures were caused by increased cranial pressure. The MRI showed that the tumors in her brain have increased significantly since the beginning of her treatment. This obviously is not what we had hoped for, but it is always a possibility when dealing with metastasized tumors."

"So what's that mean in plain English." George understood only a few words of what the doctor had just said.

"The tumors are growing."

"But I thought the treatment was supposed to shrink the tumors."

"Well, that's the general idea, but with the type of cancer Kate has, sometimes we don't always get the results we'd hoped for."

"So what does that mean?"

"It means the tumors are pressing on the lining of the brain which is causing more headaches and the seizures. Eventually, the tumors will create enough pressure that…" The doctor paused. "There's really nothing more we can do to stop it."

George grappled with the realization that her cancer was winning. When she had talked about making peace out on the boat, she had known. How long had she known?

"How long does she have? Months?"

"More like weeks, possibly days."

"Days?" George felt the air leave his lungs.

"I'm sorry, George. I really don't know what else I can tell you." The doctor placed his hand on George's shoulder as a gesture of comfort. "We will try and keep her as comfortable as possible, and I'll see to it that you can see her anytime day or night."

George closed his eyes and swallowed hard. "Thank you, doctor." He shook Dr. Gibson's hand. He wondered how often the doctor had to say those words, to give the news that someone was losing the fight.

"You can stay in here until they're ready if you'd like." Dr. Gibson smiled warmly.

"Thank you again." George sat back down in one of the chairs. He welcomed the privacy. He didn't know if he would be able to hold it together, and he couldn't bear the thought of crying in front of a room full of strangers. Days. The word loitered, unbidden, like a bad dream. He sniffed back the silent tears. He resolved that Kate would not see him cry. She needed his strength until the end.

*****

Rachel scoured her purse for her address book while Steve sped back toward Bend. Finally, after searching each pocket twice, she found the small leather-bound book. She held it firmly in her hand and paused a moment before dialing the number on Steve's phone.

"Hello?" the voice on the other line answered.

"David?"

"Hey, Rach." His voice with gruff with irritation.

"Look, um. Mom's been taken by AirLife to St. Charles."

The silence on the other end of the line only added to her discomfort.

"She probably doesn't have much time left. And it would mean a lot if you would come see her. It might be your last chance." She tried to convince him with not-so-subtle tinges of guilt. She couldn't understand why she needed to fight him on this. Why wasn't he simply agreeing to come home?

"I can't do it. Not now."

"But David?" Rachel tried to think of an argument any plausible reason other than the obvious to make him change his mind.

"Look, you've made your case, but I'm still not coming down there."

"David! Why not? This is Mom!"

"I know." He paused momentarily. Rachel hoped he was reconsidering. "I just can't."

"You mean won't."

"Whatever. But if you don't stop calling, I'm going to turn my phone off."

"David!"

"Bye, Rach."

The line went dead. She stared at the phone, unwilling to accept what she'd just heard—her brother flat out refusing to come see their dying mother. It was unreal. How could she tell her mother that David was not coming to see her? Maybe she wouldn't have to—no one knew she'd called him. Or maybe he would change his mind and show up after all. *Please, God, change his heart*. All she could do was place it in His hands and hope for the best.

Rachel looked out the window and realized they were only halfway to their destination. Rachel wanted to pray for a miracle, for healing, but she feared it might be too late for that. She didn't even know if her mom had made it safely to the hospital. *Please, God, let me see her again.*

Chapter 16

Rachel arrived at the hospital thirty minutes after George had finished talking with Dr. Gibson. He was glad she had not arrived sooner and seen him blubbering. One thing he'd prided himself on, he had never cried in front of the kids. Men don't cry—it was the anthem of his youth. His uncle had admonished him every time he shed a single tear after his mother's death. Men don't cry. So he didn't, or if he felt he couldn't control himself, he did it privately where no one would see.

"Dad," she shouted across the room.

"Rachel." He found it comforting to have someone else there with him.

"How is she?" she asked the second she reached him.

"Um. They were running some more tests, and then they were getting her set up in critical care." He recited what he'd been told and peered over her shoulder looking for Steve, Michael, and the kids. "Where's Steve and Michael?"

"Steve is taking the kids home and Michael is taking Nikki home and then he'll be right here."

George nodded. It made sense. The grandchildren shouldn't see Kate just yet. But with just *days,* they would need to come see her at some point. Rachel walked with him out to the main lobby. They sat near the window in a cozy little alcove behind the piano.

"What have they told you?" Rachel prodded.

George shook his head. "It's not good." His voice was somber.

Rachel clasped her hand to her mouth as tears formed in her eyes. "What does that mean?"

"She doesn't have very long." George fought the lump rising in his throat. "Days." He croaked out. The word still taunted him.

Rachel nodded as tears streamed down her face. George held his daughter against his shoulder as she sobbed, just like he had when she was a little girl. After a crash on her bicycle or losing the spelling bee at school, Daddy had been there to soothe the tears with a hug and words of encouragement. Only this time, there was nothing to say to ease the pain, for either of them.

They took turns pacing. The main lobby was quieter and less cramped than the critical care lobby which sat directly across the corridor from the emergency room.

"Do you know how to get ahold of your brother?" George looked her straight in the eye. He'd suspected that they emailed back and forth. The two of them had always been close, and he just sensed by her knowledge of his whereabouts that she had kept in touch. He could only hope that David could still make it in time. He should have tried to contact him earlier despite Kate's objections, but he'd thought there would be more time.

"I do," she answered quietly.

"And?" George interrogated.

"He's not coming." Rachel eked out quietly, her eyes shifted downward.

"What do you mean he's not coming?" He stared at her, stupefied by what he'd just heard. It had to be a mistake.

Rachel fidgeted a few seconds before responding. "I talked to him on the way here. He knows about Mom, and he's not coming."

George staggered backward and collapsed into a chair. He couldn't believe what he had just heard. The words pierced like an arrow straight through him. How could David refuse to come see his dying mother? What kind of person did that? It seemed so cold, callous. George shook his head in disbelief.

"Look, Dad, I know David and… He didn't tell me why. He just said…" Rachel tried making excuses just as she had every time David stormed out after some bitter argument that he typically started. Just like Kate, she tried to keep the peace, but what peace could be found in a son refusing to see his dying mother.

Michael found them in the lobby. "Man, who do you have to know to get a parking spot around here?"

"It's just the construction," George muttered.

"Yeah. It looks like a war zone out there." Michael gestured wildly toward the dust and debris outside. As he read the somber expressions, he subdued. "How is she?"

"They're moving her to critical care," George began. "And—"

"And what?" Michael interrupted impatiently.

"She doesn't have much longer," George uttered somberly. He was still digesting Rachel's revelation and hadn't given much thought on how to break the news to Michael.

"So what's that mean?"

"It means the cancer got worse," Rachel piped in.

"Can't they do something? Can't they give her more pills or more whatever? They need to do something." Michael's voice grew louder with each word. He ran his hands over his face and collapsed into a chair next to George. "How long?"

"Days. That's all we know at this point," Rachel stated calmly.

Michael slouched over his knees with his head in his hands. Red splotches began creeping across his face as they did every time he was overcome with emotion. "When's David gonna get here?"

Rachel's eyes darted at her father as if searching for approval to answer. George nodded softly. George had been stunned into silence. Michael would surely explode.

"He's not coming," Rachel said softly.

"What? What do you mean he's not coming?" Michael leapt to his feet. Rachel put her hand out in attempt to calm him, but he waved her off with a bold flail of his arms.

"Michael." She started after him. George placed a hand on hers.

"Let him go." George watched as Michael stormed off down the hall. It was a lot to absorb. First Kate, and then David's blatant disregard for them, for Kate. George still couldn't understand how he could live with himself. Kate would never see him again. Not in this life and perhaps… George didn't want to think about that.

*****

Michael returned later, after he had calmed down. George could still see anger simmering in his eyes. Just as they got settled again, Dr. Gibson found them in the main lobby. "She's ready now. George, if you'd like to come with me. Unfortunately, we'd like to keep it to one visitor at a time, for the time being."

George followed him through a corridor that led to a back hallway. They went through a set of double doors and past a sign directing them toward the emergency entrance. They turned left through another set of double doors, and he entered a code on a locked entrance as they entered the critical care ward.

A large open desk area sat in the middle with six rooms around it in a semicircle. The rooms didn't have doors but merely curtains used for privacy. It looked like a high-tech command center with monitors and computers everywhere. Dr. Gibson guided George to the room where Kate was lying in a bed. Wires monitored her every breath and heartbeat.

"Hey there, stranger." Her voice cracked as she spoke.

"Hey." He half smiled, half grimaced. He hated seeing her like this. "You gave us quite a scare."

"Yeah. I'm sorry about that. I should have told you."

"You knew?" He swallowed hard.

"I knew." Her voice was faint but firm.

"Weren't you scared? I mean, I'm scared for you." He pulled a chair right up next to her bed and sat holding her hand.

"Yes and no." She smiled at him. "I wanted to spend what time I had left living with you, not dying."

"Why go through all this, the surgery, the treatment if you knew it would end like this anyways?" He looked at her body, withered and worn by the radiation and surgery, her long fiery locks gone, her face gaunt and leathered. She had endured so much, and in the end, it had not added a single day to her life.

"The day I found out, I talked with the doctor ahead of time and asked him not to give you specifics on a timeline or odds. But I wanted to know. And when they told me. At first, I just wanted to curl up in ball. So I prayed, and I realized that if God was calling me home, there wasn't anything I could do about it. But if I had a chance, I needed to fight for you and the kids." She squeezed his hand and let out a heavy sigh. "I guess He's calling me home. But I've no regrets." She paused and turned her head away for a moment before continuing. "Except… David."

He could see her eyes searching his for answers that he now knew but wished he didn't. She didn't deserve any of this, and least of all, she didn't deserve the cruelty of David's refusal.

"He's not coming home. Is he?" The disappointment in her voice was unbearable.

George shook his head, unable to verbalize an answer without spewing hatred and disgust. Kate didn't need that now. She needed comfort and love around her. He watched as she nodded in acceptance of it. Tears glistened in her eyes. They sat silently, neither of them wanting to acknowledge David's refusal to come home and what that meant.

After five minutes of beeping and whirring, George prompted. "What can I do for you?" He held her soft hand against his cheek.

"Bring me a scarf." She laughed as the words escaped her mouth.

"All right. Maybe I'll go get them a little later, but for now, I'm sitting here with you, and I'm not going anywhere." George patted her hand.

"Good." She smiled.

After an hour had passed, Dr. Gibson brought Rachel and Michael into the room for a short visit. George took the opportunity to sneak out and stretch his legs while the kids visited with her. Hopefully, he would be able to remember how to get back through the maze of hallways. After only two wrong turns, he found the cafeteria and bought some snacks and a drink. The direction signs guided him back most of the way, and a kind nurse helped him find the right door with a phone outside to call to be let in.

As he walked by the nurses' station, he overheard a nurse discussing some patient on the phone. "She's pretty sedated for the most part. She'll be in and out of consciousness. Wouldn't really know who comes to visit her."

George found it sad to discount a person's ability to recognize their loved ones being there even if they were sedated. Kate would want her children and him around even if she couldn't talk. He felt sorry for whoever the nurse was talking about.

The curtain to Kate's room had been pulled back slightly while the nurses examined her. Rachel and Michael were still there and stood out by the command center.

"Do we take turns staying with her?" Rachel prompted, keeping her voice low.

"No, I'll stay." He looked at his watch. "I didn't realize it was so late. Rachel, you and Michael should go home and be with your kids. I'm not leaving until they throw me out."

Rachel nodded and threw her arms around him. "I'll open the store in the morning and then come in. I want to bring Braden and Jenna to see her."

"She'll want that," George agreed.

"I'll call Steve on my phone and have them draw her some pictures."

"I'll send Connor in with Rach and cover the store for you, Dad." Michael slapped a hand on his father's back before he headed down the corridor. He watched them leave before going back into Kate's room.

"We gave her a sedative, so she'll sleep soon." The nurse whispered as he passed by her. "You're welcome to stay as long as you like."

He found her sleeping already. He pulled a chair up to the foot of the bed and sat and watched her until he could no longer keep his eyes open.

*****

George woke in the chair in her room, the same chair he'd sat in right after the kids left. The whirring, clicking, and beeping of the monitors let him know that nothing had changed.

He wanted to take a shower, something he hadn't done in over thirty-six hours. He needed to change his clothes. He still reeked of bait and fish, but he was afraid to leave. He feared that if he left, she'd go, and he'd never get that time back. Whether he sat and watched her sleep or slept in the chair beside her, he simply wanted to squeeze every second of what little time remained. There would always be time to shower, but there might not be much more time with her.

Chapter 17

Rachel arrived a little after nine in the morning with an overnight bag and a little white bag from Sisters Bakery. Kate was still sleeping soundly. The nurse had been in earlier and said the sedatives would make her groggy for a while. George flipped through some *Field and Stream* magazines that the nurses had brought in for him.

"Here." She held out the little white bag, and George stood to retrieve it. "Bear claws. Save one for Mom, but don't let the nurses catch you."

"Thanks." He stepped closer and hugged his daughter.

"I called the nurses this morning to check in. They said they're going to move her to a private room upstairs later on today." Rachel looked to George questioningly.

"Yeah. That's what they say."

"So I thought it would be better to bring the kids in then," she explained. "They also said you needed some clothes, please. So I brought you a bag. There are some scarves and chocolate in there for Mom."

"Thank you," he said as he took the bag from her. He was constantly amazed by how much Rachel was like Kate, always thinking of others—and not just what they asked for but knowing what they might want or need.

Kate stirred, and they both jumped to her side, one on either side of the bed.

"Morning," she slurred. George didn't know if it was just the tiredness or the medication.

"Good morning." George smiled and patted her hand. Then one of the machines beeped and made him nearly jump out of his skin. A minute later, a nurse appeared to stop the noise. She checked the IV bag and disappeared again.

"Wow. That'll get your heart pumping," Rachel commented. "Better than a cardio workout."

Kate stayed quiet and just nodded. They hovered over her for a few minutes before the nurse returned and shooed them out of the room.

"Why do they keep doing that?" George whispered when they were out in the hall.

"Housekeeping, Dad."

He gave her a puzzled look.

"They change her sheets and things since she can't leave the bed."

"Okay." He nodded. She didn't need to explain any further.

When they were allowed back in, George let Rachel chat with her for a while, and he ate his pastry. When the nurses weren't looking, Rachel snuck part of the bear claw to Kate, who savored every morsel.

"Thanks for the contraband." Kate smiled at her daughter.

"No problem. I wish it could be more, like one of those éclairs from Rose's."

"Ummm," Kate murmured, "a piece of heaven."

George couldn't believe that they could get so excited over a pastry. "You two are easy to please," he joked.

"Yep. A little bit of chocolate, that's all it takes." Rachel laughed, and Kate joined in as if there was some private joke between the two of them that only they understood. It did the heart good to see Kate laughing.

George quietly observed their banter. Rachel talked about everything she could going on outside the hospital, outside of the cancer. The tulips in her garden had finally started to bloom. The Carlsons that lived next door finally had their twins. Susan Carlson had trouble with preterm labor, and so she had spent the last few weeks over at Emmanuel hospital in Portland, but Jeff Carlson came home yesterday to get things ready. Jill at the Coffee Shack had gotten engaged. Rachel kept up the idle chatter until the nurses came in and told them it was time for them to start the move.

While they were busy moving Kate, one of the male nurses led George to the locker room on the lower level. He was so grateful that he could clean up and not have to drive all the way home and all the way back. This way, he wouldn't have to miss any time with her at all. He'd much rather shower while they moved her than sit in another waiting room.

After a nice long scrub, he did his best to stuff his dirty clothes back into the bag, unsuccessfully. He walked the bulging bag out to his truck. He hadn't stepped outside the hospital since he'd arrived the day before. It was like a whole other world inside those doors. He hadn't watched the news or even found out who won the game. His only concern had been Kate.

*****

He tossed the bag in the rear seat where the quilt still lay from the day before, a reminder of what brought him here. He closed the truck door slowly and walked back inside. Edie, the head nurse, had told him it would take about an hour. George decided he had enough time to grab a bite to eat. Rachel had already left to go back to the store and take care of a few things before bringing Braden and Jenna in. She also wanted to give Michael the opportunity to come in for a visit. Michael's visits were short. Like Kate, he didn't idle well and particularly not in hospitals.

After lunch in the cafeteria, George checked in at the nurses' station. Edie informed him that Dr. Gibson had nearly completed his examination and had requested that George wait there for him.

"Hi, George," Dr. Gibson greeted him with a handshake.

"So what's going on?"

"Last night, we hooked up a machine called an EEG to monitor her brain activity. It was the only method we could use to really monitor what's going on inside her head without doing scans all the time," he explained. "And it shows that she's having more seizures, not the grand mal that you witnessed yesterday. They're smaller ones called petit mals, but they're coming more frequently."

"What does that mean?" George was baffled by all the medical talk. He knew Kate understood it all, but grand mal, petit mal, it meant nothing to him.

"It tells us the pressure is building. That, along with her complaints of migraine symptoms, means we're going to increase her medication," he elaborated, "which means she'll be less lucid and unconscious more."

"But she'll be comfortable? She won't be in pain?" George questioned.

"We'll do as much as we can to alleviate the pain," Dr. Gibson said sympathetically.

"Good." George nodded, trying to absorb it all. "I want her as comfortable as possible."

"That's why we moved her. Critical care has better monitoring but very little privacy. We wanted to make sure you and your family could spend this time with her."

"Thanks." George stuck his hand out and shook the doctor's hand. "Can I see her now?"

"Go ahead. She'll be awake for a little while."

Kate's new room was practically identical to the one she'd stayed in two months earlier while she recovered from her surgery. Two months. It seemed like a lifetime ago. So much had happened during that time, and time had passed in a blur. Two months. It wasn't fair.

He found Kate sitting up, talking with one of the nurses. He walked over to the window and waited until she finished talking.

"Hey, you." She smiled when he turned to look at her.

"Hey yourself." He walked over and kissed her, savoring the sweetness of her. "I see they moved you back to Shangri-la."

"Yep, I'm moving up in the world," she teased. He noticed there was a little sparkle left in her eyes. The nurse had helped her tie the scarf around her head, and it helped put the color back in her cheeks.

"You sure are." He tried to keep conversations light. He wanted her to be happy. She knew she was dying; she didn't need to be reminded.

*****

Michael stopped in with some flowers around two. Kate had just fallen back asleep. He waited around long enough to get an update but didn't stay to watch her sleep. George knew that however difficult it was on him, it was just as difficult on Rachel and Michael, maybe more so. He had the luxury of staying around, but they had families to attend to. Not only did they have to cope with their mother lying in the hospital dying, but they had to attempt to stay positive around their children. They had the burden of explaining to a young mind the incomprehensible truths of mortality.

Rachel came back at four with Braden and Jenna. Kate was awake but fairly languid. Braden and Jenna both brought her cards that they had made and some balloons. George tied the balloons to the chair in the corner and tried to help them assimilate to the hospital surroundings. He tried, as best he could, to explain the monitors and tubes. What he didn't know he made up, like the digitator that monitored when Grandma needed more medicine or the reebasacker that told the nurses when she was hungry. They seemed to like the made-up machines better than the real ones. He even caught Kate laughing once or twice. But after half an hour, Kate was exhausted, and the grandkids were bored.

"I'll be back after dinner, sometime around seven or seven-thirty." Rachel gave George a hug. "Come on, guys. Grandma needs a nap."

"Bye, Grandma," they both sang out in unison and followed their mother out the door.

"Yes. Grandma needs a nap," Kate croaked softly. She looked at George. "Why don't you go get some dinner while I nap?"

He pulled her hand to his lips and kissed it. "All right. But I'll be back." He watched her for a few more minutes as she drifted off to sleep. Her energy faded quickly. It was only a matter of time before she had no energy left at all.

Chapter 18

George stepped off the elevator onto a desolate ward stilled by night. Two nurses manned the nurses' station. Over half of the patient rooms were darkened, their inhabitants fast asleep. Earlier that day, there had been dozens of people moving around, going in and out of rooms. Now that visiting hours were officially over, the halls were eerily quiet.

A few short steps down the hall, Kate lay quietly, dominated by the monitors hooked to her frail body. The steady beep, beep, beep of the monitor assured him she was still alive. He settled into the chair next to her bed and watched her sleep. The gentle rise and fall of her chest, the little twitches of her face—all things he'd never taken time to notice before. Soft stubble had grown in on top of her head in the unmistakable shade of red that was Kate.

He wanted more than anything for her to hold on, to fight and make some sort of miraculous recovery. He wanted her to return to the vibrant Kate he knew and loved. But as the monitors beeped their rhythmic tune, he could sense the end was near. He needed to let her go, to relinquish her from the pain she most surely felt.

She stirred and opened her eyes. A smile spread across her parched lips as her hand reached for his. "There you are." Her voice was a mere whisper.

"Yep. You found me," he teased.

"Have you been here long?"

"No. I went for a walk and got a bite to eat in the cafeteria."

"You should go home and get some rest." She held her hand up to his face.

"I'm not leaving you," he said firmly.

Another smile spread across her lips, and the IV machine clicked as it administered another dose of medication. Another machine clicked and beeped as a cuff around her arm slowly filled with air and slowly released as numbers flashed on a screen. A nurse came in and recorded the numbers and checked the IV bags without mentioning a word.

Kate's eyes fluttered as she fought sleep. She fought to keep them open.

"Tell David I love him." Her eyes searched his as she said the words.

He nodded slowly, unable to respond. Her sentiment meant she knew the end was near and he couldn't bear the thought of saying goodbye to her.

"And promise me"—she gulped hard as if the words were hard to say—"promise me you'll make peace with our son."

He just looked at her as tears began to fill his eyes.

"George." Her voice grew raspy.

"I will," he said, patting her hand. "Now get some rest."

"George," she repeated. A tear rolled down her cheek. "I love you." She gripped his hand with all the strength she could manage.

"I love you too," he uttered, trying to stifle the tears stinging his eyes. He bent over and kissed her dry lips. "I'll get a nurse to bring you some ice chips." He stood holding her hand for a long moment before turning and leaving. He hadn't cried in front of Kate since they'd heard the diagnosis. He wouldn't start now. He would remain strong as long as she needed him. But it nearly killed him to hear her talking as if she'd already given up.

He waited at the nurses' station for the nurse to return. After pacing in front of the desk for a few minutes, he had composed himself. He blew air out forcefully and sniffed back any remnants of the tears that had welled up in his eyes. Just as he was about to ask the nurse to get some ice chips, a loud siren noise blared from behind the desk.

"Code Blue," she yelled to the alcove behind her, and two other nurses jumped up and began jogging past him directly into Kate's room.

The first nurse picked up a phone and dialed a number and repeated the words "Code Blue. Code blue in room 321." She hung up and followed the other nurses quickly.

George stood frozen, unable to walk the short distance back to Kate's room where three nurses frantically adjusted monitors. The elevator door rang, and two doctors jumped out and ran into Kate's room as well. George heard the doctors and nurses talking back and forth, but above their chatter, he heard the unwavering and unending *boop boop* sound of the heart monitor. He closed his eyes and could feel his heart dropping. He heard a doctor yell "Clear!" followed by a loud thumping sound. He repeated it twice more before all grew quiet, and George knew. He knew without being told. Kate was gone. One of the doctors emerged from the room. A nurse pointed toward George, and the doctor walked in his direction. The doctor came over and put a hand on his shoulder. His worst fear was confirmed. The doctor said something, but George didn't hear him. His thoughts were elsewhere. She was gone! Just like that! They had been talking, and minutes later, she left him.

Since the day that Dr. Richards had asked him to come to his office, George had thought about this day. What it would be like. How he would react. Much to his surprise, he couldn't react at all. Nothing worked. His arms, his legs seemed paralyzed. He could see people, doctors and nurses talking to him, handing him papers, and yet he heard nothing. A great numbness set in. His thoughts all focused on one thing—how could he tell the children, especially Rachel? She had only gone home to check on the kids an hour ago. She would come back to this.

Chapter 19

The details of death were overwhelming—picking a casket, a headstone, where in the cemetery to bury the body, and what to clothe her in. For the most part, George left the arrangements to Rachel. Not only did he not want to talk to anyone, particularly about Kate's passing, but he really wasn't good at arranging things. That had been Kate's job. He wouldn't have the first idea how many people would attend the service or what time of day to plan the service for. He had no idea what rules of etiquette applied in inviting or announcing the service time and place. And he certainly had no idea what type of flowers should be ordered. He didn't even know the difference between a mum and a carnation.

He wrote checks when Rachel asked him to but remained largely uninvolved in the decisions. Instead, he focused on work. Over the past month, he had spent so little time in the office that he had lost touch with the day-to-day operations of his own business. Yes, Don handled things for him, and he trusted him to do a good job, but George hadn't the slightest notion what inventory levels were or even what the sales figures were for last month. He snuck in after lunch and reviewed sales reports and initialed purchase orders.

"Hey, Dad. Here you are," Rachel said as she poked her head up into George's office.

"Yep. What 'cha need?" George leaned back in his leather captain's chair.

"I just wanted to let you know, I've scheduled the memorial service for Tuesday."

"So soon?" George didn't really know if there was an appropriate timeline, but his past experience, however limited, it had usually been a week between the person's death and the funeral. Tuesday was only four days away.

Rachel hesitated a moment. "They have services and small groups on Wednesday and, well, next Thursday… I didn't think it would…" Rachel stammered. "I didn't think it would be appropriate to have Mom's funeral on your birthday."

"No, I guess not," George said quietly. He'd been trying to forget about that detail. His birthday had always been a reminder of the tragedies he'd endured. His father had died four days before he was born—D-Day. His mother died five days after his fifteenth birthday. And this year would be his sixtieth birthday. With Kate's death, he'd just as soon forget the whole thing.

Rachel finally broke the silence. "I set up the internment for one in the afternoon. It will be just family—you, me, Steve, Michael, and Nikki. I'll get a woman from the church to watch the kids."

George nearly asked the question—*and David?* But he didn't. She would have included him if she'd been in contact with him.

"Do you want to come over for dinner?" Rachel asked quietly as if she could read her father's thoughts.

"Naw. I'm all right. I had a big lunch," he lied. Truth was, he just wanted to be alone.

"You know where to find me if you need me." She placed a hand on his shoulder and gave a small pat before retracting it and walking back to the stairs.

"Don't work too late," she said in a voice much like Kate's.

He nodded and watched as Rachel disappeared behind the stairwell wall. Her strength amazed him. She must have gotten that from Kate, the ability to just go on despite her own grief. George wanted to escape, to find someplace where he wasn't constantly reminded of her absence. Some do-gooder counselor at the hospital had talked to him about the stages of grief. The first stage was denial. George liked denial. It was comforting. It kept the cruelty of the truth at bay.

He glanced up at the clock—five o'clock—then at the small stack of paper in the center of his desk. There wasn't much more he could do, yet he didn't want to go home. He'd built that house for Kate, and now every detail reminded him of her, from the hardwood floors she'd picked out to the green granite counters he'd installed last fall. Every room had her touches in it. Now being there without her only made him miss her more.

The small leather sofa along the stairwell wall began to look inviting. He walked over to it, sizing it up and testing it for comfort. It certainly would not hold his six-foot frame in its entirety, but he could manage. There were hotels in town, but if he checked into one, it would only stir gossip in town. He knew for certain that he could not bear another night like last night. He'd shared a bed with Kate for thirty-five years. He wasn't sure if he'd ever be able to get used to sleeping without her.

Chapter 20

Tuesday morning, cars packed the parking lot at Mountainview Church. The overflow of cars lined the highway and filled the middle school parking lot. Nearly half the town showed up and some people from the clinic where Kate worked. He even saw a few children that he could only assume were patients of Dr. Lund. George glanced around the parking lot again, hoping for a miracle. Rachel had left a message on David's cell phone with the time and place of the service. George knew it was a long shot but had to hope that his son would come and pay the proper respect.

Inside, extra chairs had been set up for the service, but still some people had to stand at the back. George never could have imagined such an outpouring of love and respect for his wife. He'd attended few funerals in his life, and none of them had brought a crowd like this. There had only been ten or fifteen people at his mother's funeral. Kate's mother's service had forty or fifty mourners. And Kate's father's funeral had about a hundred people in attendance. He wondered if this many people would come to his. He doubted it.

Flowers of every type and color covered the stage at the front of the sanctuary. They surrounded an easel that held a huge portrait of Kate. There was no casket. Kate and her ornate box were at the funeral home in Bend where she would be buried later that day. Kate had requested that she not have an open-casket service, especially with her hair all shaved off. Even in death, Kate's vanity got the best of her.

George returned to his seat. Michael sat at his right and Rachel at his left. When he'd thought of the children attending a funeral, he'd always assumed he would go before Kate. He'd pictured all three of his children with their families. He'd never imagined this, attending Kate's funeral and their eldest son absent, not for any just cause but an intentional blow. He scanned the room once again, just to be certain. He reviewed each face, but no David.

The Sunday morning worship team went up onto the stage and music piped in overhead. They began singing "The Old Rugged Cross," an old hymn that had been one of Kate's favorites. Then Mike O'Connell went to the podium and began the service. He talked about Kate's service in the church, how she had been an integral part of a growing women's ministry. His words were kind and respectful. He went on to quote scripture about turning grief into joy in knowledge that she was now with the Lord, and soon all those who believed would be reunited with her for eternity. He finished his mini sermon by outlining God's plan for mourning as a community, "Mourn with those who mourn."

The worship team sang a soulful rendition of "Amazing Grace," which left the onlookers sniffing tears. George still had not wept. The same numbness he felt the night she died had anesthetized him.

After a moment of silence, Mike returned to the podium. He played a video Rachel had put together from old photographs. George watched Kate's entire life pass before him—her graduation, their wedding, her graduation from nursing school, the birth of their children in consecutive order, vacations, holidays—candid moments with her bright and shining smile. As the photos passed, a worship song played in the background.

Mike invited people to share their memories of Kate. The first woman, George recognized from the Bible studies at the house. She talked about how Kate had led her to the Lord and then spent time with her teaching her how to really make Christ the center of her life. A ten-year-old girl stood up and told about the time that Kate had come to visit her in the hospital and read her Bible stories while she received chemotherapy. Story after story revealed how much Kate cared for other people. Dr. Lund was the last to speak. He could barely compose himself as he shared that even when she knew that the cancer was terminal, she was still concerned for others.

After a lengthy prayer, the worship team sang another praise song, and then people began filing out of the sanctuary. As people left, George stood at the door with Rachel and Michael at his side. He shook hands and received hugs from attendees, oblivious to all the sentiments that people poured out in a constant stream.

*****

They kept the burial simple. Each of them held a single red rose which they laid on the casket as Pastor Mike recited Psalm 23. The entire graveside service took ten minutes. George watched as they lowered the casket into the ground, waiting for the tears to come. Still they did not. It felt surreal, as if it wasn't truly happening. As they turned to leave, he saw the thunderheads brewing in the distance. A storm was coming, he could feel it.

*****

Funerals always felt longer than they actually were. Maybe the subject matter distorted the passing of time. People always avoided talking about death or even thinking about it. And when faced with death, the inevitable conversation about mortality began. George believed wholeheartedly that there was a heaven. And he knew with absolute certainty that Kate was there now. Trouble was, she'd left him here alone, and he had no idea when he'd see her again.

George and the kids spent no more than fifteen minutes at the internment. Just long enough for a prayer and to say their final goodbyes, but it felt like hours. And the drive back from Bend felt unusually long as well. After all the ceremony, he just wanted it to be over and done with—this constant reminder that she had died.

As they pulled up to the house, cars lined the driveway, and some parked on the road in front. "What's this?" He made no attempt to mask his disapproval.

"It's customary for people to gather after a funeral," Rachel answered.

"Is it customary for them to be there when the people are absent?" George grumbled.

"Dad, Steve's mom is there. She set out everything for us while we went to the internment." Rachel turned to look at him.

"I see. Did I know about any of this?" He wasn't in the mood to see more people, let alone in his house.

"Yes. I told you, and you told me to do what I thought best."

"I'm sorry. I'm just not myself," he apologized, but really, he wanted them to leave so he could be alone.

"I know, Dad. None of us are right now."

Inside, people gathered in small groups in the living room, kitchen, and dining rooms. George spotted some of the flowers from the memorial service scattered throughout. The dining room table had various trays of snacks, and two large pots of coffee sat on the kitchen counter. Someone had gone to a lot of trouble to prepare all this. George knew he should feel grateful, but he felt like they were intruding. No one had ever cooked in Kate's kitchen except for Kate and, on occasion, Rachel. He rarely touched anything in there. He didn't even know where things were kept, like the mixer or the blender or any of those gadgets. He knew what he had needed to know, where the coffee maker was, the coffee filters, spoons, forks, the basics. Kate had a system for organizing everything and now some stranger had come into her kitchen and he didn't know if he could put things back where they belonged.

People from church shook his hand and gave their condolences. They would chat for a few moments about innocuous things such as the weather or the new stores being built in Bend. Nothing of consequence. Nothing meaningful.

He found Rachel talking with a woman he recognized from Bible studies that had been held at the house.

"Rachel, where did you find those pictures you showed this morning?" The woman asked politely.

"They were in a box my mom had."

"Well, some of those were from our women's retreat last year, and I was wondering if you could loan them to me so I could get copies. Sometime when it's convenient."

"Mom kept the box of them in her closet," Rachel said. "I could go get them right now if you'd like."

"That's okay, sweetie. Some other time would be fine." She placed her hand on Rachel's arm.

"I'll go get it." George cut in. He had been looking for an excuse to break away. All the condolences and talk of weather was starting to wear on him.

He left the people lingering in the great room and walked slowly up the stairs. Why had Rachel insisted on having the reception here at the house? When would everyone leave and let him be alone? The repetitive "I'm so sorry for your loss" was downright unbearable.

At the top of the stairs, George took a moment to study Kate's gallery. Unlike most galleries that displayed great works of art, Kate had chosen to display pictures and collages of the kids and grandkids. There were three walls, one devoted to each of the kids. Every moment captured forever by film and then framed and hung on the wall. Kate had always been a sort of shutterbug. It got worse once the little digital cameras came out. They had hundreds of thousands of snapshots of the grandchildren. Kate took the best ones and put them together in frames.

George passed by them on the way to his room. It was his room now, not theirs, his. But everything in the room was Kate—the draperies, the bedspread, the small trinkets on shelves. Everything in the house had her touches, her personality. He wasn't sure how he would ever be able to remove her from this house.

He looked in Kate's closet. All her clothes still hung neatly as if waiting patiently for her to return and wear them. A row of boxes lined the top shelf, one of which contained the pictures. George pulled down the first box and opened it. Nothing but a few pieces of tissue paper were inside. The second one was a bit heavier. He pulled it down and removed the lid. Inside were letters bundled together in groups, all of them unopened. He pulled one bundle out and discovered their mysterious origin. They were addressed from Kate to David at an address George didn't recognize in Seattle. All were marked return to sender.

George pawed through the box. The letters were grouped by years—ten bundles in all, and four letters lay loosely. He picked up one of the unbundled letters. The envelope was postmarked December. Bright-red ink marked return to sender. The envelope was still sealed shut. George flipped it over again and again, curious why Kate kept these letters. Why had she written them in the first place? What would possess her to keep writing after they had been returned? And for that matter, why would she keep them. He would have thrown them away. He never would have written them after the first one had been returned.

He flipped the letter over again and eyed the back, trying to decide whether or not to open it. He felt as if he was invading her privacy, but she wasn't here to answer the question. Perhaps the letter would be more telling. Slowly, George ripped the back open and removed the letter.

My Dear Son,

The Thanksgiving feast is over, and I've pulled the Christmas boxes from the attic. It's turned cold already. Sixteen degrees last night. Perhaps it will snow this year—a white Christmas. You and I used to secretly pray for a white Christmas. For you, it was all about the snow and building snow forts or going skiing with your friends. For me, it's a memory of my mom and me ice skating in Shevlin Park during Christmas break when I was a girl. Every year, she'd take me shopping in Portland. We'd pick out presents for my dad. When we got back, we'd spend a day wrapping presents and then go ice skating in the park. Then we'd come home and drink hot cocoa by the fire. It never really felt like Christmas until it snowed. I don't know if I'd ever told you that. There are so many things I've never had the chance to tell you, although I've tried.

Your dad is out steelhead fishing on the Deschutes with Chuck, Wayne, and Fred. He'd often hoped that one day you'd join them on their fishing trips. Your father always bragged about your angling skills, fruit of his loin or something like that. I think it would have been nice to see you with him catching fish. Of course, your fish would be the biggest as always. Unless of course I went with the two of you. Maybe someday. It's not too late.

Your sister and her family moved into their new house last month. It's a beautiful house right on Squaw Creek at the east end of town near the Redmond cutoff. Her kids are growing so fast. Braden reminds me of your father in his expressions and fascination with all things nature. Jenna is the spitting image of Rachel, inquisitive and charming. Michael is still Michael—snowboarding every chance he gets. His little boy, Connor, is two. He's so much like Michael but into all things mechanical, particularly tractors.

We're all doing fine. I hope you are well, son. I hope you receive this letter someday, and I wait for your homecoming. Merry Christmas, son. May His light shine upon you and guide you.

Love, Mom

George folded the letter and placed it back in the envelope. Were all the letters like that, just thoughts she wished she could share with David? It seemed like an exercise in futility. Perhaps that's why she never told him about them. Just as he was about to put the lid back on the box, another letter caught his eye. It appeared as if it had never been sent. Why? Had she forgotten to mail it? Perhaps it just got stuck in with the rest.

George inspected it closely to see if he had missed something. Perhaps it had been sent and returned but the markings were faint, but they weren't. This letter had not been sent yet. There wasn't even a postmark on it. She'd addressed it and even put a stamp on it but never mailed it. George carefully pried the back flap open to remove the contents. The letter was dated two weeks prior to Kate's death.

My Dear Son,

I don't know how to tell you this, perhaps you already know. I have cancer, and what no one else knows is that it is terminal. I know it, and I can feel it. They are treating as best they can, but I'm afraid I won't be on this earth much longer. Oh, what I wouldn't give to see your face, your precious face that I gazed upon when I held you in my arms when you were born. I'm certain it's changed now and grown, wearing on it the marks of time. It's been so many years since I've seen your face. I can barely remember it. There are pictures, but none of them recent. I don't say this to make you feel guilty. It's just that I miss you so much. My heart's desire is that somehow, we all could put the past hurts behind us and be a family once again. I wish that you and your father could make peace. Lay this hostility aside. You're both so stubborn, you come by it naturally, and yet both have hearts that can love. I fear now that I will not live to see that reconciliation. There are so many things I want to tell you about life, about love, about forgiveness, and healing. God loves you, my son. My biggest regret is that I didn't teach you that well enough. I pray that by some miracle I can see you again before I die. But if I don't, know this: I always loved you no matter what and always will. It saddens me to think that you might not ever read this letter as you haven't read any of the letters I've sent you before. I will continue to pray that I can see you again. Until then.

Love always, Mom

George crumpled the letter in his fist as he felt an icy hand strangling his heart. He kicked the box the letters had been in and pulled himself up from the floor. Rage consumed him. The picture taken at David's graduation still hung in the hall. He pulled it from the wall and hurled it to the floor. The glass shattered on the ground. He found another picture of David, one from high school. He tore it from the wall and hurled it at the ground. Then another and another. The rage released as each frame shattered on the ground.

Footsteps pounded up the stairs.

"Dad, are you all right?" Rachel stared at him from the stairwell. Broken glass and frames were strewn down the hall.

"How could he do that to her?" George uttered through clenched teeth. The letter crumpled and curled as his fist tightened around it. "He broke her heart, and then the coward couldn't even come pay her respect."

"Who?" Rachel furrowed her brow in confusion.

"Your brother." He couldn't force himself to say *my son*. He wasn't sure he wanted to claim David as his son. Not after this. George threw the letter to the ground and walked down the hall.

"Dad? Where are you going?"

"Away from here," he said as he passed her on the stairs.

"But you have a house full of people."

"Lock up when you leave." George ran down the stairs and out the front door. He needed to be alone, to be away from the house.

*****

He peeled out of the driveway and drove aimlessly without thought or provocation. The lines on the highway blurred through his tears. But he continued on. An hour later, he turned onto West Odell Lake Road and followed it down to Shelter Cove. He leaned into the steering wheel as he shut off the engine. His boat was still tied up at the dock. He watched boats pulling into the marina and unloading on the docks. Other boats pulled out onto the lake for an evening run. The water smoothed out to a shimmering reflecting pool as the boats moved further into the lake. This was the last place he'd seen Kate happy. He wanted to remember her happy, not the shriveling woman hooked to monitors and IVs. Her last triumph had been the day's catch—five kokanee—and they had gone to waste.

The dock swayed under him as he walked out to the edge. When people talked about their spouse, they referred to them as their other half or their better half. And even when a couple married, the scripture said the two shall become one flesh. He felt as if half of him was gone, ripped from his side. He picked up a rock and hurled it as far as he could. His heart ached. He lowered himself to sit on the edge of the dock. He slumped over and wept. Kate was gone. He was half of who he used to be.

Chapter 21

Burying the dead was an odious task but a decent paying one. It wasn't as if someone dug the holes by hand. It merely required the skillful use of a backhoe—the ability to dig and fill precisely. But digging graves, even by machine, could be tricky in Central Oregon. First, there was the terrain which in some spots was solid volcanic rock, one of the hardest substances on the planet. Then there was the climate; in the wintertime, the ground could freeze solid, more sturdy than the volcanic rock. And in the summertime, on days like this one, one minute it could be sweltering hot; the next, a storm could blow in, and within ten minutes, a single cloudburst could turn an open hole into grave soup.

Off in the horizon, the storm clouds loomed. The white caps billowed above the Cascade Mountains as the graveside service was held. They stood by the outbuilding where the machines were kept, watching from a distance. They rarely knew the people being buried or even those who attended the internments. Still they watched for timing purposes. After the last car left through the gates, then they went to work, boxing up flowers and preparing the site to be filled.

The grave attendants watched the charcoal sky as it closed in above, menacing clouds creeping nearer. In the distance, great booming vibrations echoed off the mountains.

"Better get that dirt on top of her, or she's gonna get wet," the one on the ground said.

The other one operated a backhoe. He pulled up next to the open grave. It was a fine art to dig precise holes and leave just the right amount of dirt needed to backfill the opening. He moved levers and swung the bucket, moving the dirt back over the hole. They would set the headstone in the morning. It would be dried out by then. For the time being, they covered the loose dirt with a blue tarp to keep it from turning to mud.

Just as they finished, the first drops began to fall. They headed toward the main office buildings. They took shelter underneath a work shed just as the skies opened, pouring out cold rain toward the ground. Brilliant white flashes lit up the sky to south and east, and the wind whipped up dust against the driving rain. They had finished just in the nick of time.

Across the cemetery, they saw him ambling toward the grave, unaffected by the streams of rain and light. The shadowy figure walked directly to the new grave. He set something on the grave and stood there in the downpour. The guy had to be crazy or suicidal to stand out in the open in a storm like this. A brilliant flash hit the ground across the highway in a spectacular spray of sparks and fire. Their attention shifted to the display. When they turned back to see if the man had wised up and taken cover, he was gone.

Chapter 22

George was completely unaware how long he'd sat on the dock. The storm had passed over and the rain had stopped. People always talk about the calm before the storm, but not much is said about the calm after. The clouds moved northeast, revealing a bright-blue sky in their wake, and the water started to smooth out where the white caps had been only moments before. He too began to feel a calm come over him. He needed to let go of the pain he'd bottled up—the anger, the frustration. Reading the letter set him off. He was so angry, not just at David but at Kate, at God, and at himself. Kate should have told him, prepared him. For the past few months, he'd been operating on the premise that she would get better, that she had more time. God should have given her more time. He had prayed so often for nothing. God just wasn't listening. Now she was gone. His heart felt so heavy at times he found it hard to breathe. She was without a doubt the best thing that had ever happened to him.

George moved his legs, and the wet fabric of his suit clung to him uncomfortably. It was the first he noticed that he was soaked to the bone. Perhaps the time had come to go up to the house and get a change of clothes. In the rush of that day, Rachel had left all their clothes. He stood and turned. He saw the figure of a lean younger man coming down the dock toward him, his features obscured by the mist. For a moment, he let hope rise up. David had come after all to apologize, to set things right. Hope was quickly dashed the second he recognized the unmistakable swagger and tufts of red hair of his youngest son.

"What are you doing here?" George wiped his eyes, trying to keep his face slightly hidden from his son.

"Mac called Rachel. We were worried about you." Michael looked sorrowful.

"I wanted to be alone. If I had wanted you to know where I was, *I* would have called." George didn't mean to sound so harsh. He felt ashamed to have his son find him like this weeping like a child.

"Why? You didn't want us to see that you're human?"

"I wanted to grieve your mother alone, and I couldn't do it there with a house full of people," George said curtly.

"So why'd you go berserk on us?"

"Just something set me off." He kept his answer purposefully short. He really didn't feel like discussing it now.

"David?" His invidious tone spoke volumes about the resentment he felt toward his brother. George couldn't blame him. David had disappointed all of them.

"I expected to see him today. And…" George hadn't verbalized that yet. He had clung to the last shred of hope that David would have had the decency to at least make an appearance today. It was one thing to refuse to see her in the hospital. But to skip her funeral was cowardice at its worst. It spoke volumes about how little concern David had for them.

"I still can't believe he didn't show. How low do you have to be to skip your own mother's funeral?" Michael ranted. "But hopefully, *now* you can see he's not the perfect son you always made him out to be."

"I never thought David was perfect." George was stunned by Michael's comment.

"Yeah. Then why did you love him more than me?"

"I… I didn't. I don't." George was stunned. Just when he thought the emotional tidal waves had subsided.

"You could've fooled me. When he left, you left us too. Maybe not physically, but you did." Michael turned his head for a moment before continuing. "You know, I can't even remember once…you throwing the ball with me or you asking *me* to go fishing."

George stared at his son, the full weight of just how much he'd hurt him hitting him. He'd never intended to do so. Had he been so caught up in trying to figure out why David disappeared from their lives that he'd ignored his family? Michael had become an unwitting casualty in this ongoing battle of wills between David and him.

"I'm sorry. I just never thought you wanted to. You were always off skiing or snowboarding with your friends up at Hoodoo or Bachelor. And..." George picked up a rock and skimmed it across the water. The anger had seeped back in. "I didn't want to push you. I guess I pushed David too hard. I had to have done something wrong, otherwise he wouldn't have..." George shook his head. He tried to rationalize his actions, although he had no excuses for taking so little interest in Michael. "Anyways, I didn't want to make the same mistake with you."

"I always thought it was because David was your favorite," Michael said flatly.

"Oh, no. Son, I love you. I just didn't want to repeat my mistakes. I guess I can't win for losing." George shook his head. It was the first time either of them had honestly talked about how they felt with one another. Kate had always acted like a buffer. Without her there, they were forced to sort out their differences on their own. Maybe Kate should have asked for him to make peace with Michael. That at least was feasible. "So do you want to go fishing now?" George nodded toward the boat still tied up at the end of the dock.

"Are you serious?" Michael looked surprised.

"Why not?" George clasped his arm around his son's back and led the way.

They climbed down into the boat. George still wore his drenched suit. He started up the engine and pointed the boat toward Breezy Point. It was the first time that just the two of them had gone fishing, and it felt good. Father and son, just as it should be.

They motored out onto the lake, and the clouds cleared. George trolled the waters where Kate had caught her fish just over a week before. Within minutes, Michael landed a nice-sized kokanee. Golden light radiated from behind one of the clouds, streaming down in luminous rays. Kate was in heaven with God, and they were smiling.

After their impromptu fishing trip, George sent Michael home to be with his family. Michael had caught three fish to George's one. It turned out to be a good end to an extremely bad day. In one day, he'd buried his wife and came to the realization that David may never come home again. David had hurt him for the last time. He wouldn't waste any more energy on him. He wasn't worth it. If Kate had only known what kind of gutless wonder he'd turned out to be, she never would have asked him to make peace. It was an impossible task and one he had no intention of carrying out. The only good that came out of David's absenteeism was it allowed George the opportunity to reclaim a relationship with Michael. He lost one son and found the other.

To avoid the perpetual pity that surely awaited him at home, George decided to stay at the lake house for a couple of days. Rachel and Michael could handle the store for that long. He wasn't ready to deal with other people just yet. His employees, his customers, they would treat him differently, especially with his birthday just days away.

As he opened the door to the house, he realized that he had never stayed here alone, not merely without Kate but without anyone. Not once in the thirty-seven years he'd been coming to this place had he stayed here by himself. There had always been someone else here to help fill up the silence.

Slowly, he meandered from room to room, wondering if it had been a mistake. The house contained no television, no telephone, and no distractions. And every nook and cranny held a memory—the first time he met her parents, the day he proposed, the day he taught David to swim and then Rachel and Michael, and the awful day he drove from this place to the hospital.

He needed a plan. He needed something to do. In the kitchen, he took stock of the supplies and made a quick list of what he needed from Shelter Cove in the morning. He would fish for mackinaw, something he hadn't done in years. But he would need new tackle.

The challenge of finding the elusive fish would serve as the distraction he desperately needed.

After he had a list, he forced himself to go into the room where they had stayed. It was exactly as it had been when they left it just the week before. At the foot of the bed, his clothes still hung out the sides of his bag. He was relieved to see them. Anything would be a welcome change to the damp suit that still clung to him.

Once he changed, he sorted through the mess on the floor. Kate's book bag had spilled its contents all over the floor—books, magazines, scarves, and hats. A card envelope addressed to him hung out of the pocket on the front of the bag. He removed it and studied it curiously.

He stared at the outside of the envelope, afraid to look inside. The card sat here while she lay in a hospital bed dying. She never mentioned it. The entire time he sat in her room with her, not one word about it. After much deliberation, he opened it. Inside, the card read,

> To My Loving Husband on His Birthday

Kate, even in the midst of her illness, had taken the time to plan for his birthday. As he flipped the card open, an avalanche of papers fell from inside. He picked them up off the floor, inspecting them. Then he nearly fell to the floor himself. She had bought him a fishing trip on the Kenai River in Alaska—his dream vacation, one they'd talked about for years—plane tickets, a reservation sheet, and a brochure on the guided fishing trip.

He held the tickets for two in his hand. For two? Had she planned to go with him? When had she purchased the trip? It was too much. Pangs of grief swirled around him and engulfed him once again. Why? Why had God taken her? She was so beautiful and as close to perfect as he would ever know. Her heart amazed him. And now she was gone.

Chapter 23

During the summer months, Patterson's Hardware could barely keep enough inventory on hand for the onslaught of contractors doing work in and around Sisters. To make up for the lean winter months when snow made it nearly impossible to build anything, contractors took full advantage of the longer days to squeeze in as much work as possible. Business was booming. George scarcely had a moment's rest. But it hadn't always been like this.

The economic recession of the 1980s hit Bend with both barrels. The slowdown in housing, coupled with environmentalists screaming about endangered species, brought the logging industry to a complete standstill. Like many men in Bend, logging and millwork were all George had ever known. He had worked odd jobs, but it had been Kate's income that sustained them. He hated that! Relying on her. He was the man. He needed to provide for his family. They had three kids, one still in diapers, and the horizon looked bleak. George had no job prospects until Old Joe Davis hired him to help out at his hardware store in Sisters. A spry eighty-two, Davis needed help running the store. Old Davis had lost both his sons to war—his oldest in Korea and his youngest in Vietnam—and wanted someone he could trust to take over for him. He taught George all there was to know about the hardware business, about seasonal inventory and building customer loyalty. The only sage advice he'd passed on, "God didn't give us the golden rule for nothing. If you treat people—and by people, I mean customers—if you treat them the way you want to be treated, they'll always come back."

Old Davis died in the spring of 1985. His widow kept George on at the store as manager. Two years later, George bought the store. He thought of keeping the name Davis Hardware, but then he thought of his two sons and the legacy he wanted to leave for them. When George bought the store, he didn't know that being an entrepreneur meant giving your life to the store. He had seen years where he couldn't keep enough inventory to keep up with sales and years he couldn't give stuff away. The 1990s brought a building boom like none he'd ever seen. Then people stocked up for Y2K. After that, things quieted down for a year or two, but then the building kept coming. Now they were busier than ever. The new housing developments in Sisters kept a steady stream of contractors in the store throughout the day.

George welcomed the onslaught of business. It occupied his mind with something other than missing her. He spent every waking hour at the store, devoting every spare second to inventories and delivery schedules. No detail was overlooked. He worked from the time the sun peeked over the mountains until he could no longer keep his eyes open. Some nights he slept on the couch in his office rather than make any effort to drive home.

Sundays offered his only respite during the week. Then he could be found somewhere on the Metolius River with a fly rod in hand. He began trying new spots on the river, venturing further north toward the Indian Reservation. There were pools with fish as thick as thieves. He perfected his cast and identified which patterns worked best in which spots. He even went so far as keeping a journal of where he fished at what time of day and what nymphs he used and what he caught.

Other than work, he made every effort to avoid spending time in town. He shopped at Costco in Bend once a month rather than go into Ray's. It had been a little over a month since Kate had passed, and people still looked at him with pity because of it. And every time he heard the words "I'm so sorry for your loss," he cringed. It reminded him she was gone, and he didn't need any reminders.

*****

In mid-July, Pastor Mike O'Connell stopped by the store. He stood at the contractors' counter where George was working and waited while he completed an order for Bill Rogers, a local builder.

"Hey, George." Mike stepped up to the counter in front of George.

"Hey, Mike. What can I do you for?" George was still scribbling notes from the order he'd just taken.

"I'm not here for lumber or anything." Mike waved his hands in a nullifying motion.

"Then what are you doing here?" George returned to scribbling notes. It was too hectic for a social visit. Four major orders had been placed that morning alone. He had been on the phone with one of his vendors trying to get a rush on a special-order beam for one of the big developers in town. His call to Weyerhaeuser directly followed to see how quickly they could ship him fifty thousand board feet of two-by-six studs. And he still hadn't decided what to do about the trip Kate bought him. He only had a week or so left before he forfeited the trip entirely.

"We haven't seen you in church lately," Mike said in the pat, concerned pastor tone.

"Well. We've been busy." He gestured to the bustle of men in the store. *Great, just what I need, the pastor hounding me about church.* Going to church meant seeing people who felt sorry for him. They'd want to ask how he was doing or, worse yet, talk about Kate. It hurt too much to talk about her.

"I thought maybe it had something to do with…" Mike stumbled over the words. "Maybe you weren't ready to attend church solo."

"You thought wrong," George snapped back.

"Could I buy you some lunch, and we could chat?"

"About what?" George said, exasperated.

"Life and things."

"Why would you want to do that?" George tapped his pen on the counter in a nervous irritated manner.

"Some friends and family are a little concerned."

"Rachel." He shot a censuring glance over his shoulder and caught her looking out at him, then looked down quickly.

"Yes. She's concerned," Mike confirmed.

"She worries too much. I'm fine really." George shuffled some papers, trying to look busy. He was busy. There were no less than twenty things he could do instead of going to lunch with the pastor of the church.

"What's the harm in lunch?" Mike persisted. "A man's got to eat."

George realized the pastor wasn't going to leave unless he agreed. "All right." George gestured to Rachel that he was leaving and walked outside. The sultry dog days of summer had already begun. The thermometer on the bank read eighty degrees by noon. Before the day ended, it would be a hundred. Still, George and Mike walked the six blocks to Coyote Creek Café.

Sisters had plenty of places to eat in town, but only a handful actually had seating for more than twenty people. One of the nicer restaurants in town, Coyote Creek Café offered air-conditioning in addition to the meal. Nikki was working and sat them at a nice booth close to the air vent. She brought over ice water. They ordered without even looking at the menu.

"You know after my wife died, I sort of retreated for a while," Mike broke the silence.

"I didn't know you'd been married."

"We were married fifteen years. She was killed six months before I moved to Sisters."

"I'm sorry. I didn't know."

"Not many people do. It's been five years now, and sometimes the wound is so fresh it feels like just months have passed. It gets less a little each day, but some things remind me of her, and it feels like just yesterday I kissed her before she headed out for work."

"How did she die? If you don't mind me asking."

"I don't mind. I wouldn't have brought it up if I did. She was killed by a drunk driver on her way to work. She was a schoolteacher." Mike quickly looked out the window as if the memory were still painful.

"I'm sorry." George truly meant it. He knew that pain. He was living it.

"Yeah, me too. Not just about my wife but about yours. You know, the thing that I couldn't stand was everyone treating me with kid gloves. They did it for six months. And I'd get upset or defensive. I really didn't know how to accept sympathy from others. Looking back, I was pretty volatile. I'd blow up for no reason at all. I ran off half the membership of the church I was leading. It's natural to be angry when we grieve."

"So that's what this is all about." George knew that there had to be a point to this conversation, a sermon somewhere in the visit.

"Rachel said you've been a little upset. She told me about the incident at the house after the funeral."

"Look, I know Rachel put you up to this. But honestly, talking about David isn't going to help me be any less upset."

"It might. Sometimes talking about things help us deal with them."

"What's there to talk about? David chose not to come see Kate while she was still on this earth. His choice was spiteful and mean-spirited. Kate went to the grave with a broken heart. He did that." George's words were fueled with the anger that still simmered beneath the surface.

"Maybe he had a good reason." Mike shrugged.

"There's no reason good enough. Even men in the armed forces are given a furlough to see dying family members. And as far as I know, my…" George stopped short of saying "my son." It hurt to call him that. "David is not bound by anything as restrictive as the army that would prohibit him from coming."

"George, you can't let David's actions do this to you."

"Do what?"

"Make you bitter and angry."

"What would you suggest then, good pastor?" George said mockingly. His blood pressure had risen just from the conversation about David. But the pastor had insisted on talking about it.

"How about forgiving him?"

"What? Why would I? How could I?"

"Forgiveness is a process. You don't just forgive someone, and it's over. That's what Christ meant when He said to forgive your brother seventy times seven. You forgive a little each day."

"But why should I forgive him?" George knew that Mike was doing his job, but he was barking up the wrong tree. David hadn't even asked to be forgiven and probably didn't even see anything wrong with what he'd done.

"If I can forgive the piece of human trash that killed my wife, Connie…" Mike stopped and responded to George's look of surprise. "Connie was killed by a drunk driver. The guy didn't even have a license because he already had three prior convictions. But I forgive him daily."

"Why? Why would you forgive him? What about justice?"

"God is just, and He forgave me," Mike said calmly.

George didn't have a response to that.

"God forgives us because He loves us. We are supposed to forgive others because we love Him. But see, the beauty of forgiveness is, it isn't about the other person. It's about us not allowing their actions to make us bitter." Mike paused a moment before continuing, "Maybe if you came to church—"

"Look, I know you want to help," George interrupted. He knew where the pastor was headed, and he'd heard enough. "Church was Kate's thing, not mine. I went because she wanted me to go. The truth is, I'd rather fish than go to church."

"I see. So you don't need God to help you with your grief."

"I didn't say that. I believe in God and His Son, Jesus Christ. I just don't particularly like church, all the singing and the hugging. It's not really my thing." George said. "Besides, Jesus's disciples were fishermen. It may sound strange to you, but I actually feel that fishing is my way of worshipping. I feel close to God when I'm out there alone with Him."

"I see. I actually hear that a lot from men, especially men who have lost their wives. Not necessarily fishing but some sort of outdoor activity. But see, the church can offer support. The church is a body that helps one another in times of need."

"And what is it that I need? A bunch of well-wishers telling me how sorry they are for my loss? No, thank you." George didn't mean to sound so glib.

"I hear you there. After my wife passed, I got so sick of the sweet sentiments and the well-wishes. I remember thinking they just have no idea the pain I felt every time they said her name. It just reminded me of her even more."

"Yep. I don't need it." George shook his head.

"What do you need?"

"I don't know. I don't know what I need. I've just been taking it one day at a time and working as much as I can." George wasn't sure why he was telling Mike all this.

"Nighttime is the worst?"

"Yeah." George looked at him incredulously. It was eerie how he knew.

"I couldn't sleep for the first year. I still wake up every once in a while and think she's there, until I reach over, and her side of the bed is cold."

Mike's honesty surprised George, but at the same time, it was comforting to hear another man say the things he was feeling. He felt so weak and ashamed of missing her so much. The only other man he ever really knew who had lost his wife was Kate's father, and he had isolated himself and drank himself to death within two years of his wife's death. He knew he didn't want that. He'd practically promised Kate he wouldn't do that.

"Here you go." Nikki interrupted, sliding plates in front of the men. George half expected Mike to bow his head and say a long-winded prayer right there in the restaurant, but instead, he dove right into his sandwich. George had ordered the prime rib sandwich, a Coyote Café delicacy. Mike had their famous BLT. The men ate in silence.

Once finished, Mike slid his plate to the side. He waited for George to do the same before resuming conversation.

"Listen, do you think you might be able to teach me to fly fish?"

"Seriously?" George couldn't see it. The pastor in slacks, a button-down shirt and tie, fly fishing? He didn't strike George as the outdoorsy type.

"Sure. It seems to be a part of the Central Oregon experience. I sort of feel like an outsider, not knowing how."

"Okay. When?" George offered, wiping the remaining crumbs from his hands.

"How about next Saturday?"

"All right. I'll meet you here in the Coyote parking lot at four-thirty."

"In the morning?" Mike sounded skeptical for a minute.

"No." He watched the pastor let out a sigh of relief. "In the summertime, the bite is best in the evening, from six till dark."

"All right then. I'll meet you here at four-thirty *PM*, Saturday."

George nodded. "Okay. And thanks for lunch." He stood. "But I really do have a lot of work to do."

George walked off and waved to Nikki as he exited through the lounge entrance. Lunch really hadn't been as bad as he expected. He ambled slowly back to the store, mulling over the lunchtime conversation. Mike seemed like a decent enough fellow. The whole spiel about forgiveness was a bit preachy, but maybe he had a point. Being angry with David didn't help him any. It just made him angry. He hoped that he hadn't made a mistake inviting the pastor to go fishing. Would their entire day be like lunch had been?

Chapter 24

Saturday afternoon, George met Mike in the Coyote Creek parking lot just as they had arranged. George hardly recognized him at first. Apparently, Mike had gone to one of the outdoor stores in Bend and purchased all-new gear. He was clad in a new logo T-shirt, though George suspected Mike didn't even know what the logo was for. He also wore just-out-of-the-box water sandals and a pair of hiker shorts that prominently displayed his tanless legs, in a shade George could only describe as day-glow white. To top it all off, Mike had purchased a multipocketed fishermen's vest. George tried not to chuckle as Mike climbed into the cab of the truck.

George brought along the fly rod that he had taught both of his boys to fish with. David had taken to it almost immediately, but Michael lacked the patience or finesse for fly fishing. Michael had fought the rod and the line every time they went out. He would usually end up with line wound around him instead of the reel. Still, the rod was good for beginners. It was a good choice to teach position and poise. Since Mike had never really been fishing before, George thought it best to take him to the Crooked River, out past Prineville below Bowman Dam. The water there was flat and easy, and the fish weren't all that finicky.

The drive took an hour, and the men chatted about baseball and fishing. They arrived at mile marker 17 at ten to six—perfect timing all in all. It afforded them three hours of fishing—two hours for Mike to learn and an hour of solid fishing when the bite was good.

George led Mike to the riverbank. "Now first things first," George said as he got the rods set up. "The first thing you need to do is forget anything you might already know about fishing."

"I don't know much. I've been fishing two, maybe three times before." Mike watched closely as George handled the flies and tied them to the end of the line.

"Good. Fly fishing is considered a gentlemen's sport. It is about finesse, not strength, and timing is everything," George began. He held the boys' rod in his hand to demonstrate. He took a step out into the water. The cool water was refreshing on his feet after the long drive. "All right, first I want you to watch, and then I'll get you started. Most instructors will tell you to cast by moving your rod between ten and two, but I'm a firm believer in keeping it between eleven and one." George pointed to the dial on his watch and then demonstrated with the rod.

George eased the rod through the air in a smooth continuous motion. He gripped the rod firmly in his right hand and the line in his left. With each cast, he gently loosed the line from the reel and threw more line further out across the water, letting the fly gently rest atop the water and glide easily on the current toward him. After about five or ten minutes, he pulled his line back in and handed the rod to Mike.

"Do you have the general idea?" George searched his student for any sign that he might have paid attention.

"Yeah. I think so."

"Don't worry, we have some time. And remember to let the rod do the work. You're not trying to force the line out with brute strength. If you keep a nice smooth motion and keep your loops nice and tight, inertia will do the rest," George instructed.

He stood back and watched Mike with the rod. His first few casts were stiff, and the line whipped across the water, but after a few tries, he began to find a rhythm. George had purposefully tied a bogus hatch on the line. He wanted Mike to learn technique before trying to figure out how to reel in a fish.

After an hour or so of practicing, Mike pulled in the line and sat up on shore for a few minutes with a cool drink. "It's hard work." He rubbed his arm.

George was so accustomed to the sport he'd forgotten that while fly fishing didn't require brute strength, it did require controlled movements. Until Mike developed a feel for the line and the rod, he would use muscles he didn't know he had. But he had picked it up rather quickly, probably since he'd never really been fishing before and didn't have to unlearn spinner casting. George switched the nymphs on the end of the line. He grabbed his rod and headed down to the water. It was time for Mike to learn the thrill of landing a fish.

Not five minutes after his first cast, the tip of the pole began nodding as the line went taut.

"What's wrong? What do I do now?" Mike asked, panicky.

"Pull back lightly and start pulling in the line like I showed you," George responded. He quickly gathered in his own line to help Mike who looked completely out of his element.

"Why?"

"You have a fish on." George tried not to laugh. He began walking over toward Mike as he drew in the last bit of line for his own rod. He stood right behind Mike, guiding him through every step. Luckily, the fish didn't put up too much of a fight.

Mike practically fell into the river, trying to keep hold of the slippery beast he held in his hand. George demonstrated how to remove the hook without hurting the fish or sticking the hook into a finger. And then George showed Mike the fine art of bonking. It was much more humane than letting them suffocate in a cooler. The fish was a beautiful rainbow. Not a trophy or anything, but good sized.

After that, Mike confidently walked back into the river and cast over and over again. He caught one more fish before they called it a day.

"I can't thank you enough." Mike lamented as they loaded their gear and prized fish into the truck. The sun had long since set, and dark shadows were beginning to make their way across the road.

"No problem." George actually enjoyed the company. It had been awhile since he went fishing with anyone. He had plenty of fishing buddies, but he had avoided even them since Kate died. Perhaps it was time to stop avoiding people.

"I was astounded. I mean literally awestruck by the beauty of God's creation today," Mike began pouring out on the drive home. "I know everywhere around here is beautiful, but standing in the river and just being there, now I understand."

"Understand what?" George knew that catching the first fish often had a certain adrenaline rush associated with it. But he had never been out with a guy who immediately attributed his catch to God. Then he'd also never been fishing with a pastor before.

"Why you do it. Why you go fishing to be near God." Mike looked as if it were his first time seeing the mountains. "I was thinking while we were standing out there fishing that maybe this year, our retreat should be like a fishing, camping kind of thing—sort of a fishing fellowship. What do you think?"

"I'd go. If it involved fishing and outdoors, I'd go. I'm not the kind of guy who likes sitting inside and relating. That's women's stuff." George turned back onto the highway. The light began to fade over the mountains.

"Would you be willing to help me set it up?"

"I don't know about that," George answered skeptically. He didn't know how to plan or arrange things—especially not a retreat for a bunch of men.

"Well, could you at least give me pointers on where and who to contact, what rivers? What time of year?" Mike rattled off details.

"Sure. I can do that." The sun finally took its last light, leaving the quiet darkness. The road hummed beneath the tires on the road. The conversation had ended. Both men quietly reflected on the day. George had found a way to fit into church. For a fleeting moment, he suspected Kate in heaven still orchestrating, nudging God's shoulder to get George involved in the church.

"You know, I can't thank you enough, George," Mike said as they pulled into the parking lot at Coyote Creek.

"No problem. I'd say anytime, but it's our busy season, and I've also got a trip coming up." George wasn't sure why he'd mentioned that. He was still undecided.

"I know. Rachel told me about your dilemma, that Kate purchased the trip for two to Alaska. She said that you were having trouble deciding whether or not to go."

"She talks a lot." George didn't know if he should be embarrassed or upset.

"You don't have any fishing buddies?"

"None of them can get away. Fred's the sheriff, and he's understaffed. Chuck's the football coach, and they're starting practices next week. And Wayne's a builder. He's as busy as we are." George didn't know why he explained so much.

"And your son Michael?" Mike prodded.

"I offered. He didn't want to. He's not *really* interested in fishing." George had actually thought that after their impromptu fishing at Odell, that Michael would be the most likely candidate to go, but he turned him down.

"I think you should go." Mike paused a second. "Seeing you fish today. It's your passion. Kate wouldn't want you to pass up the opportunity. Maybe you're meant to go alone."

George nodded quietly. He'd never considered that. It seemed like such a waste of money. The package was for two, and there were no refunds. But it was paid for, and maybe Mike had a point. He'd been so focused on trying to find someone to go with him he hadn't considered going alone. It was ironic. He'd spent the past few weeks trying desperately to be left alone, yet the thought of taking a vacation solo had never occurred to him. What would it hurt?

Chapter 25

When George stepped off the plane in Kenai, Alaska, he knew he'd made the right decision. He would thank Mike when he got back. The view from the airport was spectacular beyond imagination. On the flight in, he saw wilderness so breathtakingly beautiful he was certain he'd never encounter the likes of it anywhere else. Snowcapped peaks fringed the water that reflected a sky so deep and blue that it felt as if the heavens were nearer somehow.

A shuttle from the lodge met him at the baggage area to take him the ten or so miles from the airport to the lodge. The scenery along the road resembled some of the more remote areas of Oregon, lush and green. But here, the colors were more vibrant; even the river looked like a precious stone glimmering in the morning sun in a shade of blue green he'd never seen before. On the horizon, towering mountains stood sentinel around the valleys like a protective shield.

The lodge was amazing, a hand-hewn log lodge. Not cabin. Lodge with six thousand square feet to roam inside. Two great rooms, both adorned with floor-to-ceiling rock walls housed huge fireplaces to gather around after a day of fishing. His hosts, Bob and Cindy Handley, met him in the foyer and gave him the tour. After notifying them of his dilemma the week before his arrival, they rearranged everything for him, including the fishing trips. Kate had booked them with bigger outfits which required a two-party minimum, but since he was solo and an avid fisherman, they had arranged a private guide for three days. Bob led George to his room upstairs, nothing fancy, just a nice clean room, with a bath and a balcony overlooking the river below. Bob left George with an itinerary of what they had planned for him. George had an hour or so to settle in before his first float. As he looked out his window at the river rolling by, the excitement of it all finally kicked in. He was in Alaska about to embark on a trip that was the best the sport of fishing had to offer. He could hardly wait to hit the water.

*****

Per the arrangements, George stood on the front deck at one o'clock and waited. A few minutes later, Bob walked up with another man, who George could only surmise was the fishing guide.

"George. This is Phil Havens. He's usually booked this time of year cause he's one of the best," Bob introduced the guide.

George eyed the man with a gray beard and salt-and-pepper hair. George wasn't sure what he had expected, maybe a Grizzly Adams type given the untamed wilderness around him. But Phil looked like any one of the men that frequented his store, clean-cut, tan, just an average Joe. He shook his hand and followed him out to a truck hooked up to a drift boat.

Phil drove east toward a place called Cooper Landing. George lost all sense of time as he watched the scenery around him in awe. Every bend in the road exposed more splendor. They turned down a gravel road and followed it to a small boat ramp. Phil stopped the truck to unload the boat. George followed his lead and helped unload the gear.

They boarded the drift boat and pushed away from shore. A half mile downstream, they spotted two brown bears on the riverbank devouring their spoils. Around the next bend in the river, a moose craned his neck down to drink. High above them, a bald eagle soared, announcing its presence with high and loud cries. George took in all the sights and sounds. Never before had he encountered so many species in one place at one time.

"So, George, where'd you say you were from?" Phil began the conversation once they had settled in the boat and had begun floating.

"Sisters, Oregon." George half expected the usual—where's that or is that near Portland. Very few people outside of Oregon had ever heard of Sisters.

"I know a guy from there. What did you say your last name was?" Phil seemed intrigued.

"Patterson, George Patterson."

"George Patterson, any relation to David Patterson?" he asked casually.

George nearly fell out of the boat. The odds of a fishing guide arranged by his hosts in Alaska knowing his son had to be on par with winning the lottery ten times in a row. "He's my son."

"Oh. So you're David's dad." Phil grew quiet for a few minutes and rowed the boat. "I'm sorry to hear about your wife."

"How'd you know about Kate?" George looked at him incredulously. It was uncanny this man, someone he didn't know from Adam, not only knew his son but had seen him recently enough to know about Kate.

"David was up here about a month ago. He stayed with friends and camped up along the Russian River," Phil explained as if it were no big deal.

"I see." The whole idea that this man had seen David recently was mind-boggling.

"He talked a lot about his mother, something I'd never known him to do in all the time that I've known him."

"*How* exactly did you know my son?"

"He was one of my students at UW. I helped him get into grad school and helped him with an internship with Alaska Fisheries Science Center," Phil explained as if George should be familiar with at least some of what he was saying.

George didn't know how to respond. He was both curious and fearful of talking to this man about his son. He wanted desperately to ask questions but afraid of the answers, if he knew them. He'd already told him more than he'd known for the past eleven years, like the fact that David had interned in Alaska and had gone on to graduate school. Until that moment, George had no idea what David had done after graduating college. Phil offered the first glimpse into David's life.

"Why would he come here and not come home?" George heard the words escape his mouth, although he hadn't intended to ask them.

"I don't know exactly why David came up here. I think maybe because of my history with cancer," Phil responded, not realizing George hadn't meant to ask. "I've had a double dose. My wife, Rene, died of cancer two years ago. And I was diagnosed with prostate cancer five years ago."

"But you look so healthy." George remembered all the patients at the cancer center; even those who were winning their battle with cancer still looked unhealthy. And Phil looked as if he could compete in a triathlon if he wanted to. "How did you do it?"

"Are you a religious man, George?"

"I guess you could say that. I read the Bible and go to church." George was never quite sure how to answer that question, especially when he didn't know where the conversation was going.

"See, I believe that it's only by God's mercy and grace that I'm still here. When I was diagnosed, my prognosis was—well, it was pretty grim. But chemo worked, and I've been in full remission for three years." He turned the boat down a channel past another river that poured in from the north. He deftly guided the boat through the current before the water slowed again, and the conversation resumed. "Rene wasn't so lucky. She went through a round of chemo and a round of radiation before she succumbed. So I think David knew I'd relate."

"I'm sorry. Here I am rambling away, and I didn't even realize."

"No worries. I'm on the other side of grief, where I can remember how great she was and all the adventures we shared." Phil's face lit up as he said it. Then his face turned somber as he looked at George. "But I remember the beginning. The part where you're afraid to run into someone because it will remind you of her, and then the hurt comes at you like a freight train."

"How'd you do it?" George eyed this man who appeared healthy and happy. How had he not only overcome the odds of cancer but then been able to move past the grief of losing his wife to the same dreaded disease?

"It's gonna sound crazy, but I started talking to her as if she were right there. I'd done it for so long. Every day, she was there to talk to. I guess that's what I missed most, her listening to me. So I talked to her, and over time, I could remember her without missing her so much I wanted to die. Eventually, I got to the point that I could be thankful that God let me know her while she was here."

George nodded quietly. They drifted silently through the water around another bend in the river. Phil pulled the boat up onto a bar in the middle of the river. He directed George to a large pool on the south side of the bar. He followed Phil's lead. The pole was heavier than he was accustomed to and the flies much larger than anything he'd ever used before. But the rhythm, the movement was the same. Phil had tied on a fly he called the Battle Creek, and George could see the fish rising toward it in the light-blue-green water. Within thirty minutes, George landed the largest sockeye salmon he had ever seen. It had to have weighed at least ten pounds. Phil prodded and pushed the fish into the cooler and returned to the water's edge. Another twenty minutes passed before George landed the second one. It wasn't much smaller than the first. Phil switched flies and moved George down the beach where he hooked into a coho. After he landed his sixth coho, he set down his rod, his heart still pounding with the exhilaration of the catch. For a fleeting moment, he forgot his grief and simply enjoyed the best day of fishing he'd ever had.

With his limit met, they got back into the boat to drift back toward the lodge. During the float, Phil pointed out the various noteworthy sights. Kate would have loved the scenery and solitude. She would have fallen out of the boat trying to get pictures of the bears and the moose. The past two months, he'd spent hiding from Kate's memory, trying to escape the pain associated with it. But maybe, Phil was right. The point wasn't to try and forget. He knew he'd never be able to do that. Maybe healing occurred when he could embrace her memory and be thankful he'd known her at all.

George remembered the last conversation he'd had with Mike before he left. "God leads us down a path. Our job is to follow by faith and listen to what He is telling us." But what was God telling him? What was he supposed to do with what he was learning on a drift boat in the middle of the Kenai River?

*****

After dinner, George went and sat on the pebbled beach of the river. Even though the clock read ten to nine, the sun still shone just as bright as midafternoon. The beach was quiet, and the bright aqua-colored water flowed past swiftly. The solitude of the beach was welcoming. He surveyed the panoramic vista and stopped as his gaze fell upon the mountain range to the north that Phil had pointed out during their float.

He picked up a handful of the small pebbles and let them slip through his hand. "You would have loved it here, Kate." It was the first time he had spoken to her since her death. He felt silly doing it, but simply saying her name as if addressing her felt cathartic. "That hill over there is called Resurrection Pass. There's a trail over the top of it that miners used during the gold rush. On the other side is a town called Hope. When Phil told me that, I could hear you plain as day saying, 'How fitting because the only hope is in the resurrection.' How many times did you tell me that? I told Phil, that's the guide, I told him you would probably want to climb it. And you would, wouldn't you?" He picked up more rocks and, this time, threw them across the water. "I saw some bears today and a moose. They say there are even some caribou around here, but I haven't seen any. And Phil, he knows David. Pretty well. David came up here last month, but then you probably already knew that. Did you know before? I wonder. But you couldn't have." He sighed heavily. He was rambling. He never thought about what he would say to her; he just talked. "I miss you, Kate. Not just the big things but the way you'd hum when you did the dishes or the little notes you'd leave on the fridge. So many things." He felt the tears slide down his face as he watched the aquamarine water flow by.

The next day, Phil took him to the Lower Kenai River in a twenty-foot aluminum boat with a covered drive and seat area. To catch the big kings, they needed to troll rather than fly fish. Trolling moved slower than drifting, not as much action. Kings were pernickety fish. Gear and just the right bait were key to catching them. Phil had told George that for most people, it took forty hours of fishing to catch one king. So they killed the time talking. They chatted more about fishing and about what Phil actually taught, fish sciences, rather than dead wives or an absent son. An hour into their trip, George got lucky. His pole began to dance, and he fought the monster fish for fifteen minutes before they pulled it onto the boat. George felt that same rush of adrenaline that he felt after catching the first fish. His arms would certainly be sore in the morning, but the prize was worth it. When they pulled into the marina at Soldotna, they weighed the enormous fish—all sixty-five pounds of it. The fish weighed more than Braden. He posed for a picture with his trophy catch.

*****

As he packed to go home, George carefully wrapped the souvenirs bought for Michael and Rachel and the grandchildren. Bob had helped him pack the fish the night before—all 150 pounds of it. Kate would have been amazed by the bountiful catch. She would have already started thinking of new ways to prepare it and figuring out how much they could smoke to give to their friends. Though she hadn't been able to go with him physically, she had been a part of every minute of his dream trip.

He helped load his bags into the van and took one last look around. "Thank you, Kate," He whispered softly. Thanks to Phil, he had started to make peace with her passing.

George sat in the airport terminal waiting for his flight. David invaded his thoughts unbidden. Try as he might, George simply couldn't clear David from his mind. George still hadn't forgiven him for what he'd done, or rather not done. Phil had given him the first glimpse of a son he didn't know. Maybe he wasn't as bad as George had thought. Maybe there was a good reason he didn't come home. He scanned the faces around him, taking careful notice of men in their twenties and thirties. None of them bore any resemblance to

David. But subconsciously, he continued searching the crowds for him. It was strange to think that David had been there just weeks before. The stewardess announced the boarding. George stood in line to go home. Would David ever come home? If Kate's funeral couldn't bring him back, what would?

Chapter 26

The first Saturday in October, George agreed to go with Rachel, Steve, Michael, and Nikki to dinner in Bend to celebrate Rachel's Birthday. They had spent so much time dwelling on death. Now it was time to celebrate life. Summer had come and gone without so much as a family get-together. They had let birthdays and holidays pass without the solace of family. Instead of the usual barbecue and firework bonanza, Rachel and Steve went camping with some friends for the Fourth of July, while George had hit the river alone. Their normal family vacations and barbecues were put on hold while they grieved Kate. For the first time in thirty-five years, the Pattersons had not vacationed at Odell in August. Without Kate, it felt like an intrusion. But Rachel had turned thirty, a major milestone, and they could no longer put life on hold to grieve.

George offered to spring for dinner so long as they went to the Pine Tavern. He didn't want to try some new bistro; he wanted something he could count on. Rachel called and made reservations for the back dining room for six o'clock. George circled downtown just after five-thirty, searching for a parking spot, and finally found one between Minnesota and Oregon Streets. He had promised to meet them at the restaurant ten minutes early. Rachel had been adamant that he not be late.

He couldn't remember the last time he had been in downtown Bend. New businesses had followed all the new houses with all the new people. He hardly recognized the historic area of Bend. The buildings were the same tired-looking brick buildings that had been there since the 1920s, but the store fronts and businesses had changed. A bunch of uppity restaurants and bistros had replaced coffee shops and corner diners. There were still a few spots from the town he remembered, but most had been replaced with new and improved stores. Even the Old Mill District, the very heart and soul of the logging community that once was Bend, had been completely rebuilt into a fancy new shopping area—one of those outdoor esplanade-type malls. It was odd to see people shopping where the sawdust piles used to sit.

He met up with Rachel and Steve at the corner up the street, and they walked together. Pine Tavern was only a few blocks down toward Mirror Pond. George was eyeing some of the new construction when a man leaving an ATM caught his eye. He turned his head and then glanced back to be certain. The resemblance was uncanny. Could it really be David, or had he become so consumed by thoughts of David since his return from Alaska that he had begun imposing David's features on a stranger's face? He scanned other passersby for evidence that this might be the case, but no one else resembled David. He glanced over his shoulder once more, but the man had disappeared around the corner. He dismissed the encounter. He promised Rachel he would do his best to enjoy the evening, and he was determined not to let anything interfere with that, not even some random man that looked like his son. Besides, how would he know if it was David? The last time he'd seen his son, he had been a fresh-faced twenty-one-year-old about to graduate college. How would he recognize his thirty-two-year-old son even if he did run into him on the street? The thought of not knowing his own son disturbed him more than the thought of seeing David's face on every stranger in the crowd.

"What's wrong, Dad?" Rachel asked, placing a hand on his shoulder.

"Nothing. I just thought I saw someone." George shrugged, and they continued on to the restaurant. How could he explain it? He hadn't told Rachel or Michael about meeting Phil and his knowledge of David. The only person he'd told about it was Pastor Mike. Besides, this was Rachel's night—a night to celebrate Rachel's life as it was meant to be celebrated. Today, she turned thirty years old, and this year had aged her far beyond her years. If anyone deserved a night on the town, it was Rachel. Why ruin it by bringing up a sore subject like David?

"Here we are." Rachel gestured in a dramatic ta-da fashion.

He hesitated at the door. The last time he'd been to the Pine Tavern for dinner had been the night he found out Kate had cancer. It hadn't occurred to him when he asked Rachel to make the reservations. He tried to force a smile to hide the melancholy mood brewing inside. They had spent many celebratory dinners here, and the last real night out he'd spent with her was here. George tried to push it from his mind. He'd been trying for months to find a way to not miss her every time another memory blindsided him.

Inside, Nikki and Michael were waiting for them.

"Wow. Is this my present? You're actually here on time," Rachel remarked sarcastically.

"That's all you wanted? Good. I can take the present back," Michael kidded.

George wondered if they would ever grow out of the juvenile sibling bickering that they had mastered. The hostess waited for a pause in their banter, then led them to the back room, past the old ponderosa that grew right up through the middle of the dining room. Their table had a breathtaking view of Mirror Pond glowing in hues of pink and orange as the sun set.

Despite the bittersweet memories, George actually enjoyed going to dinner with the kids. He worked with Rachel and Michael every day, but at work, they were constantly busy helping customers so much that they rarely talked about anything other than work. He missed the barbecues and the get-togethers. He missed the laughter and the sardonic banter. He hoped that by the holidays, they could be together without it turning into a memorial.

After dinner, as they waited on dessert, George pulled the envelope and box from his coat pocket. He waited until he had Rachel's full attention before sliding it across the table.

"Dad, what's this?"

"Just open it." He didn't want to ruin it ahead of time.

Rachel started with the card and gasped when she came to the inscription. Kate had left specific instructions not to give them to her until her birthday. Through tears, Rachel carefully undid the bow and unwrapped the small box. Inside was a telltale pale blue box. Rachel's hand shook as she opened it. Inside, the beautiful diamond-and-sapphire necklace sparkled in the candlelight. Rachel held her hand to her mouth.

"I can't believe she did this?" Rachel used her napkin to blot her face. "We saw this on our last…our last shopping trip. At Tiffany's." Her voice faded out as she wept. "I can't believe she bought it."

George swallowed hard to force the lump in his throat down. Kate had arranged so much in her last month of life. Her lawyer was still working out some of the details. George had been meeting with him once every two weeks or so just to sign papers for this or that. The only difficulty had been accepting her wishes for David. Not once did she think of excluding him. Kate had made her final wishes and final gestures out of love. Soon the kids would know just how much. To fulfill those wishes, he would somehow need to get David to come home.

Book 2

David

Chapter 27

Early fall in Central Oregon brought with it many changes. The leaves turned from a pale green to vibrant red and orange, redefining the landscape. The mountains once again coated themselves in white. The tourists changed from summer campers to hordes of hunters covered from head to toe in camouflage with their similarly painted Polaris four-wheeled ATVs in the back of their trucks. But fall also brought the revered steelhead southeast down the Columbia into the Lower Deschutes River. Avid fishermen sought after the elusive steelhead like hunters after the trophy bull elk. Steelhead are a finicky fish; some days they won't even so much as look at the line in the water. The next day, it's impossible to keep them off the hook. And pound for pound, they fought harder than any other fish around the Northwest. The best reason of all to catch them was how delectable they tasted no matter how you cooked them. Every year, George waited for steelhead season like most men wait for football season.

For twenty some odd years now, George and his fishing buddies—Chuck Fisher, Fred Bricker, and Wayne Rogers—would drift down the Deschutes above Maupin every first Sunday of the month. Like clockwork. They didn't have to call to check; they had standing plans where to meet and at what time. The only time that any of them had ever been late in the twenty or so years that they had been fishing together was when Fred, being the sheriff, had been called out to a DUII early in the morning. But he still found a way to meet them at the river two hours downstream from the put in point.

*****

The first Sunday in October, Fred Bricker pulled into Chuck Fisher's driveway. Fred lived a half mile up the road from Chuck. To split the cost of gas, they often rode together. Fred sat in his truck and looked at his watch for the umpteenth time. He'd waited five minutes, and the lights hadn't even turned on inside. He glanced at his watch again. If it hadn't been so early, he might have laid on the horn to get Chuck to move a little faster, but at four thirty in the morning, he couldn't justify disturbing the neighbors. He waited five minutes longer before he turned off the truck and walked up to the porch illuminated by the outside flood lights. He opened the screen and found the door unlatched but not opened. Fred knocked lightly before pushing the door open slowly. The interior of the house was dark and quiet. An alarm went off deep in his gut, perhaps thirty years of law enforcement told him that something was amiss. Fred unsnapped his off-duty holster and retrieved his service pistol. Better to be safe than sorry. He reached inside the door and flipped on the light switch.

"Chuck," he called out as he stepped inside. "You here?" After no response, he inched inside and saw nothing out of place. He walked down the hall toward Chuck's bedroom. "Chuck?" he called out again to no response. Fred paused at the door before opening it. Chuck hadn't mentioned any recent girlfriends or the like, but he certainly did not want to embarrass himself by walking in on Chuck and a female companion. Fred pushed the door open slowly and found the bed empty and no sign of Chuck. Fred scratched his head. Chuck didn't mention anything about going anywhere, and he'd just seen him Friday night at the football game. Fred walked back down the hall toward the door. He was just about to holster his gun when he caught a glimpse of something lying on the kitchen floor. Fred flipped on the light in the kitchen and approached cautiously. Fred took one look and then turned his head; he knew without any doubt that it was Chuck, and he was dead. Chuck was lying in a pool of blood. Bullet holes dotted his chest like polka dots. Fred quickly moved back around through the living room, making sure not to compromise the crime scene, still moving cautiously to ensure the house was clear.

Once outside, he ran to his truck and grabbed his radio and called in for assistance from the Sisters' Sheriff's Station. Someone there would relay the call to the deputies in Bend and to the Oregon State Police.

"Sheriff's office." Fred recognized the voice as Drew Webber. Drew joined the force in July as a deputy. He was young but had good instincts.

"This is Sheriff Bricker. I'm at 14500 Bluegrass Lane. Chuck Fisher has been shot. By the looks of things, probably sometime yesterday. I need dispatch to get a detective from OSP out here."

"Coach Fisher?" Drew repeated.

"That's affirmative," Fred replied. "I'll guard the crime scene until you can get here."

"I'm on it," Drew replied.

Fred hung up the radio. He hated homicide investigations. He'd spent his entire career keeping the peace. He was one of the lucky ones. In Central Oregon, an average day's work might include a drunken disturbance, maybe a shoplifter, or even a domestic dispute. And lately, they'd even had to deal with a few more drug issues as meth found its way into their corner of the world. He considered himself blessed that he only had to deal with the more brutal aspects of the job a handful of times. But nothing he'd ever experienced was quite as heinous as this. Over the years, he'd witnessed countless car wreck victims and even investigated one or two homicides over infidelity or greed. But this was different—an unwarranted savage attack on an unarmed man in his own home, a man that he knew personally.

He knew Chuck Fisher. They had a history. They'd been part of a fishing foursome for years. Now Chuck would be referred to as the victim, and they would search through his personal effects with a microscope while they tried to piece together why he was killed—and more importantly, who did it.

He grabbed his cell phone from the clip on the visor and dialed the number for George Patterson. He would much rather be fishing than dealing with this.

"Hey, Fred. I was just wondering about the two of you. You and Chuck on your way?"

"No, we're not," Fred hesitated. He couldn't tell George the reason just yet. He couldn't even tell him that Chuck was dead. He searched for some excuse but could find none. "Look, I'll call you later and explain, but Chuck and I won't make it today."

"Everything all right?" George sounded concerned.

"I'll explain later. Catch a big one for me," Fred said quickly. The less he said the better.

"Okay."

Fred hung up the phone. No sense in ruining George and Wayne's fishing. He couldn't tell them anything, not until they'd processed the crime scene and notified the next of kin. He knew that Chuck had a sister that lived in LaPine. Other than that, he wasn't certain if Chuck had any other living relatives. Then he would need to notify the school. He wasn't looking forward to telling Principal Powell that he lost the best football coach Sisters ever had.

The first rays of light streaked the sky with yellow and pink just as Drew drove up. The weather was perfect—a crystal-clear blue sky, not a cloud in sight. The wind was light out of the west. It would have been great fishing on the Deschutes. He probably would have limited out. Chuck too. But now it was going to be a long, long day. Fred kicked at the gravel in the driveway.

"Morning, Sheriff. I stopped and got you a tall one. Thought you might need it." Drew handed Fred a tall white paper cup filled with steaming coffee. He sounded exceedingly cheerful for the task they had ahead of them.

"Thanks. Where's the rest of the crew?" Fred took the cup from Drew and took a big gulp.

"On their way. OSP is sending a detective unit from the crime lab. I brought a crime scene kit with me so we could get started. Oh, and Earl Pritchard is on his way too," Drew reported.

It was certainly refreshing to have someone as on the ball as Drew, especially for as young as he was. Drew had followed protocol to the letter. He'd even called Earl, which usually fell on Fred since no one else wanted to talk to the cantankerous old so and so. Earl was the only medical examiner in Central Oregon. He covered Deschutes, Lake, and Crook counties. Most of the time, he was called in after a welfare check turned up an expired elderly person or an occasional accident victim whether by water or road. Rarely did they require his services for a scene as grisly as this.

"You're either brave or stupid," Fred said as he walked around to the trunk of Drew's squad car. "At this time of the morning, even I wouldn't want to call and wake Earl."

"He's not that bad. You never met my grandfather. Now he's cantankerous. He was a colonel in the army. He fought in two world wars and 'now those pretty boy politicians have let this country go to pot. Why if Ike or Truman were still around, they'd show those boys a thing or two.'" Drew lowered his voice and tried to make it sound raspy and cranky.

"Sounds like my kind of guy. Does your grandpa go fishing?" Fred purposefully tried to keep things light, given that they would soon have to face the severity of the crime scene inside the house.

"No. He's got some shrapnel in his leg from Iwo Jima."

Fred opened the black plastic toolbox labeled crime scene. The box contained everything they needed for gathering evidence. Fred removed a pair of latex gloves. "So is this your first homicide investigation?" Fred inquired as he snapped the latex gloves on.

"No, sir. I trained with the Gresham Police Department for two years before moving over here. We had at least one a month." Drew reported like a private reporting to a drill sergeant in boot camp.

"Really?" Fred was surprised to learn he had an old pro on his force. "Well, then let's get started."

He grabbed a roll of yellow tape, and Drew held one end as he rolled it around trees to quadrant off the property. Just as they were finishing up, the OSP officers pulled up. Fred could see the neighbors were starting to rouse, and he saw a few standing in their front yards trying to catch a glimpse of what was happening. They would have to work quickly if he was going to keep the investigation under wraps. Everyone in town knew or knew of Coach Chuck Fisher, and rumors would spread faster than a forest fire in late August.

When the other officers arrived, he assigned duties so they could process the scene quickly. In order to avoid any finger-pointing or mishaps, he assigned one of his deputies to work alongside an

OSP detective. Drew and Detective Williams worked inside. Fred had no desire to be around the body on this one. Deputy Paul Brown worked with a Detective Taylor, dusting for prints and photographing both entries to the house.

Fred had two other deputies help him keep the crime scene secure. Neighbors by nature were nosy, and with bright-yellow crime scene tape, they'd naturally gravitate toward Chuck's house. Fred hoped that they would have enough time to process the scene and maybe find some real leads before the media arrived and the newshounds added their spin, contriving a story of their own.

Chapter 28

George pulled the boat off the water and helped Wayne secure it to the trailer. They'd gotten skunked; not a single fish all day. The only consolation was that no one else around them had caught one either. They heard a myriad of excuses—the weather, the sea lions at Bonneville, the water levels. But George knew fishing was like gambling; it was more about luck than skill. He could have all the right gear and do all the right things, but if the fish weren't biting, they weren't biting.

Now it was time to go home with their tails between their legs. Just as he turned south onto Highway 97, his cell phone rang.

"Hey, George," Fred began.

"Hey, Fred. Sorry you couldn't join us, but you didn't miss much. Not even a single bite all day," George rambled, completely missing the severity of Fred's tone.

"Look, George. I wanted you to hear from me before you saw it on the news."

In an instant, George's mind raced with all the horrible possibilities that could follow the sheriff telling you those words. He thought of Rachel and Jenna and Braden or Michael and Connor. He imagined visions of twisted steel. He wasn't sure he could handle any news that followed. "What?" He heard the word escape his mouth.

"It's Chuck. He's dead. He's been shot."

At once, he felt relieved and shocked. He didn't want to discount the tragedy of losing a friend, but at the same time, he breathed a sigh of relief that nothing had happened to his family. He wasn't certain that he could take another loss, not this soon after Kate. "Chuck. How? Where?"

"We're still investigating, so all I can tell you is that he was shot at home. I wish I could tell you more, but right now, we don't have a whole lot."

"Sure, I understand." George now grappled with the thought that Chuck had been murdered in his home. In any other town, that might seem commonplace, but not in Sisters, Oregon. "Thanks for calling and letting us know. I'll tell Wayne."

"Thanks, George." And the call ended.

"You'll tell me what?" Wayne turned to look at George.

"That was Fred. You're not gonna believe it. Chuck was shot and killed at his house. Fred's there investigating."

"You're kidding, right?" Wayne looked at him in disbelief.

"Nope." George was still trying to grasp the enormity of the news himself. He saw Chuck on Friday just before the game. He'd wished him good luck, and they talked briefly about the trip planned for today. "Fred doesn't kid about stuff like that."

"I know. It's just hard to believe. He was supposed to join us today. It's just kind of weird. Do they know who did it?"

"Fred didn't say much. He said he didn't want us to hear about it on the news. They're still investigating. That's all he said." George tried to relay as much detail as he'd been told, but Fred hadn't told him much.

Wayne just shook his head, then turned and stared out the window. George could almost read his thoughts. How could something like this happen to someone they knew? You read about stuff like this in the papers happening to people in bigger cities like Portland, Salem, and Seattle. George couldn't remember the last homicide in Central Oregon. It must have been two or three years since someone had been shot, and that had been in Bend. He couldn't remember the last time someone had been shot in Sisters.

The strangest part was that someone killed Chuck. Of all the residents in Sisters, why Chuck? George couldn't think of a single reason anyone would want to harm him aside from a rival coach tired of losing, but that was certainly no reason to kill. Who on earth would want to kill Chuck?

*****

The trouble with crime in a small town is that everyone knows everybody else. It wouldn't take long before everyone would start asking questions. First, they would look at outsiders with suspicion and mistrust. Then they would start looking inward until they would ask the inevitable—"How could this happen in our town?" Then their scrutiny would turn toward law enforcement. What could *they* have done better? And more importantly, what are *they* doing now? The onus to solve the crime and put the suspect behind bars would be laid squarely on the shoulders of one man. In this case, that man was Sheriff Fred Bricker.

Sheriff Bricker called together an interagency task force to work solely on this case in order to bring it to an expedient conclusion. The longer the case dragged out, the longer rumors would fly, and the ability to cipher through fact and fiction would become more difficult. He stood at the head of a large oval cherry table and scanned the faces of the men he had hand selected for the task force—two detectives from OSP, one with crime scene experience, the other some new guy assigned to Central Oregon; the forensic lab supervisor; and two deputies from his force, the only two with any homicide experience.

"Needless to say, we need to keep a tight lid on this one," he started without any formality or introductions. "Our killer is still out there. This was a personal crime, not some random act."

"What makes you say that?" one of the OSP detectives inquired. Fred couldn't keep their names straight. Both had only been in Central Oregon a little over a year. One was named Williams and the other one Taylor, but he had no idea which was which.

"Autopsy results are in." Sheriff Bricker passed around copies of the report, a simple two-page document. "Cause of death was obvious. They pulled eight .45 caliber rounds from his chest. Eight. This was personal."

"Who are we looking for?" Deputy Brown looked up from his copy of the report. Brown had been with the sheriff's department for over ten years, and he could probably count on one hand the number of homicides he'd investigated.

"We're looking for someone who hated Chuck Fisher, and I mean pure unadulterated hate for the man," Sheriff Bricker said. "The thing is, I knew the victim—Chuck Fisher. I can't think of one person who disliked him, let alone hated him enough to do this."

"Why do you say that our perpetrator hated Fisher?" the younger OSP Detective asked.

"I've been around a lot of gruesome crime in my time. The brutality of this particular crime screams hate. When a wife finds her husband cheating on her, she shoots him once, maybe twice, and drops the gun. That's a crime of passion—passion from love. When a robber enters a home, gets caught, he shoots once, maybe twice, enough to kill the other person—that's a crime of indifference. When you unload the clip and possibly keep shooting after you run out of bullets…that's hate."

"Do we have any suspects?" Deputy Brown asked.

"Not a one. The only lead we've got is a mysterious red sports car with a rental agency sticker in the window. Martha Binkard lives across the street from the victim's house, and she saw the car leaving the vicinity shortly after 7:00 p.m."

"Did she get a look at the driver?" the older OSP Detective asked.

"No. It was too dark outside, but there aren't many cars rented this time of year, so we'll work it from that angle."

"What if it wasn't even rented here?" the other detective piped in.

"We'll cross that bridge when we come to it," Fred answered firmly. He could only hope they'd get lucky with what little evidence they had to go on.

"Did anybody hear the shots? I mean eight rounds. It's not like someone dropped a pot." Deputy Brown looked around the table for confirmation.

"He lived in Crossroads. All the houses are on at least an acre, and the whole thing is surrounded by national forest land. His nearest neighbor is at least fifty yards, and the shots were fired indoors," Fred explained. "No one heard a thing. Earl Pritchard places time of death sometime between five and eight pm on Saturday. Forensics found multiple prints throughout the house. There was a clear set on the front doorknob. The backdoor's prints were too smudged to lift. And we printed every surface we could inside."

"Problem is, I don't think our guy is in AFIS. So we'll need a suspect to match prints to. If this is as you said a hate crime, our guy hasn't likely done this before," the forensics guy explained.

"True," Fred agreed. This case wasn't going to be easy unless they got lucky. He had very little physical evidence and no suspects. And they had no leads on the big question—why? What motive could anyone have for killing Chuck? He was at a loss to figure it out.

"And our preliminary shows at least twenty-five different sets of prints inside the house," the forensics guy added.

"He was a high school football coach. I'm sure some of the players have been to his house." Fred knew for a fact that football players often went to Chuck's house to go over plays or whatever.

"So where does that leave us?" the older OSP Detective inquired, looking directly at Fred.

"Up the proverbial creek unless we get a break in the case. Let's get on it and remember, keep a tight lid on this one. Folks are already talking. We don't need a lynching if we don't have a case on anyone." Fred picked up his copy of the report and nodded to adjourn the meeting. They all took his cue and left.

When he returned to his office and checked his email, he slumped back into his chair. They had their first break in the case. The car rental agency had only rented one red car. They officially had a suspect, although he hoped that their information on the suspect was wrong.

Chapter 29

Since Kate's death, George had moved most of the creature comforts into his room in the shop. He could tie flies while listening to music or catching sports highlights on the news. Or he could relax in his La-Z-Boy without having to go inside. The house felt so empty without her. Everywhere were touches of her, from the furniture to the pillows. But the shop had always been his domain. He felt more comfortable out here. After work, he went straight to the shop and turned the channel to the local news, wanting to hear if they had anything new on the coach's death.

"And now for our top story," a pretty blond said in the flat newscaster tone. "Police have identified this man"—George practically fell from his chair as the picture appeared on the screen—"David Patterson."

She said the words just as the reality sunk in. It had been David that he saw at the ATM Saturday night. George was not prepared at all for what followed.

"As a person of interest in the ongoing homicide investigation in Sisters," The newscaster continued.

George stared blankly at the screen, not hearing any of the news that followed. He tried to wrap his mind around the idea of David being involved in Chuck Fisher's murder. The whole idea of David killing anyone, let alone Coach Fisher, it was ludicrous! David could barely bonk a fish he caught. How could anyone think he killed the coach? Yet the news identified him as a person of interest—what was that anyway?

The phone rang and interrupted George's thoughts. "Hello," he managed to eke out.

"Dad?" George could tell simply by the tone of her voice that she had seen the same newscast.

"Rachel?" He exhaled heavily at the sound of her voice. He'd practically jumped out of his skin when the phone rang.

"Dad, did you see the news?" Rachel asked hysterically.

"Yeah. I was just watching." George was still stunned by the report.

"Did you know David was in town?"

"No. But I thought I saw him in Bend at an ATM near the restaurant," George admitted.

"Why didn't you say anything?"

"I thought I was seeing things." George thought back to that moment on the street. What would have happened if he had simply called out to David when he saw him? That was the night Chuck died.

"Do you think he saw us?"

"I don't know." George hoped not. He hoped that his son would have at least said something to him if he had seen him on the street. Any more, he didn't know.

"Dad, how can they think that David did this?"

"I'm not sure. I'll call Fred Bricker and see if he can fill me in."

"You don't think he's involved, do you?" he could hear the uncertainty in her voice. He shared the same suspicions and doubts, but he didn't divulge that information.

"Rachel, it's been fifteen years since David set foot in this town, eleven since any of us have seen him. Right now, I'm not sure what to believe," George admitted.

"He couldn't, Dad. You know that." Rachel tried to sound convincing.

"I know." He too tried to sound more certain than he was.

"Keep me posted."

"I will. I'll see you tomorrow," he said as he hung up the phone.

Chuck Fisher's murder was hard enough to accept. Now to even contemplate that David had any sort of involvement—it was preposterous! First of all, David was incapable of hurting anyone, least of all Coach Fisher. David had been one of Sisters's star quarterbacks. He led he Outlaws to a state championship his senior year. And David had idolized the coach. He spent weekends over at the coach's house helping stack wood, trimming trees, and watching countless hours of football tapes, all to improve his game. What possible reason could David have? After all this time, to come back here to kill him, it was pretty far-fetched.

But the timing—what was David doing in town? George had to admit, no matter how much he wanted to believe in David's innocence, the timing of David's arrival and Chuck's death proved to be an awfully intriguing coincidence.

George dialed Fred's number but merely got his voice mail. He thought of leaving a message but was afraid it would sound something like, *Hey, Fred. I saw my son's face on the news, you know, the one I haven't seen in over ten years. The reporter said he's a person of interest. Call me.* George hung up rather than leave a message. He would talk to Fred in the morning.

Over the years, at least a million scenarios of David's return had run through his mind. Not a single one of them played out like this, with David the prime suspect in a murder. George looked toward the house and all the memories of Kate. She would have remained unruffled, unphased by the news, and wait until they found out more information. "Oh, Kate. I wish you were here. You would know what to do. What am I supposed to do now?"

Chapter 30

The next morning, news vans lined the side streets of Sisters. A crowd of reporters stood outside the store before it opened. George avoided them by sneaking in through the side door. He went straight up to his office, set down his coffee, and pilfered through the stack of invoices on his desk. Nothing required immediate attention. Through the window in his office, he could see the news vans hanging around town. The media would interview anyone who could answer questions regarding David. Person of interest—the words hung in the air like the stench of old salmon roe. It was completely absurd, to think that David had killed the coach. Why would he? What possible reason could he have for killing Chuck?

George removed the bands from his copy of the *Bend Bulletin* and slowly unfolded it, afraid to see what news they might have about David being a person of interest. The headline nearly leapt from the front page. "Abuse Allegations May Provide Motive for Coach's Death." Stunned, George read on to try to make sense of what allegations they were referring to.

> *Amid the investigation into the circumstances surrounding the homicide of Sisters's head football coach, Chuck Fisher, allegations of sexual abuse among past players has surfaced. One source cited that players for teams dating as far back as the mid-1980s were coming forward with allegations of sexual abuse by Coach Fisher. Though Fisher had never been formally charged with any wrong-*

doing, several complaints had been filed with both the school district and the state child welfare offices. The complaints never produced enough evidence to warrant a full investigation. However, parents of some victims claim that it was the coach's winning record that kept the school from performing a full investigation.

One ex-Outlaw player stated, "The coach had a distinct pattern of selecting his victims. They were usually the star player for that year, his favorite players."

Another source commented, saying, "Once he got his hooks into you, it was hard to back away from it. The guilt and shame sort of fed his sick games."

The district had no comment on any past or current allegations of wrongdoing by the coach.

The Sheriff's Department only commented that no formal charges had ever been made against Fisher.

One source stated that the sheriff's person of interest in the ongoing homicide investigation, David Patterson, 32, fit the profile of Fisher's pattern of abuse. Police are now investigating this as a possible motive.

George felt the room spinning wildly. His stomach lurched as he set the paper down. Chuck accused of sexual abuse? It had to be a mistake. He'd known Chuck for nineteen years, since he'd first moved to Sisters and started coaching. They had fished together, camped together. He'd been to their house for Christmas dinner, during years that the snow had kept him from driving to his mother's in Eugene. Sure Chuck had been a little different. He never had any serious relationships. Still he dated women, lots of women. Certainly, he couldn't have been a pedophile as the news report suggested.

And David, one of his victims? It simply wasn't possible. George searched his memory, trying to remember if there had been any indication. They fought so much of the time that maybe... He felt the bile at the back of his throat. It couldn't be true. George leaned forward and rubbed his temples, then pulled his hands across his face. *Dear Jesus, please, this can't be happening.*

George stood and paced the floor of his office. He wanted to find David, to make him talk, to clear this up. The reporter had to be wrong. David would have told him. David wouldn't have kept it secret all these years and come back to murder Chuck. And why now? Why not years ago? He needed to find David. He needed to know the truth. George picked up his keys from the desk.

Just as he readied to leave, Fred Bricker arrived. "Hey, George."

"Hey, Fred." George eyed Fred suspiciously. Fred was in uniform. The last time Fred had visited his store in uniform had been in official capacity. A clerk had caught a young boy shoplifting, and Fred wanted to give him a talking to. "What can I do for you?"

"George, you and I go way back." Fred took off his hat and sat down on the couch.

"Yeah, we do." George looked at him, perplexed.

"I mean you were there when I married Midge." Fred sounded strange, almost nostalgic.

"And you were there the day I met Kate. So?" George wasn't sure where this conversation was headed, but he was almost certain it had something to do with David.

"So did you read the paper this morning?"

"Yeah, and I can't believe it. You knew Chuck as well as I did."

"Yeah, but under the circumstances, I had to follow up on it."

"And?" George searched Fred's stone face for answers.

"And there were complaints filed and"—Fred paused, rubbing his balding forehead—"and he had a record in Spokane."

George sank back in his chair, his stomach churning with disgust.

"Because of our friendship, I wanted to tell you myself, in person." Fred placed his elbows on his knees and leaned slightly forward. "George, we're charging David with Chuck's murder."

"No. Fred, come on." George took one look at Fred's stolid look and knew. "You're serious."

"As a heart attack." Fred looked at the floor. "I've known you practically all my life. I watched your kids grow up, and David and Kevin were in little league together. I didn't want to believe it myself, but I can't ignore the evidence."

"What evidence?" George demanded.

"We've got his prints at the scene. Martha Binkard saw him driving away from Chuck's house around the time of the murder. And now"—Fred paused for a moment and pointed to the paper sitting on George's desk—"now we've got motive."

"That doesn't sound like enough to arrest someone."

"There are some other little things, but it all points to one thing. David shot Chuck."

"I don't believe it." George shook his head as if he could shake the words out. It had to be some kind of nightmare. This couldn't really be happening.

"Look, George, he's been away a long time. You said yourself that you didn't even know him after what he did—not showing up for Kate and all. I have to do my duty and go with the evidence. I came here to let you know out of respect for our friendship. I didn't want you finding out on the evening news." Fred toyed with his hat nervously. George could only imagine how hard this must be for him. He knew Fred wouldn't arrest David without reason.

"Thanks, I guess." George still shook his head in disbelief. "What's next? I mean, what happens to David?"

"He'll be arraigned tomorrow morning. The judge will set bail, and uh, he'll need a good lawyer."

George suddenly found himself speechless. He simply nodded his head. Fred seemed to pick up on his inability to speak and took it as his cue to leave. "I'll be seeing you around George."

Fred stood and quietly disappeared down the stairs. George made a small waving gesture. The events unfolded like one of those crime dramas that Kate used to watch on television, except this was real. David was in real trouble, and George didn't know what to do or what to believe.

Chapter 31

The very first call George made following Fred's visit, even before telling Rachel and Michael, had been to Kate's lawyers. They informed him they were business lawyers and handled primarily wills, trusts, and real estate.

During the months following Kate's death, George learned a lot about lawyers—what they do, how they work, what they cost. He had learned more than he cared to. Kate's death forced him to meet with her lawyers at least once a month to sign papers and make decisions about her estate. Kate's parents had left her with a substantial inheritance, which included not only the house at Odell Lake but two other properties in Bend. She had never fully dealt with her inheritance and left specific instructions on her desires for her estate. She named George as the executor in charge of it all.

Right now, George needed a criminal lawyer, and they were few and far between in Bend, Oregon. Then he remembered that Neil Cohen had moved back to town. Rachel had been talking about how strange it was having her high school sweetheart playing golf with her husband. Years ago, before the mill closed, George had worked with Neil's father. A few years later, Neil came to work as a stock boy at the store. And during Rachel's junior and senior years of high school, she and Neil had dated. He even took her to prom. Then Neil earned a scholarship to some prestigious school back east and went on to law school somewhere in Washington, DC. George didn't know most of the details, although he suspected Rachel did.

George found Neil's office in one of the newer office complexes on the river in the newly refurbished Old Mill District. It took up the northwest corner on the first floor. The office was small but very nicely decorated. A middle-aged secretary welcomed him from behind a desk in the reception area. Shortly after he arrived, she showed him back to Neil's office.

"Hey, Mr. Patterson." Neil stood from behind his desk and extended his hand.

"You can call me George." He shook his hand. George could still remember the fair-haired boy that knocked on his door every Friday night to take out his daughter.

"That seems kind of strange given history. But George it is. Please sit." Neil motioned for him to sit.

George took a seat in one of the chairs across from Neil's desk. He was right it did seem strange. Neil was Rachel's age, and coming to him for help did seem a little backward. But at the moment, Neil was the only chance he had to help David.

"Like I told you on the phone, I would love to help, but I don't think I can do it. Right now, I only have a secretary. I don't even have a full-time investigator." Neil tried his best to dissuade him.

"I don't know where else to go. I hate to stick him with a public defender." George didn't want to sound desperate, but he was running out of options. David's arraignment was in the morning, and he needed some type of representation. George didn't know where else to turn if Neil wouldn't take the case.

"No, you don't want to do that," Neil said. "They'd probably just plea his case out for a lesser sentence just to avoid the death penalty."

"The death penalty?" George hadn't even considered that aspect. He'd been solely focused on getting David out of jail. He completely put it out of his mind that if David was found guilty, he could face the death penalty.

"Yeah. Oregon is a capital punishment state. It's usually reserved for the more gruesome crimes. Unfortunately for David, this one fits the bill. From what I understand, Coach Fisher was shot multiple times at point-blank range."

"The death sentence. Now what do I do?" George leaned back against the chair, the severity of David's trouble hitting him fully for the first time.

Neil sat back in his chair and rubbed his temples. "I shouldn't. I can't guarantee the outcome."

"You're the best chance he's got," George urged.

Neil let out a heavy sigh, still shaking his head to the negative. "It won't be cheap."

"I know." George had been ready for that. The lawyers, the business ones, were at least informative about money matters. They had explained that he should expect no less than a million dollars for bail if the judge even set bail. In murder cases, the judge could hold the defendant over until trial without bail. But if bail was set, then George would need to pay the court 10 percent for a security release. That was just the bail. A lawyer for a criminal case could run upward of a hundred thousand dollars. George had made arrangements to pull enough money from Kate's estate to cover the costs.

Neil sat quietly contemplating. Then he extended his hand toward George. "I may hate myself…because this isn't going to be easy."

"You'll do it?" George shook his hand, hopefully sealing the deal.

"You've got yourself a lawyer." Neil looked as if he'd just signed up for the marines the day before being deployed into war. "My secretary will draw up the retainer agreement. That should get me an investigator. But David still needs to agree to my representing him."

"Thanks." George shook Neil's hand again. He wanted to hug him. He'd just thrown David a lifeline, but would David be smart and take it, or would he sink?

*****

Coach Charles "Chuck" Fisher held the undisputed distinction of being the winningest coach in Sisters football history. In the twenty years he coached varsity football, the Outlaws had fifteen winning seasons and won eight state championships. The school had attained legendary status under his tutelage. Boys seeking athletic scholarships actually transferred schools from Redmond and Bend just to play on his team. Despite the allegations in the morning news, the entire town had rallied for his memorial service. Principal Powell had thought it only fitting to hold the memorial in the new football stadium.

Cars filled both the high school and middle school parking lots as well as lined the highway. People poured into the football stadium as if it were another championship game. George tried to blend into the crowd. At first, he didn't want to attend. His emotions over Chuck's death ran the gambit. Chuck had been a friend, one of his fishing buddies. But what if the accusations in the newspaper were true? What if he had done those despicable things? And to David? He prayed they weren't true. He kept expecting this to be some nightmare and to wake up at any moment.

Hordes of people filled the stands. He passed by some familiar faces, and he caught glimpses of people whispering. Ever since the announcement of David as a person of interest, George had noticed the discerning glances of friends and neighbors. Rachel had called the night before in tears because some women were speculating about David's motives and inevitable guilt at the grocery store. "Hope he gets the chair," Rachel had repeated. It was hard to hear people speak so cruelly about his son.

George moved along with the crowd making their way up into the grandstands. He didn't want to talk to anyone. He merely wanted to pay his respects and then get out of there.

"I'm surprised to see you here," Sally Jensen said with a note of condemnation in her voice. Sally was a clerk at the grocery store.

George looked up and felt as if all eyes were now watching him. "Chuck Fisher was my friend," he defended.

"So does your son go around killing all your *friends*?" Her voice held the smugness of judgment.

George started backing down the steps. It had been a mistake to come. "He didn't do it," he said with all he conviction he could muster.

"That's not what I heard. I heard they got him dead to rights," Bill Porter added. He was sitting next to Sally. Bill owned the gas station.

"Whatever happened to innocent until proven guilty?" George had stopped moving, and now the people behind him were watching the conversation.

"That's what I'm saying. He's been proved guilty." Bill pounded his hand in his fist to drive home his point.

"By who, the media? He hasn't been proven guilty in court. You let my boy have his day in court before you go convicting him." He tried to sound confident. He didn't want anyone to know he was wavering in his belief that David was innocent.

George scanned the small group around him. Their eyes narrowed as they looked at him. These people had been his friends, some even went to his church. They had convicted David without so much as seeing him or hearing even an inkling of his side of the story. They had judged him without mercy and would surely lynch him if given the opportunity.

George turned and left. Chuck was dead. Nothing would change that. It didn't matter if he attended his memorial or not. He noticed Fred as he walked out, a look of remorse and pity in his eyes as he caught sight of George. As much as he wanted to, he couldn't blame Fred for any of this. He was simply doing his job. George just wanted answers. Perhaps tomorrow he would have some after David's arraignment.

*****

There had been relentless media coverage of the coach's murder and David's subsequent arrest, every angle covered, every stone overturned in their pursuit of a story. One paper had printed a follow-up article to the now infamous one in the *Bulletin*. The reporters had discovered that Chuck Fisher had been previously convicted of sex abuse and had served two years of probation for that offense. That had taken place in Washington before he moved to Sisters. Another reported that David had been in a drug rehab center two years ago, and that recently, he did not attend his mother's funeral. Nothing, it seemed, was too personal or too trivial to report.

The morning of David's arraignment, the media descended upon the Deschutes County Courthouse like vultures on a day-old carcass. Many arrived before dawn and camped out across the street. All of them waited impatiently for David's arraignment. Some already planned their stories based on the presumption that he would plead not guilty since George had hired Neil for the defense.

Due to the deluge of interest in the case, the judge prohibited all cameras in the courtroom to prevent his courtroom from turning into a circus, also, to prevent the district attorney from grandstanding. Bruce Heywood had been elected district attorney in the last election. He was the youngest DA in the state, and he had political aspirations beyond the confines of Central Oregon. Some people suggested he might run for governor; others said he would run for the senate. In either case, he needed a solid conviction record to stand on. Chuck Fisher's murder trial would be no exception.

When George arrived at the courthouse at ten o'clock, he made the mistake of parking out front. Immediately, he was swarmed by reporters. Cameramen followed him around as newscasters shoved microphones at him. All of them asked the same question he'd been asking himself—"Do you believe your son is innocent?"

He wedged through the sea of reporters, creating a path and forcing his way through the pandemonium to the safety of the courthouse. Neil was waiting for him outside the courtroom.

"Hey there, George." Neil came up and shook his hand. He looked like a lawyer in his navy suit and slicked-back hair, unlike their first meeting where he'd been the same kid he'd always known in jeans and a sweater. Neil's appearance gave George more confidence. He could handle David's case. He was a professional.

"Neil." George acknowledged him and then let out a heavy sigh, glad to have escaped the reporters.

"Because of all that"—Neil nodded through the window toward the mass of reporters across the street—"the judge decided to move David's arraignment to three o'clock. He had to move some things on the docket around because he's not going to allow any cameras in the courtroom."

"Three this afternoon?" George hadn't expected to be gone all day for this.

"Well, the bright side is it gives me an opportunity to actually talk to David before we stand before the judge." Neil looked down at his watch, then back at George. "Look, if you want, you could just go home or back to the store, and I could call you when it's all over."

"No," George said definitively, "I'll come back and be here at three o'clock."

"Okay. I'll see you then. But you might want to park on the back side of the courthouse." He winked and then turned and walked down the hall.

George glanced at his watch and suddenly found himself with five hours to kill. He looked up and down the empty hallways, then out the window at the swarm of reporters waiting to pounce. He needed to unwind, to escape all the hoopla for a while and gather his bearings. He just needed to find a way to sneak past the reporters. Luckily, the DA loved the cameras, and he distracted them long enough for George to slip out unnoticed.

George left downtown with no particular destination in mind. If he had more time, he could go up to Maupin and try his luck on the fall steelhead run. Unfortunately, by the time he would get there, he would have just enough time to turn around and drive back. As he neared the turnoff, he made his decision. An hour later, he stood knee deep in the Metolius. The bull trout had been running hot and heavy. He cast his line out over the pool just beneath Canyon Creek Camp. The tranquility of his surroundings offered a much-needed reprieve from all the chaos in town. He felt as if it had been a month since the last time he'd hit the water, even though it had only been days, four days, four very long days. The trickling water calmed his nerves. As he took another step along the rock-covered riverbed, he began conversing with God.

"It's always quiet out here. It brings me back to You," he began. "Please tell me there's a point to all this—to Kate's death, to David's sudden return, to the trouble he's gotten himself into. I need to know there's light at the end of this tunnel. Please, God, show me some light."

*****

At quarter to three, George pulled around to the rear entrance to the courthouse as Neil had suggested after George's run-in with the press earlier.

George found Neil in the same spot he had that morning. He stood outside the courtroom, waiting to go in. "It shouldn't take long, maybe fifteen or twenty minutes. You can sit in the gallery and watch."

"All right." George nodded.

"I got to talk to David for about five minutes this morning. Just so you know, we are officially going to plead not guilty."

"Thanks." George wanted to ask how David was holding up, but before he got the chance, a petite brunette in a deputy's uniform appeared through the courtroom doors and waved Neil inside.

"Here we go," Neil muttered quietly. He held his hand up with his fingers crossed. George followed him inside and sat in the last row. He wasn't sure he even wanted to watch this. Slowly, the large wooden doors closed behind him.

Neil had already explained to him that the arraignment was simply a formal proceeding for David to acknowledge the charges brought against him and to respond to them. Then he would formally declare his counsel or have counsel appointed if need be. Finally, the judge would determine appropriate bail considering any extenuating circumstances. Neil had already submitted his petition for bail, but ultimately, bail was up to the judge. That was the part that worried George. What if the judge denied bail, and David had to remain in custody until the trial? George hated to think of his son locked away with real criminals.

George caught a glimpse of a man in a bright-orange jumpsuit being escorted by two deputies. He couldn't see the man's face. George could only assume it was David. He sat behind a desk with Neil.

The side door to the courtroom flew open, and Bruce Heywood emerged with an entourage behind him. George recognized him from his campaign ads and his many appearances in parades and local events. Bruce was a politician and looked like one of those Hollywood hero types. Everything from his hair to his shoes screamed position and power. Bruce and two members of his entourage sat at the desk on the other side of the courtroom. The remaining followers sat in the gallery, up front.

The bailiff stood and gave the formal announcement, and everyone in the court stood. George stood along with them. The judge appeared through the same door that Bruce had emerged. He walked directly to the bench without so much as glancing at anyone else in the court. The judge rapped his gavel to bring the court to session.

The entire process took forty-five minutes. Most of which, George didn't understand. The judge and the lawyers all bantered back and forth in legalese—some sort of foreign language that only legal professionals understood. George grasped the charge of murder in the first degree. He also understood when Neil said, "Not guilty." The rest was Greek. Once the word *bail* was mentioned, George heightened his attention, carefully listening. Neil and Bruce primarily did the talking, arguing. As predicted, Bruce made a case for no bail based on David's absence from the community for the past fifteen years. He sounded like a preacher delivering a sermon. Neil butted in a few times, and finally, the judge pounded his gavel on the desk and pronounced bail set at two million dollars. George wanted to stand up and shout *no*, but he refrained. He had only set aside enough funds from Kate's estate to cover what Kate's lawyers had said would be the worst-case scenario—one million, not two. It was four o'clock Thursday evening, and if he didn't work quickly, David would have to spend the weekend in jail.

With bail set, the arraignment was over. David was led out one of the side doors, and people began filing out through the rear. George sat and waited while the reporters and spectators all filed out of the courtroom. Neil came and sat down next to him as everyone else tried to get a quote or comment from Bruce.

"All right. The good news is the judge set bail, despite Bruce's long-winded summation as to why bail should be denied. The bad news is…he set it a two million dollars. That means you need—"

"Two hundred thousand dollars," George said, disheartened.

"Correct. If you can't post bail, David will remain in custody until the trial. The judge was gracious enough to give us eight weeks before jury selection begins."

"That's a long time. I'd better find a way to raise the bail."

"Yeah. Then maybe David could help explain a few things. Now let's get out of here before the reporters finish with Bruce."

Chapter 32

George had waited in the jail reception area for hours. He'd been surrounded by men and women, whom he could only presume had been there more than once. Then at long last, David emerged, haggard and weary. George stood back and took a long look at David. He had aged significantly. But underneath the whiskers and the fine lines of sun damage, he saw the same boy he'd always known.

"You posted bail?" David looked at him skeptically.

"Yes," George answered. He didn't know why David was so surprised.

"How? I know business can't be that good."

"What does it matter? You're out, and you can come home."

"If it's all the same. I'd just as soon stay at the hotel," David shot back.

Nothing had changed. David was still as belligerent as ever. George tried not to let his disappointment show. "If that's what you want."

"That's what I want. But I could use a ride to the hotel."

George nodded and led the way out to the parking lot. He unlocked the truck, and both men climbed in. He pulled out of the parking lot and headed south toward the center of town. David watched out the window without saying a word.

"The town has changed a lot," George attempted to make small talk.

"Yeah. Progress," David said snidely.

"They built another high school over on the west side off Century Drive."

"Hmm." David nodded, seemingly disinterested in anything George had to say.

George turned onto the parkway. It would take mere minutes before they arrived at the hotel. George felt as if he were running out of time. He wasn't sure what he had expected when he posted bail, perhaps a thank you or any sign of gratitude. Instead, for his trouble, he was treated with indifference.

"Neil Cohen agreed to represent you." George fought the urge to tell David what it was costing him and how he'd practically had to beg Neil to take the case. But David was already agitated, and he didn't want to make it worse.

"Yeah. I kind of caught that at the arraignment. I thought he went back east somewhere DC or New York?"

"He did. But apparently, he's moved back. Your sister's husband, Steve, plays golf with him." George tried to be as casual as possible. He didn't want it to seem as if they were pushing Neil on him, even though at the moment, Neil might be his only chance out of this mess.

"Rachel married a guy that plays golf?" David smirked.

"Yes, she did, and they're happy." George was pleased to hear David taking any kind of interest, even if it was scoffing at his sister's choice for a husband. David had always made fun of the golfers in Bend; he used to call them the uppity yuppitys.

"Good for her," He said, thick with sarcasm.

"Neil wants to meet with you early next week. I can get you the number if you need it. Will you call him?" George wasn't trying to intrude or nag. He merely wanted his son to have a chance.

"Look, Dad. I'm a big boy, and I can take care of myself. I've been doing it for fifteen years now. I think I can manage calling a lawyer," David spat acrimoniously.

"Son, I wasn't trying to…" George stammered. He didn't want a fight. He wanted to help his son get out of the predicament into which he had stumbled. "I just want you to know I'm here to help."

"I'll let you know if I need any."

George pulled to a stop under the covered drive at the hotel. David hastily unbuckled his seatbelt and jumped out.

"See ya, Dad," David said quickly and closed the door before George could respond.

"See you, son," George said quietly as he watched David enter the hotel. He put the truck in gear and headed toward home, a gnawing ache consumed him. How could he support a son who wanted nothing to do with him? "Help me, Lord. I can't make peace with someone who hates me," he said under his breath. "I'm trying, and I'm not sure I can get through."

The sun sank slowly behind the mountains ahead of him. Darkness stretched from the east, covering everything in thick black shadows. George felt the shadows creep across his heart. His brief time with David gave him no indication of whether David was innocent or guilty. And he knew that if David didn't soften before his trial, regardless of his guilt or innocence, he would spend the rest of his life in prison or worse—be sentenced to death.

*****

George went into the store early the next morning. He'd endured what he suspected would be the first of many sleepless nights until this ordeal ended. He replayed the conversation with his son over and over in his mind. David's complete disregard for him was disturbing. Even after he'd posted bail for him, David had treated him coldly. He didn't expect David to jump up and down with excitement or fall at his feet with gratitude, but he'd never anticipated the apathy David had shown. It was as if he had no feeling left in him. George tried to suppress the nagging feeling that maybe David was guilty. He didn't want to believe it. He couldn't believe it. And yet…he couldn't deny the fact that he didn't really know his own son. He shuddered at the thought that his son could be a cold-blooded killer.

Maybe the people in town were right. The evidence did speak volumes, but David had told Neil that he didn't do it. Could he believe that? If it was anyone else, would he be willing to believe in their innocence? George stood at the contractor's counter and shuffled some papers, looking for something, anything to take his mind off it.

Michael was the first to arrive.

"You posted bail?" he spat right off without so much as a hello or good morning.

"Yes. But how'd you know?" George hadn't told anyone, not even Rachel.

"It's on the news, Dad," he said as if George should know.

"Are you serious?" It was surreal, having your every move being broadcast for the whole world to see. With everything else that was going on in the world, the news chose to report that he had posted bail for his son.

"Where'd you get the money? I heard you put up two hundred grand." His anger was palpable.

"Well. That was the 10 percent to—" George started to explain.

"Two hundred grand. Dad, that's insane. What if he did it? Did that ever occur to you? What if the lowlife actually did it? What if he decides to skip town? Then you're out two hundred grand."

"But he didn't do it!" George protested.

"What if he did? What did you do? Mortgage the house? The business?"

"Not that's any of your business, but I sold the house at Odell." George had wanted to tell them earlier but never found the right time. He still hadn't finished with all the arrangements of Kate's will. He had thought that telling them about the house after they'd received their trusts would soften the blow. This was certainly not the way he'd intended for them to find out.

"What?" he practically screamed. "How could you? For David?"

"No, not for David. I sold it a month ago to pay off your mother's hospital bills."

Michael grew quiet, but his face was still red with anger.

"Still you used the money for him. Didn't you?" Michael shook his head and stormed off.

George watched him stomp off toward the yard where the delivery truck was parked. For a moment, he thought of going after him to explain. But he didn't. Michael needed time to cool off.

George turned to head up to his office, and there stood Rachel.

"He'll cool off eventually. He always does." Rachel smiled.

"I know. But he didn't let me explain, and now he thinks that I sold the house just for David. And it's not true." George wondered how much of the argument she'd heard.

"Why did you sell it?" Rachel was much calmer about it.

"Like I told Michael, to pay off the hospital bills, the cancer center." George wanted her and Michael to understand. He wanted to sit them both down and tell them everything, but parts of Kate's plans were still waylaid in probate. The Odell house had been the asset he could sell to cover the medical bills. And after his short stay following Kate's funeral, he knew he could never stay there without her.

"I suppose it was your house to do with as you saw fit." He could hear the disappointment in her voice.

"Yeah. Well, I don't think he's as upset about the house as he is about David." George knew it wasn't about the house or even the money but that George had used the money to post bail for David. That was what had upset Michael. "He's got a point somewhere in there. David may not be worthy of our loyalty. He certainly doesn't act as if he wants it."

Rachel fidgeted uncomfortably. "Dad, David is going to be staying with us, me and Steve."

"What?" George stared at her in disbelief.

"He called this morning and was asking about places to stay that were less conspicuous. He was talking about Camp Sherman or something. Then I offered to let him stay in the guest room above the garage," Rachel rambled nervously.

"I see. He's okay with staying with you. Just not me." George didn't even attempt to mask his resentment.

"Dad?"

"It's okay, Rachel. I just pay the bills." George grabbed some papers and headed up to his office. He wasn't sure who he was more upset with—David for refusing to stay with him or Rachel for opening her home up to him.

Chapter 33

After fighting with her father at the store, Rachel returned home early to set up the room for David. The house was quiet for the moment. Steve took the kids and Conner pumpkin hunting. Amid the chaos, Steve was her pillar; first when her mother died and now with the trouble with David. It had actually been Steve's idea to invite David to stay with them. But once David agreed, she realized just how much work lie ahead of her. They had lived in the house for almost a year and never used the spare room. When she opened the door, she could still smell the fresh paint and new carpet. She opened a window to air it out. The bed still sat in pieces with plastic wrapped around the mattress. She muscled the pieces together and then made up the bed with clean sheets. Then she went to work on the adjoining bathroom, scrubbing paint splatters and dust. An hour later, the room was ready.

Shortly after noon, Steve and the kids returned with an assortment of pumpkins. All three kids buzzed around, trying to give their version of their adventures at the pumpkin patch. Rachel sent them upstairs to wash up while she made grilled cheese sandwiches and tomato soup. All three kids devoured their lunch as if they hadn't eaten in days.

Just as they finished lunch, David pulled into the driveway. Steve showed him to the guest house, which was actually a studio apartment above the garage. Steve had built it in case his brother came to stay with them—which hadn't happened. Steve's brother was no closer to his family than David was to hers.

Steve took the kids upstairs to watch a movie and take a nap, while Rachel cleaned up the lunch dishes. She placed the last plate in the dishwasher as David came in through the back door and sat at the table in the breakfast nook.

"Hey there, stranger," Rachel said with a smile.

"Hey, sis. Thanks for letting me stay here. I didn't want to tell Dad, but the hotel was more than I could afford."

"No problem. But you could stay with him too."

"Don't start," he warned, shooting her a searing glance.

"I'm just saying—"

"Look, I didn't come back to town to see him. I stayed in Bend to avoid that very thing."

"Why?" She hated being caught in the middle, trying to make peace. She wondered how her mother did it for so many years.

"He and I are never going to see eye to eye on anything. I don't know why he thinks we can be all buddy-buddy. Sure I appreciate him posting bail and all, but I think it's sort of hypocritical for him to act like there's no animosity between us. We're just never going to get along, and that's all there is to it."

Rachel dried her hands on a towel and leaned up against the counter, towel still in her hands. "So that's it. You won't even try."

"What's the point?" David shrugged.

"The point is what both of you are missing out on, especially you. He tried to call you when Mom got sick. Then again after Mom died."

"Look Rach—" he started.

"No. You look and listen. You're the one who left. You're the one who started this fight between the two of you. You're the one who's missed out. You missed my graduation. You missed Michael's. You missed both of our weddings and the births of your niece and nephews. You've missed a thousand moments—for what? To prove some point to Dad? What about the rest of us? What about Michael? He took it the worst when you didn't come back home. Every summer, he'd wait and watch for you. He idolized you, you know. It crushed him when you never came back. He was never the same and refused, I mean refused, to play football."

"Good," David said emphatically.

"Good?" Rachel couldn't believe her brother could be so callous.

"About the football. I didn't know about the rest," he explained quickly.

"No, you wouldn't know. You wouldn't know what it's like to explain to a three-year-old why there are pictures of a mommy's big brother hanging at Grandma and Grandpa's house. Or why that same brother never comes home for Christmas or Thanksgiving or Easter," Rachel ranted. She didn't want to belabor the point, but it was the first time she had been able to talk to David. She hoped he would listen. "Then you stroll back into town, and a cloud of fury follows. And everyone thinks you're guilty. Why? Because you can't explain why you're here. You can't give one good reason why you came back. You haven't even explained why you missed your own mother's funeral."

"Who says I missed it?" David shot back.

"What?" Rachel looked at him incredulously.

"I came to the graveside service. I sat up on the hill above the cemetery and watched. Then after you all left, I came down and laid a rose on her grave," David said calmly. "And I called and talked to the nurses at the hospital a couple of days before she died. A nurse told me she was sedated most of the time. I really didn't see much point in coming down to see her sleep."

"But why? Why didn't you just come see her?"

"It wasn't the right time. I didn't want to show up and everyone expect that Dad and I would make up just because of everything that was happening."

"But *now* is the time?"

"I didn't say that. I didn't come home to see him."

"Then why did you? Just tell me that. Why now?"

"It's complicated."

"Well, then uncomplicate it for me. Does it have to do with that article in *The Bulletin*?" Rachel could tell by the look on his face that it did. Her heart sank. When David looked at her, she now saw what he couldn't say. His eyes weren't filled with hatred but pain, pain caused by Coach Fisher. "You need to tell Dad."

"I don't know what you mean." David looked away quickly.

"Yes, you do. It's eating you alive. It's made you bitter and resentful. Talk to him. It's the only way to end this fighting."

David grew quiet and nodded in agreement. He stood up from the table. "I think I'm going to go for a walk."

"Okay." Rachel nodded. She hoped that by some miracle, he took her words to heart. As he headed for the door, she softened and added, "I'm making lasagna for dinner. We eat at six."

"I'll see you then." David smiled.

Through the window, Rachel watched him walk down the driveway and turn onto the sidewalk. She set down the towel and propped herself against the counter, letting out a heavy sigh. *Jesus, please help him. He needs You.* She felt the tears stinging at her eyes as the realization of their conversation hit her. All this time, instead of feeling resentful about his absence, she should have been reaching out.

*****

David cut through the new development area and walked down through the main area of town along Highway 20. So much had changed in fifteen years. He grew up in this town, watched it gradually change over time, a dozen or so houses built a year. Not very many considering the vast wilderness that surrounded the town. During his absence, the topography of the town had changed. Everywhere he looked, houses or condos stood in what once had been empty fields. Now rooflines obstructed the panoramic views. His senior year they had just completed the new high school. Now it housed the junior high. A newer larger high school had been built to accommodate all the people moving into town.

He walked past a new building complex with a day spa and movie house, a fancy term for a theater. Never would he have thought he would see the day when Sisters had its own movie theater. So much had changed. Of course, he had changed too. He'd left this town fifteen years ago, a fresh-faced punk filled with dreams and aspirations, none of which he had fulfilled. He'd gone off to college the town hero with the idea that he'd play college ball, become an All-American, maybe even win the Heisman. Then he'd be drafted into the NFL and live the life all men dreamed of—houses, cars, toys, and women. He'd bury the past under the success of his future. But the past wouldn't stay buried, and the bitterness and resentment brewed until a fistfight with one of his college teammates forced him to quit playing ball. He did everything he could think of to try and forget. He changed his major and took up causes that he'd always dismissed but knew would outrage his father. He studied Eastern religions in attempts to find the inner peace they promised. When all else failed, he began to drink more and more until he could no longer remember why he drank.

He'd been sober now for two years. His advisor back at UW offered him a job on one condition—he quit drinking. He did quit and hadn't so much as thought about a drink until he got that email from Rachel about their mom's diagnosis. Then Tyler Green called about the investigation into the coach. Without the booze, the anger and resentment festered unchecked. Then came word that his mother had died. He should have come home. He just couldn't. And he added guilt to the bitterness. He'd survived all that without one drop. How? He didn't know.

Now here he was, back where he started, in Sisters and in a world of trouble. More trouble than he'd ever known. He'd read the article that Tyler wrote, the one he'd helped Tyler get. It practically gave him permission for justifiable homicide. But for some reason, people in town didn't see it that way. They looked at him with daggers and skittered off when he walked by. He was no longer their long-lost hometown hero but an outsider who'd returned and turned their town upside down.

He walked along the main drag, and once again, it felt like his hometown. There was comfort in the familiarity of it all. There were a few new shops, but the cornerstones were still there, Leavitts Western Wear, The Sisters Hotel, Sisters Drug, and Sno Cap Drive-In. This was the town he remembered, the buildings with the Old West theme, board sidewalks and wooden facades atop the stores.

Once he got past all the shops, he discovered the entire landscape of the west side of town had changed. Condos had gone up in what once was an empty field next to the elk farm. Even the roads had changed. The city had rerouted McKenzie Highway so that it no longer came in next to the gas station but, instead, looped around by the condos. Some of the houses where his old high school friends lived still stood. They were mixed in with the new homes, the bigger homes all with the northwest signature craftsman style.

He thought of turning back, but for some reason, he pressed on. The old high school, the field where he played, wasn't much further. He crossed the road and cut across the field. He sat on the bleachers and watched as thirteen-year-old boys scrimmaged on the field below, the same field where he had won so many games for the Outlaws. He had been the hometown hero, and now some other kid had earned that title. In recent weeks, David had learned that Coach Fisher had taken the Outlaws to five more state championships after he graduated. That made him a legend in this small town, whether he deserved it or not. He watched the young boys passing the ball. Once football had been his life; it made him that hometown hero, the prom king. It won him a scholarship to University of Washington. Now it was just a game he had played when he was younger.

David climbed down from the bleachers and decided to head back to Rachel's house. He cut across the field and saw the church next door. He hesitated a moment before turning toward it.

David entered the empty sanctuary. A man was setting up chairs near the front.

"Can I help you?" he asked warmly.

"Um. No. I was walking around town and thought I'd come in and look around," David began, looking around the large sanctuary. They had finished the new addition. Other than that, it was exactly the same. "I used to go here a long time ago."

"Then feel free to look around. I'm Pastor Mike O'Connell if you need anything." He continued setting up chairs.

"Thanks," David said.

"Do I know you?" The pastor turned to get another look.

"I don't think so." David lowered his head, hoping the pastor would let it go.

"You look familiar."

"Maybe I'd better go." David turned to leave.

"No. I didn't mean to scare you off. It's just I could swear I've seen you before."

"Probably on the news," David admitted. He heard the door close behind them and glanced over his shoulder but didn't see anyone.

"You're David then," Pastor Mike inquired.

"Yes. I'm David Patterson."

"Come sit." Mike pointed to a chair.

David hesitated at first, but then he sat in a chair at the aisle. He looked up at the stage with the pulpit and the life-size cross at the right side of the stage, just as it had been when he attended church in his youth. He remembered sitting in a chair next to his mom during the morning service. She'd always brought a pad and pen so he could doodle during the message.

"Pastor. Um…" David started but couldn't remember his name.

"Mike. Pastor Mike O'Connell."

"Pastor Mike, are there any unforgivable sins?"

"I'm not sure I get what you mean?" Mike looked at him quizzically.

"Are there sins that are so bad God won't forgive them?"

"Say like murder?"

"Sure. Something like that."

"God's word is clear on that. He says that if we confess our sins, He is faithful and just to forgive us our sins and to cleanse us from all unrighteousness," Mike explained.

"So… He forgives just like that?" David heard the side door close. He looked but didn't see anyone. "Even the big ones?"

"Even the big ones. To Him, sin is sin. Men are the ones who rate the gravity of the sin, but to God, it makes no difference—sin is sin."

"Just like that?" David responded skeptically.

"Just like that." Pastor Mike pointed to the cross as he said it. "Christ took all our sins and paid the price. The Bible actually says that once God has forgiven us, it is as if our sin was no more. All we have to do is confess our sins and believe that Christ is Lord." Mike paused and looked at David. "But I think you already knew that."

"But"—David paused a moment, trying to choose his words—"what about the other big ones? Say like the one about having no other gods?"

"That is a big one, but if you return to Him sincerely, then He'll forgive you."

In the quietness of the sanctuary, he remembered the Bible verse he'd learned in this very church. He knew in his heart that what the pastor had said was true, except for one part, repentance. To ask forgiveness required repentance. "Thank you, pastor." David stood and stretched out his hand. He shook the pastor's hand.

"Anytime. And if you feel like talking to someone, I'm always here."

"Thanks." David took one last look around as Mike returned to setting up chairs. David let his gaze hover at the cross, absorbing the words that Pastor Mike had shared. During his youth, he'd been imbibed in the teachings of the Word. And then like everything in his life, he turned his back on them. He took one last look, turned, and walked outside.

"You *did* do it!" Michael exclaimed, appearing out of nowhere.

"What? What are you talking about?" David watched his brother get closer.

"I heard you in there." Michael nodded his head toward the church. "Unforgivable sins, huh?"

"What? Are you following me?" David eyed his brother with disbelief.

"Maybe. But that doesn't change the fact that you did it."

"Did what?"

"Killed the coach," Michael exclaimed.

"You don't know what you're talking about."

"All right then. What was all that in there?" Michael nodded back toward the church.

"None of your business."

"Oh, I'm making it my business." Michael got up in David's face. He could feel the spittle hit his face as Michael ranted on. "First, you leave us all 'cuz you're too good for us. Then Mom gets sick, and you're too lily-livered to come home and just see if she's okay. Then she dies, and you can't even show your face. You, gutless wonder. But you're here now, and the coach is dead. It doesn't take a rocket scientist."

"You're making an assumption about something you know nothing about."

"So now I'm stupid too." Michael pressed in closer, and David shoved him backward. Michael came back at him, his right hand clenched into a fist. David felt a blow to his right eye. He fell backward into the gravel, and Michael tumbled on top of him. He tried to wrestle free, but Michael kept trying to pin him down.

Pastor Mike pulled Michael off. "That's enough," he scolded. "What's gotten into you?" He directed the question at Michael.

"Ask him," Michael spat angrily. He wiped the dust from his pants as he walked off toward his truck. He jumped into his truck and left quickly, his tires throwing gravel into the air.

"What was that all about?"

"Beats me," David lied. Michael had a right to be upset with him. He even understood why Michael might suspect him. Everyone else did. If he was an onlooker, he'd probably suspect himself as well.

"Do you need a ride somewhere?"

"No. I'll be fine." David dusted off the dirt and lightly brushed the blood from a cut on his lip. Maybe he should just lie low until the whole thing blew over, but would it ever be over? Everyone in town, even his own brother, believed he killed Coach Fisher. Some probably even thought he'd be justified in doing so. Normally, he wouldn't be so concerned what everybody else thought, except twelve of these people would soon become the jury that decided his fate. And if they were anything like his brother, he was a dead man.

Chapter 34

Michael's truck screeched to a halt in front of the house. Rachel called from the foot of the stairs for Steve to bring Conner down. Michael's perpetual tardiness annoyed her, and this time was no different. The agreement was that he would pick up Conner between twelve and twelve-thirty. It was almost two. He didn't even bother to carry a cell phone. He didn't want people to find him. As he walked in the front door with his clothes all mussed and scrapes and scratches covering his face and hands, Rachel's annoyance turned into concern.

"What happened?" She looked at him wide-eyed.

"Nothing," he muttered.

"No. Something happened."

"If you must know, I got into it with David," he admitted reluctantly.

"Got into it as in argument or as in a wrestling match?"

"Both."

"Michael," she said disapprovingly.

"Look, Rach," Michael said, "David is my brother too, but all the evidence points to the fact that he killed Coach Fisher."

"Circumstantial evidence," Rachel clarified.

"You've been watching too much CSI." Michael shook his head. "He did it. Get over it."

"I just can't believe it. Not David."

"You weren't there at the church. You didn't hear him—unforgivable sins and all that. He practically confessed right there. I don't understand why you and Dad blindly defend the guy. This is the same David that didn't show for Mom," he ranted.

"It's just…" she started. But how could she explain that she just had a gut feeling, a sixth sense, he didn't do it. "It just doesn't make sense. Why now? If David wanted to kill Coach Fisher, why now?"

"You'll have to ask David that one. 'Cuz I don't know. And frankly, I don't care."

"You don't mean that."

"Maybe I do. Maybe David's getting what he deserves for giving the coach what he deserved," he said angrily.

"Now, I know you don't mean that," she chastised her younger brother.

"Rach, how can you stand there and defend him after all he put this family through? All the heartache he brought Mom and Dad? And now all this too."

"Because he didn't do it, and maybe, just maybe, God brought him here at this time so he and Dad could finally make peace." She'd been praying as she tried to make sense of it all since the news first broke labeling David as a person of interest. She knew that God used everything for good but couldn't seem to find the good in this. "Just please try not to make things any worse."

"Tell that to your other brother."

Conner appeared at the bottom of the stairs with Steve who held the diaper bag. Michael picked up his son and snatched the diaper bag before leaving in a huff, letting the screen door slam shut behind him.

*****

George pulled up just in time to see his son peel out down the street, leaving long black rubber marks on the pavement. "Do I want to know what that was all about?" George asked as he came in the same door Michael had just slammed.

"He and David got into a fistfight at the church. Then he came to chew me out about it," Rachel shook her head. "But what brings you here?"

"Steve asked if I could drop these by." He handed her a couple of books.

"I could have got them Monday."

"I suppose. But he said he needed them, so I thought I'd drop them by."

"Are you sure you didn't come to see David?"

"No. Besides, he probably doesn't want to see me." George turned to leave and then swiveled back around. "By the way, why did Michael and David get into a fistfight?"

Rachel explained from what little Michael had told her during his rant fest.

"I see. So Michael is convinced that David is guilty." George shook his head. He'd known that there would come a time that the two would butt heads, given Michael's animosity toward his older brother. He had no idea it would turn into a fistfight. "Well, I best be getting. See you later, kiddo." He forced a smile and walked back down the sidewalk.

"Bye, Dad." Rachel closed the door and went back inside.

When he reached his truck, he paused at the door and looked back at Rachel's house—a house they bought just the year before when everything had been wonderful. Now it seemed one calamity after another happened to his family. The stress of David's trouble was taking its toll on all of them. He wondered when the turmoil would end.

Chapter 35

For months, George avoided going to church because of Kate's passing. On Sunday morning, he nearly skipped it again, this time because of David and people's reactions when he showed up to Chuck's funeral. He didn't want a repeat of that experience. But he needed to talk to Mike, and Mike was at church.

He waited until they began the worship music, then slipped in unnoticed and sat in the back. Pastor Mike's sermon was on judging others. *How appropriate*, George thought as he listened, watching people who had been gossiping all week wriggling in their seats. Then Mike recited scripture from Matthew about removing the plank from your own eye before removing the speck from your neighbor's eye. For some reason, he felt as if Mike were talking to him at that moment. He had been angry with the people of this town for judging his son, and yet he had his own doubts and suspicions as well.

He waited until the service ended. He wandered the grounds until nearly everyone had left. Then he found Mike in his office. After Rachel had told him about the scuffle between his two sons, he needed some answers, and the only person he could trust to tell him the truth was Mike.

"I understand David came to see you last night."

"He did," Mike said as he looked up at George. "Please have a seat."

George sat down in a chair across from him. "Can I ask what you talked about? I mean it's not like you're a Catholic priest or anything."

"True, but I still like to keep things confidential. I can tell you that I don't think he killed Chuck."

"What makes you say that?" George was curious how he could know in such a short time.

"Just a gut feeling."

"Well, a gut feeling isn't going to prove he's innocent."

"True." Mike nodded in agreement.

"So what do I do?"

"I honestly can't tell you what to do or not do here. I've never encountered a situation like yours before. All I can do is offer some friendly advice. Have a little faith."

George guffawed.

"Not only in God, but in your son," Mike continued. "You and Kate raised him, and those values are buried in him somewhere. So have a little faith."

"It's not that easy. I trusted God with Kate, and see how that turned out."

"You tried bargaining with God for Kate. You didn't trust Him. You need to trust in God's plan."

"But—" George started to protest.

"I know it's a difficult thing to do. Trust." He stood and walked around and sat on the edge of his desk. "When Connie died, I felt so lost. I felt like a complete failure because I lost some of my faith."

"You?"

"Yeah, me. I couldn't understand why God would take her from me. He didn't, but He allowed it. And I simply couldn't understand why?" He paused. "But then after I lost my church, I really felt like God was hitting me upside the head with a two by four. So I spent time in the Word really reading it like I had when I was in seminary. And I found I had been on autopilot, doing the things I was supposed to do but not really trusting God. And it all boils down to a matter of trust."

"But how? How do you trust Him after everything?"

"You just do because He commands it, because He loves us and has plans for us."

"I wish it were that simple."

"It is. Because if Connie hadn't died, I wouldn't have come here, and I wouldn't have been able to serve this church in a way that I never could have served before. And look at you. You and I have a connection in our grief for our wives. That was all His doing."

"So what? I just trust that God will save David? How?"

"You trust. And you pray that God will give you wisdom and understanding."

"For what? To watch my son go to jail?" George longed to have the kind of faith Mike talked about. He wanted to trust that God had a plan; sometimes that was all that got him through. But lately, when George thought he could see bottom, it fell again. How could any of this be part of God's plan?

"I don't know. Only God knows. But I don't think David going to jail is part of God's plan." Mike raised his brows in emphasis.

"What makes you say that?"

"Talk to David. And trust him." Mike looked George squarely in the face as he said it.

George pushed up from the chair. "Thanks."

Mike smiled compassionately. "I'll keep you in my prayers."

"I'd appreciate that." George turned and left. He walked out of the church. All the talk of God's plans made him think of his chance encounter with Phil. Maybe the meeting hadn't been up to chance at all. Maybe it had been part of God's plan all along—one step along the path. But where was the path leading? And what would happen to him and to David along the way? He had trusted God to save Kate. Could he trust Him to save David?

*****

After chatting with Pastor Mike, George considered trying his luck with the fall hatch on the Metolius. Instead, for reasons he couldn't explain, he drove straight home. When he arrived, he found David's rental car parked in the driveway. George checked the house and shop but found no sign of David. Then he peered over the edge of the rim and saw a lone figure on the rocks at the bottom of the canyon. He started down the path, watching his footing as he went.

He crossed the log and rounded the tall ponderosa at the bottom of the steep incline.

"You know, I used to find your brother down here all the time," George said as he sat down on a boulder a few feet from David. "Anytime he got upset, which was a lot of the time, he'd come down here and throw rocks in the water, just like you're doing now. In fact, he came down here the day you left for college. He sat down here for hours," George elaborated.

"I don't really remember." David didn't even bother to look up.

"He idolized you. Wanted to be just like you, until you left and didn't come back." George wanted David to understand how deeply they had all been hurt by him, and he was still hurting them with his caustic indifference. He wanted him to see that Michael wasn't simply a hothead, although that was part of it—Michael had years of pent-up resentment to release.

"I never knew that." David's tone remained cold.

"That's part of the reason he's so upset with you now."

"Oh, I know why he's upset with me." David rubbed the bruise around his eye. "I just wish I could make him *understand*. I wish I could make everyone *understand*."

"Understand what?"

"Never mind."

"No. You want us to understand, but you're not saying anything. How are any of us supposed to understand if you don't tell us anything?"

"I don't know." David plunked a large rock on the ledge on the other side and let it fall into the water. He sat quietly, avoiding the question.

"Maybe I should go back up to the house." George started to get up.

"Dad. Wait," David stalled. "We do need to talk."

"About?" George prompted as he sat back down.

David turned back toward the creek. He picked up a few more rocks and threw them at the water with all his might. "It's true—the article about Coach Fisher."

George's stomach dropped, fearful of what might follow. His heart began pounding so hard that he could feel his pulse throbbing in his forehead. Since the first time he'd read that article, he'd dreaded the possibility it might be true. Try as he might, he was unable to convince himself it had been a mistake.

"It started out with him just buying a couple of us guys from the team some beer," David started, throwing the rocks harder into the water as he spoke. "Then he'd invite us over and get us drunk and we'd watch movies—movies you'd never approve of." David hesitated. "And each time, it sort of escalated, and I don't even really know how or when he started manhandling me. I just remember afterward, I'd feel sick and dirty and angry."

"Why didn't you tell us?" George was trembling. His emotions ran one into another—disgust, loathing, heartache, and disappointment. His son had just confirmed that Chuck had molested him.

"I don't know. I guess I was ashamed. What kind of man lets that happen to him? And I honestly didn't think you'd believe me."

"David, you're my son. Of course, I would believe you."

"Really, Dad? Do you remember how much we fought? I was constantly in trouble. You didn't believe me half the time."

"I would have believed you," George said firmly, not knowing if that was entirely true. At some undefined point in the past, his son had lost the capacity to confide in him, with any sense of surety that George would listen. Consequently, David had carried this secret with him, allowing it to simmer, turning into hate. That hate is what kept him away all these years. George couldn't help but feel that he shared some culpability in that. If only he'd been more…more what? He'd done all he'd known how to do as far as David was concerned, and it wasn't good enough.

David turned to look at him. For the first time, George looked beyond the caustic attitude and saw the pain in David's eyes. George wanted to scoop him up in his arms like he had when he was Braden's age. He wanted to take the pain away, but it was too late; the damage was done.

"Yeah. Well, I guess we'll never know, will we?" David stood abruptly, taking George off guard. "Not that it matters anymore, anyways." He stared down at George, with contempt brewing in his eyes. "What gets me is that you think I did it. You've always been willing to think the worst of me. You try and hide it, but it's there. At least Michael is honest about where he stands. But you…you're trying to be all supportive. All the while, you think I did it."

*****

Before he had a chance to respond, David had hiked halfway up the path. His heart literally ached from all he'd just learned. Even after David left, his words lingered. George replayed them over and over in his mind. Chuck Fisher had broken every cardinal rule of manhood, of trust, of friendship—not to mention God's laws. Right under his nose, this devious pervert violated his son, destroyed his innocence, stole his faith in all that is good and right, and hardened his heart.

George could never mend the irreparable damage done. The contempt, the utter hate that David had coursing through him all stemmed from it. Why hadn't George seen it? Why hadn't he been able to stop it? Now he knew why David hated him, and he didn't blame him. He should have been able to protect him, to keep him safe. He had failed as a father.

And now Chuck Fisher was dead. He felt complete ambivalence about that fact. Just days before, he had mourned the loss of a friend. Now he didn't care. No, that was a lie. He cared. He was glad Chuck was dead because he might have killed him himself if he had known about this while Chuck was still alive. The only part of his death that bothered him was the fact that he would never be able to confront him, to look him in the eye and denounce their friendship. Maybe it wasn't very Christian like, but he relished in the thought that Chuck Fisher burned in hell.

David had been right about George thinking or at least considering the possibility that David had done it. The question tormented him because he didn't know with absolute certainty if David was guilty or innocent. Mike had said to have some faith, to trust. Trust—that tenuous thread between belief and unbelief. But how could he trust in his son's innocence if he was uncertain what he himself might have done if he had known before.

Chapter 36

David got directions to Neil's office from Steve. Surprisingly, Steve turned out to be a decent guy. He kept David entertained, while everyone else was busy accusing and mistrusting him. Steve had a pool table in the game room, and they shot pool and talked about football and the upcoming World Series. It offered a nice diversion from everything else.

At first, David took a wrong turn on the roundabout at Powers Road. His wrong turn landed him in the parking lot of a movie plex and a shopping mall. While he'd been away, all the creature comforts of big city life had moved into the small town of Bend. He still couldn't believe how much Bend had changed. The population when he left had been somewhere in the neighborhood of thirty thousand people, and now it was more than double that. After an unintentional scenic detour through the west side of Bend, David finally found Neil's office. Neil's secretary escorted him back to Neil's office.

"Please sit." Neil gestured to the chairs across from his desk. "Can I have my secretary get you some coffee? Water?"

"No. I'm fine thanks." David sank into one of the chairs.

"Let's cut to the chase here. I've been reviewing your case, and there's not a lot of physical evidence, which is good for us. Their only basis is finding your prints at the scene and the eyewitness account that places you at the scene near the time of the murder. The crime scene was pretty clean, but I'll send over my investigator just to check things out. There's no DNA, no weapon recovered, and without the gun, they can't prove conclusively who did it. Normally, with this type of circumstantial evidence, I could get the case thrown out. In order to get an acquittal, I need to create reasonable doubt in the minds of the jury. Our job is to ascertain what most likely happened and who other than you had motive, means, and opportunity. Because that's all they have you on right now. If we can show that someone else had just as strong of a motive and had the opportunity, then we have reasonable doubt." He flipped open a leather-bound legal pad and scribbled something at the top of the page. "All right then. Let's start with your account of that evening."

David shifted slightly in his seat. He hadn't talked about it yet. The whole thing gave him the creeps. "Let's see. I pulled up to the house sometime around seven that evening. The porch light was on but no lights inside. I thought for a moment about turning around and going back. But then I knocked on the door. No answer. I looked around. I um, I think I peeked in one of the front windows. I knocked again, and the door was unlocked, so I went in."

"It wasn't locked?" Neil questioned.

"No. The coach never locked his doors. A lot of people around here never lock their doors."

"You went inside?" Neil coaxed.

"Um. Yeah. I opened the door, and it was dark inside. I reached down the wall and flipped on a light."

Neil flipped through some papers quickly. "That's odd. The police report shows that they only found your prints on the doorknob. Exterior. They said no matching prints were discovered inside." Neil looked at him dubiously.

"I don't know what to tell you. I flipped on the light."

"What next?"

"Um. I heard a noise toward the kitchen. I thought it might be Coach, and that's when I saw him on the floor. There was no doubt he was dead." David paused for a minute. "There were bullet…um…what do you call them…shells?"

"Casings," Neil answered for him.

"Okay. There were casings scattered on the floor. I was pretty freaked out seeing the coach like that and then I thought I heard the screen door and I ran out of there. I peeled out of the driveway, and that's when old lady Binkard saw me leaving."

"Why didn't you call the police?"

"I don't know." David looked at the floor. "I honestly don't."

Neil flipped through some more pages. "You said you turned on the light."

"Yes," David answered quickly.

"Did you turn it off when you left?"

"No." David shook his head. "I was just so freaked out about Coach, so I just ran."

"Hmm." Neil jotted down something on the legal pad and underlined it.

"What?" David tried to peek at Neil's notes over the top of the desk.

"It's just odd. Sheriff Bricker states in his affidavit that when he entered the house, all the lights were out. *He* had to flip a light on, which might explain why your prints weren't found. Still that's odd."

"What is?"

"Well, you said you thought you heard the screen door. That might mean someone else was there."

"That's sort of what I thought, and I saw what they did to the coach. I didn't want to stick around and find out what they might do to me."

Neil scribbled some more on his legal pad and flipped through the file again. "And you said you saw casings?"

"Yeah."

Neil flipped through the pages in the file on his desk. "There's nothing in the police report about casings. They would be considered physical evidence. You're certain you saw them?"

"Yes," David asserted. "I stepped on one when I entered the kitchen. I'm pretty sure I heard it roll across the floor."

"Hmm." Neil rubbed his brow and made some more notes. "Where'd you go after you left Coach's?"

"I drove back to the hotel in Bend."

Neil scribbled some more notes. Then he looked at David directly. "Why did you go out to Chuck Fisher's house in the first place?"

David hesitated before answering. He wasn't certain how much to entrust with his lawyer—enough to keep him out of jail. The rest, Neil didn't need to know. "I was helping Tyler Green with an exposé on Coach Fisher. He'd been working on it for some time."

"Yeah, I thought so."

"What?"

"You don't just throw a story like that together," Neil explained and then returned to questioning. "How exactly were you helping Tyler Green?"

"I called Coach. He agreed to meet me at his house to talk. I don't know really what I hoped to accomplish. I just thought that I might be able to figure out who some of his other victims were to give Tyler more collaboration."

"Why? I mean what's it to you?"

"He thought that the more sources he had, the more credible the story and"—David slipped his hand over his neck, rubbing the base while he decided how much to tell—"we were hoping to figure out if he had a current victim. The statute of limitations has already expired on what he did to me and few others. I wanted to see him go to jail."

Neil looked down at his notes. "How did Tyler uncover the coach's history?"

"I'm not 100 percent certain on that." David remembered Tyler mentioning something briefly about how he got turned on to the story, but David stopped paying attention after Tyler mention the coach's name and molest in the same sentence. "Something about his brother married a girl from Sisters. He didn't give many specifics. But it didn't take him long to track me down."

"How many other victims did he know of?"

"Why?"

"Because they have the same motive as you, and maybe one of them pulled the trigger." Neil closed his legal pad and folded his hands on top of the leather binder. "I think I have enough for now. I have someone checking out the crime scene."

"So what now?" David looked down at his watch. The entire interview had taken only fifteen minutes, less time than it took to drive in.

"I go to work. Somebody out there knows something."

"Do you think you can get me off?" The way people in town looked at him, he was almost positive he was headed to prison if they didn't lynch him first.

"Yes. But I need you to keep a low profile. Don't say anything to the press, even your reporter friend Tyler. If you want the jury to believe you're innocent, then you need to act innocent. So please, don't draw any attention to yourself."

"Anything else?' David didn't like being told how to act even if it was in his best interest.

"Yeah. Lose the attitude. This brooding loner act doesn't help you. The DA already has enough to feed the jury, including your reluctance to make an appearance at your own mother's funeral, a woman whom, by all accounts, was practically a saint," Neil scolded.

"What's that got to do with anything?" David couldn't believe that Neil was throwing it in his face as well. He'd already heard enough from his family. He didn't need more guilt trips from his lawyer.

"It goes to character. The DA can sway the jury by showing a history of lack of concern for others, including your mother," Neil explained.

"But that has absolutely nothing to do with the coach's death," David argued.

"Look, there's very little physical evidence in this case. The jury is going to base their decision on whether or not they believe you were capable of committing the crime. Your fate is going to be in their hands, and they need a reason to believe you didn't do it. While your past actions have nothing to do with the crime of which you're accused, it does suggest your ability to commit the crime. Understand?"

"Yes." David still didn't like it, but there was nothing he could do about it.

"All right. Then I better get to work." Neil stood.

"Thanks." David shook his hand. As much as he hated it, Neil was right. His past could not only come back to haunt him, but it might even convict him.

Chapter 37

George found it hard to suppress the overwhelming curiosity. He was eager to find out what David had told his lawyer. Work provided little distraction. In fact, it had the reverse effect. David's troubles now distracted him from work. He'd looked at the same invoice six times and still couldn't say who it was from. He wanted desperately to help David, but how could he if he didn't know what was going on or how to help him?

After meeting with David, Neil had called and requested a meeting with him and Rachel. Neil said there were a few things that they might be able to clear up. That only intensified the curiosity. How could they possibly provide any answers?

Neil arrived around noon. George led him upstairs to his office so they could talk without everyone in town knowing about it. He was certain that some of his employees subscribed to the opinion that David was guilty. Gossip had been flying all over town since they first showed his picture on the news.

"You've added to the collection." Neil pointed to the array of antique logging tools George hung on the wall. He had started collecting them shortly after he bought the store. It was his way of making the store his own. Neil had been gone for a while, and George was surprised he remembered.

"I bought a few new implements at an auction over in Eugene a couple of years ago," George explained as they walked up the stairs.

"I forgot about the tools and stuff. My dad used to love coming in here and talking about the old times with you guys."

"How is your dad these days?" George felt bad that he hadn't even asked Neil anything about his family since all this began. He'd been so focused on David. Neil had practically been part of the family. Before he went off to law school, he half expected Neil and Rachel to marry, and now he was treating him like hired help instead of the friend that he was.

"He's doing quite well. He's the operations manager for a Weyerhaeuser mill in Washington."

"Good to hear." George found it comforting to have Neil handle David's defense.

Neil settled onto the couch, scooting over to make room for Rachel. She opted to stand by George's desk. Maybe it was too close for comfort. George sat in his chair and placed his hands on his desk giving Neil his full attention.

"Thanks for meeting with me. I wanted to talk to you about David's case, see if there are any details you can help me with." Neil cut right to the chase. "Later, if need be, we can formalize them at my office."

"Sure, whatever you need," George offered.

"Let's get started. George,"—he looked directly at him as he spoke and pulled out his pen and legal pad—"you and Chuck were still pretty good friends, right?"

"Yeah, you could say that. We went fishing about once a month." George couldn't believe it had only been a little over a week since that day he was supposed to go fishing with Chuck. It felt as if a lifetime had passed in that one week.

"Did you happen to notice if he had been jumpy or nervous lately?"

"No, I don't think so."

"He never mentioned David?"

"No. Never." George began to get uneasy. He wasn't sure what he expected when Neil said he had a few questions. He hated to think that Chuck talked to David or even thought about David.

Neil jotted down some notes before continuing. "When was the last time you saw Chuck Fisher?"

"Friday afternoon. He came in and bought some cleaner and sealant for his back deck. Winter's coming, and he wanted to get something on it before the weather started. He liked to do little projects before a game to help relax."

"And he didn't seem at all edgy or nervous?"

"Not that I could tell. Maybe a little jittery about the game. Why do keep asking?"

Neil wrote down some more notes and then looked up to address George. "It just seems to me that with all the poking around for the story that Tyler was writing, that Chuck might have caught wind of that. I thought if Chuck knew about it, he might act a little weird around you."

"I didn't notice." His brow wrinkled as he tried to recall anything unusual. He'd been doing that a lot, looking back, trying to see the signs he might have missed. How do you not know that your friend is abusing your son? And now, how could he have missed that Chuck knew David was going to be in town and never once mentioned it?

"You were going fishing with him on Sunday?"

"Yeah. We had standing arrangements. The foursome went every first Sunday of the month from September to December."

"Who else knew about that arrangement?"

"It wasn't a secret. We've been doing it for years."

"The same foursome?"

"Yeah. What 'cha getting at?"

Neil set his legal pad down and scratched the back of his head. "I don't know. Just this gut instinct." He shook his head as if debating how to proceed. "I think someone wanted Fred to be the one to find him. That someone knew Fred would be there Sunday morning."

"That's strange."

"Yeah, well, this is a strange case." Neil picked his pad back up. "Who else knew?"

"Everyone here at the store. Wayne's wife and sons for sure. Wayne's a contractor, and he's been real busy. His sons complained about him missing one day a month. Um. I guess Midge, Fred's wife, and I don't know who else."

"But you said it wasn't a secret."

"Neil, you lived here. You know that everybody knows everybody else's business. The four of us went fishing the same place, on the same day, for I don't know fifteen, twenty years." George shrugged. He couldn't imagine that Neil's theory was correct. It didn't make any sense for someone to kill Chuck and set it up so that the sheriff would be the one to discover it. But then none of this made any sense.

"Well, that narrows down the list of suspects," Neil said with a hint of sarcasm. He scribbled on the legal pad quietly for a minute.

"Do you think you'll find the real killer?" Rachel piped in.

Neil looked up at her. "That's what I'm hoping. I'm headed out to the crime scene after this."

"So you think David has a chance?"

"I won't make any promises, but I can make a really strong case for reasonable doubt. All I have to do is make the jury see that someone other than David could have committed the crime. Now that would be easier if I could find someone with a motive and means." Neil then turned his questions to Rachel. "Rach, you're the only one in your family who had been in contact with David. When was the last time you'd heard from him?"

Rachel glanced at George before answering. "A month ago."

"Did he mention anything about being in town?"

"No."

"He hadn't mentioned anything about an upcoming article or about the coach?"

"He didn't really confide in me like that. I emailed him pictures of the kids, and he'd email me internet jokes. That kind of stuff."

"Did you happen to notice any changes in Coach Fisher lately?"

"I can't say that I paid that much attention to him."

"Probably not." Neil scribbled a few remaining notes and then put away his legal pad. "I guess I'm off to Coach Fisher's. I'll let you know if I find anything."

Neil stood. George walked him out. He stood in the parking lot and watched as Neil drove off. *Please God, let him find something that proves David didn't do this.*

*****

This was Neil's first trip to Sisters since he'd moved back to Bend. He'd moved back in mid-July but hadn't taken the time to come out this way. The closest he'd come was a round of golf at one of the nearby golf courses. He hadn't been by the house he grew up in or any of his old hangouts. He'd been busy setting up his practice and his new condo. He'd had to buy all new housewares, towels, pans, dishes.

His ex-fiancée, Patricia, kept almost everything when he moved out. He took his clothes, CDs, and books. Everything else, he left for her. He didn't want to fight over who got what. Besides, she'd already spent a small fortune on the wedding, a wedding that wouldn't take place.

He should have ended things earlier. He knew it wasn't right when she insisted on moving in after they were engaged. It went against everything he believed, but she had been so convincing. So he went along with her, and she moved in and redecorated. Then she had a prenuptial agreement drawn up. They had a huge fight when he refused to sign it. Things were said, and he moved out. It was a matter of principle, a piece of paper saying their marriage was destined to fail, and here's the safety net. He hadn't wanted her money; he proved that when he left.

He would have stayed in DC, except Patricia's father was a well-respected fixture in the political scene and sought retribution for his little girl's embarrassment. Neil's position at the big law firm was terminated, and the rest, they say, is history. At least recent history. It was for the best. Neil never really fit in with the hobnobbers and the socialites—the country-club scene. He missed real people, hard-working people that earned a living with the sweat of their brow, not by browbeating some official into some legislation that allowed larger profits. He missed barbecues in the backyard instead of cocktails on the yacht. He missed the comfort of community over the status of a house in the right neighborhood. But most of all, he missed church. An associate in a large law firm is expected to work no less than eighty hours a week which, for most means, working not only Saturday but Sunday as well. The payoff is making partner if they don't burnout.

When he left, only one destination came to mind. He knew the legal scene in Bend, primarily real estate deals, and no one worked on Sundays. When he returned, he never expected to have a case like this one. Not in a million years would he have guessed that he would wind up defending David Patterson. When he first left for college, he'd always imagined that one day, he'd return to Rachel and be part of the Patterson family. But time and distance eroded their relationship, and both found new people to share their lives with. His just didn't work out. But here he was, drawn back into the Patterson clan. He only hoped he could live up to their expectations.

*****

He took in all the familiarity of the scenery as he drove out McKenzie Highway to the Crossroads turnoff. Crossroads Community had the feel of one of those picture-perfect neighborhoods portrayed in 1950s sitcoms—every house with a fenced yard only placed in a wooded landscape. A playground had been built smack dab in the middle where kids could climb and swing after school. Older couples could stroll down the winding streets day or night without fear. Most folks left their houses unlocked without fear.

The remnants of yellow crime scene tape strewn around the enormous pine trees looked strangely out of place at the house on Bluegrass Lane. Neil pulled into the driveway. Sheriff Bricker had given him a key. They had changed the locks on the house and gave keys only to investigators.

Neil entered through the front door; black print powder still clung to the doorknob. Inside, nothing looked out of the ordinary, except the mess in the kitchen. There were no signs of a burglary or even a struggle. Whoever did this came with the sole purpose of killing Chuck Fisher.

Neil pulled a pair of latex gloves from his pocket and snapped them on. One thing he'd learned working in Washington, DC, was not to contaminate any possible evidence. Even then, getting it admitted could be tricky. When he moved back to Central Oregon, he liked the idea of a slower pace, less investigating. He had worked for a large criminal defense firm in DC and handled multiple cases involving burglary, rape, and murder. Coming home, he'd hoped to leave that all behind him. Yet here he was in the middle of maybe the biggest case of his career.

"Neil." A familiar voice rang out.

"In here," Neil said over his shoulder.

"Hey bro." His brother Matt came up and clasped him in a hug.

"Thanks for coming." Matt lived in Seattle and worked as a full-time investigator there. He'd been an officer for the Oregon State Police but budget cuts took his job. Now he *freelanced* for lawyers in Seattle.

"Hey. This beats tailing a deadbeat dad or running down plates. So what do we got?" Matt asked, looking around.

"I'm not sure yet. But David said he saw casings on the floor, and when the police did their investigation, there weren't any." Neil had already filled in Matt on most of the particulars when he'd asked him to come down and help him.

"That's odd. You sure your client didn't make it up?"

"He didn't even know what they were called. I talked with Rachel—" he started.

"Wait a second. David Patterson. That David Patterson? Rachel Patterson's brother?" Matt let out a raucous laugh.

"Yeah, don't give me hard time." Neil felt the heat rush toward his cheeks.

"David couldn't shoot straight to save his life. I mean he went out with the guys once in a while back in high school and we'd shoot and he'd watch. The sheriff's got the wrong guy."

"Huh." Undeterred by Matt's comment, Neil pulled a flashlight from his rear pocket. As he turned it on, he aimed it under the cabinets in the corner. Then he got down on all fours and looked under the fridge. "Aha."

"What did you find?" Matt asked as he came up behind him.

"A casing." He stood and motioned for his brother to help him move the fridge back. Underneath, there was an assortment of bottle caps, dust bunnies, and one bullet casing. Matt snapped a picture with his digital camera. Then Neil used his pen to scoop it from the floor and place it in a bag Matt held open for him.

"You still have buddies at OSP crime lab?" Neil asked as Matt sealed the bag shut.

"Yep. And one of them owes me a favor." Matt grinned as he said it.

"Good." They slid the refrigerator back into place and continued to walk around.

"Now what are we looking for?"

"I don't know." Neil walked slowly, and his foot stuck slightly to the floor like on a movie theater floor. He lifted his foot twice more in the same spot, testing the stickiness. He looked at the floor and saw a couple shiny areas about the size of a man's foot.

"Did you bring your kit?"

"Yeah."

"Let's get a sample of this sticky stuff."

"On it." Matt turned and went back out toward the driveway.

Neil walked past the bloodstained area quickly. The police would have focused their efforts on that area. There was no need to cover it again. He opened the door to the back porch. A couple of footprints stood out in the finish on the deck, and as he turned, he saw a pair of shoes in front of the door. He inspected the bottom of the shoe and found the tread to be different than that of the design in the finish. He snapped a few pictures on his digital camera. Then he went back inside.

The living room appeared completely untouched, just a few dots of fingerprint dust. In the corner, he found the coach's shrine, a bookshelf with photos and game balls and trophies. The bottom shelf held yearbooks from Sisters High School all the way back to 1985, the year Chuck Fisher started teaching there. Neil had read that in the background information on Chuck. Neil thumbed over them and discovered two years were missing—1988 and 1989. The books were pushed together, so the missing books weren't conspicuous. He looked around the rest of the memorabilia to see if anything else looked out of place, but since he'd never seen it before, he would have no way of knowing if anything else was missing.

"What did you find?" Matt entered the room.

"I'm not sure. Maybe nothing. But let's get a sample of that stuff and take a sample from the deck too."

"All right. Didn't the police already do that?"

"There's no notation in the report."

Matt looked at him with raised eyebrows. "Sloppy police work."

Neil stood back to get a better viewpoint of the trail of sticky stuff on the floor. The path started at the back door, went through the kitchen, and stopped in front of the fridge before turning and crossing back over itself. It could simply be the coach's footprints coming in to get a drink, but the coach would have the presence of mind to remove his shoes first. Therefore, the footprints could be the killer's. If the killer was smart enough to remove the casings from the crime scene, then he'd also be smart enough to enter and leave through the backdoor where he could come and go unseen, under the cover of the national forest which butted up to the coach's property line. Chuck Fisher had no fence between his yard and the labyrinth of trails cutting through the forest. The police had questioned neighbors on who they'd seen coming and going on the road out front. But who would have been looking or even paid attention to someone walking on the trails? Neil walked to the back door and looked out at the acres and acres of ponderosa and lodgepole pines. The killer was clever enough to sanitize the crime scene except the one casing. It was the only real piece of physical evidence. It proved that either David was telling the truth, or he had cunningly let it slip to cover his tracks. Neil prayed it was the former and not the latter.

*****

The police were still investigating, even though David Paterson had already been charged. Framing David had not been part of the plan. Still, letting him take the fall worked out beautifully. Everyone assumed he killed Coach Fisher, especially after that article came out in the *Bulletin*. It couldn't have gone better if it had been planned. The entire town thought David was a victim semijustified in killing Coach Fisher. Even members of his own family thought he was guilty.

David had been released on bail. His family hired some lawyer that used to work back East somewhere, DC or New York. The lawyer asked lots of questions and even went out to the coach's house to investigate himself. Even the neighbors were watching with more scrutiny now, paying attention to everyone coming and going, probably even writing down license plate numbers. Too many people were asking too many questions. With that lawyer nosing around asking questions, it could ruin everything.

The question was, how much did David know? So far, he hadn't talked. If he did, it could be just a matter of time before the whole thing unraveled. Then all the meticulous planning would be wasted. Well, maybe not wasted; Coach Fisher was dead. He was in hell where he belonged. But going to jail for delivering justice was not part of the plan.

What did David know, if anything? What had he seen that night? If he did, and he talked… No, David wouldn't talk, even if it meant silencing him permanently.

Chapter 38

Neil met Matt at Papandrea's Pizza. They hurried to a booth in the corner, trying to be inconspicuous. Most people in town assumed David was guilty. He had topped the ranks of their most despised. And now thanks to the news, everyone with a television knew that Neil was defending him. That made Neil persona non grata simply by association. Matt ordered the pizza and some drinks and quickly retreated back to their table.

"Did you get the casing to your friends?"

"Yep. We should have something in a day or so. He did say it came from a .45 caliber. And he took a look at the markings and said they were consistent with the firing pin of a 1911-1A."

"Isn't that a military pistol?" Neil looked at him curiously. Who would have access to a military pistol? David certainly didn't. They wouldn't be able to prove that the casing and the slugs retrieved from Chuck's body came from the same gun unless they found the gun. Still, it opened the door for reasonable doubt. How would David have gotten a military handgun?

"Yep. And there was a nice print on the shaft." Matt took a swig from his root beer.

"I went to the *Nugget* office today and pulled up this." He pulled a piece of paper from the file he had brought in with him and handed it to Matt. "Can you follow up on it?"

It was a photocopy of an article retrieved from microfiche about the suicide of a former Sisters Outlaws football player, Chris Sanders. Sanders had been the quarterback in 1988. Matt read it quickly. If the guy had been one of coach's victims it was too late; he died in his college dorm room in 1990. "Sure. But how does it tie in?" Matt placed the article in his folder.

"I'm not sure it does. But it's the only thing I could find that would tie in with the missing yearbooks. David didn't have any ideas. He didn't think that the missing yearbook had anything to do with the murder. He could be right, but let's check it out anyway."

"All right, I'll get on it."

A young waitress brought the pizza over to the table and dropped it on the table without so much as a second glance. Matt and Neil dove in. Papandrea's Pizza was legendary. Toppings were stacked high and deep on each piece, and they used real mozzarella, not the preshredded, prefabbed stuff, the kind that pulled apart in a stringy, gooey mess.

As they devoured the pizza slice by slice, a deputy walked in and placed an order at the counter. Then he made a beeline for their table. Neil didn't recognize him, but then he hadn't worked many criminal investigations since his return.

"Howdy." The deputy flipped a chair around and sat at the end of their table.

"Can we help you?" Neil snapped his folder shut quickly.

"Rumor has it you two have been snooping around town." The deputy looked at Neil as he said it.

Neil just looked at the young deputy stone-faced. "It's my job."

"Sheriff Bricker just wants us to cooperate with the two of you in any way we can." He looked from Neil to Matt and back to Neil.

"Is that so?" Neil didn't trust the young deputy, and he wasn't sure if it was his false sentiments or if he'd just grown accustomed to mistrusting people bearing gifts from all the years in DC around the payoffs and the politics.

"Yeah. Well, Sheriff Bricker wants to make sure that you have everything you need for a proper defense in light of his friendship with the family and all," he said politely. "And I'm sure you want to cooperate with us as well."

Neil couldn't tell if it was a veiled threat or just a friendly reminder that any evidence they found needed to be shared with law enforcement. If he wanted to use anything they found in court for the defense, the police would need to know about it. But that's what he had Matt for. He was an insider. He used to be in law enforcement. He knew just how far they could bend the rules without breaking them.

A teenage girl waved a white box behind the counter.

"Well. That's my order. See you guys around." The deputy stood and returned the borrowed chair to its table.

Neil watched the deputy pick up his order and talk briefly with the cashier before he left.

"I don't trust that guy," Matt said it first as if reading Neil's mind.

"Me either, and I'm not sure why. I know this much. I've known Fred Bricker a long time. He's one hard-nosed son of gun. He wouldn't send a deputy to make nicey-nice with us. If he wanted to know what we were up to, he'd hunt us down and ask us."

"Then what's up with that guy?"

"I'm not sure. Maybe he's trying to impress Sheriff Bricker, or maybe he's like everyone else around here and believes my client is guilty and doesn't want us finding some way to get an acquittal."

"Do you think he's trouble?"

"Who, the Barney Fife wannabe? I don't see how. The evidence from the scene has already been submitted. If new evidence shows up with his name on it, then I'll worry." Neil dropped a couple of dollars on the table for tip. "In the meantime, we've got work to do."

Matt stood and finished the last swallow of his drink. "All right, I guess I'm off to Eugene."

Outside, Neil found a parking ticket on his car marked "*parked in handicapped zone.*" He looked and saw his tire had crossed the line onto the handicapped parking spot. He shook his head. How had the deputy known which car was his? At least, now he knew the deputy's name.

*****

Business had slacked off, not enough to be detrimental but enough to be noticed. George didn't know how much of the slowdown was due to the normal seasonal change and how much could be attributed to David's predicament. By noon, there were only two customers in the store. It was eerily quiet when Neil burst into the store unannounced.

"Where's David?" Neil practically shouted.

"I'm not sure." George looked to Rachel for answers.

"Beats me." She shrugged.

"His cell phone's message says that he's outside the service area. Does that help?" He looked pointedly at Rachel.

"Hey, I'm not my brother's keeper. He is staying in our guest room. But he's a grown up and comes and goes as he pleases," Rachel said defensively.

"How am I supposed to defend him if I can't find him?" Neil threw his hands in the air to stress his point.

"Did you have an appointment or something?" George asked.

"Not exactly, but something has come up."

"Then what's this all about?"

Neil took some calming breaths, and his face softened from red to light pink. "The DA faxed over David's cell phone call logs for the past month. He's submitting it as evidence, and I need to talk to David about it. ASAP."

George and Rachel looked at each other, not sure how to respond. George didn't want to pry, but he didn't see how David's cell phone records could cause such a commotion.

"If you see him—" Neil started.

"Wait," George interrupted. "I might have an idea where he is." He grabbed his jacket and keys and led the way out to his truck. He only hoped he was right about his son's whereabouts and that he hadn't actually jumped bail. He could see it in their faces. Rachel and Neil both secretly suspected it if only in a fleeting manner. The thought had crossed his mind as well.

The wind nipped at his face outside. Even though the sky above didn't show signs of a single cloud, it had turned cold outside. In another few weeks, winter would be upon them. They could see snow in a couple more weeks if it kept up like this.

The two men climbed into the cab of his truck, and George immediately started the heater. He knew, within minutes, warm air would replace the bitter cold. He turned onto the highway and headed west.

"This news isn't good. Is it?" George could tell just by Neil's demeanor that it wasn't, but he needed to ask.

"Not really, but I don't know the extent of it until I talk to David." Neil had quieted down.

"How bad is it?"

"Let's just say I don't like being lied to, and I can't build a defense if I don't know the facts." Neil's voice was piqued with indignation. He turned to look out the window. George took that as a sign that he didn't want to talk.

The aspen leaves had turned bright gold and stood out among the crimson and olive green of the forest. George turned up the radio to mask the silence.

Doubt crept back in. Neil hadn't said much, but what he had said spoke volumes. David had been evading questions and giving short answers all along. George hoped he was right about where his son had gone. It would prove that he still knew his son to some extent, that David hadn't become a complete stranger. Still, he worried that David wasn't as innocent as George wanted him to be.

Teach your children in the way of the Lord, and they will return to it. George couldn't remember if that was a psalm or a proverb. Kate had always said it whenever the kids got into trouble. He hoped that it was true. He prayed that David was not so far gone that he couldn't be saved.

They approached the turn, and George slowed. Just after the entrance to Camp Sherman, beyond the schoolhouse and the small resorts, a bridge crossed the Metolius over a wide and shallow bend in the river. On the other side of the bridge, the road diverged in various directions toward camping, the head waters, and Wizard Falls. But directly to the right, a short gravel road led to the Camp Sherman Store and a cabin resort. The bridge at the bend had a wooden walkway and a series of observation decks built right above the bank of the river. The deck looked out over the water in such a way that the fish could be seen in the shallows as well as under the bridge. It provided the perfect setting to contemplate life's big issues.

George pulled into the parking lot at the Camp Sherman Store. David's car was parked right in front. George put the truck in park.

"Could you give me a minute?" George asked Neil.

Neil nodded the affirmative. George got out and crossed the road and walked down onto the deck. There David stood, tossing Cheetos into the water.

"Thought I might find you here," George started.

"I was getting claustrophobic at Rachel's. And it's utterly unbearable to go into town. Everyone whispers and watches, and clerks give you dirty looks if they'll even help at all." David grabbed another cheese snack and threw it into the water. "I tried a few casts, but I couldn't remember what pattern to use, so I came down here."

George leaned over the deck just as David threw yet another snack into the water and watched as two large trout fought to gobble up the prize. "I see you haven't forgotten everything."

David smiled a little. It was the first smile George had seen on his son since his return. "I'll never forget the first time you brought me here. I don't know if I was more excited about the fact we were eating chips and soda for lunch or that the fish actually ate Cheetos." He poured out the remaining crumbs and threw them out on the water. "And the day you brought Michael down here for the first time. What was he, four or five? At first, it scared him when that hog jumped out of the water. It had to have been twenty-six, maybe thirty inches long. I thought he was going to wet his pants. However, you calmed him down and told him the fish only eat Cheetos."

George let out a chuckle. "Yeah. I wouldn't have had to calm him down so much if you hadn't told him that since his fingers were so small, the fish were liable to bite them off."

"Yeah. Well, what's a big brother for?" David wiped his hands together to remove the excess crumbs. "I doubt you came out here to reminisce."

"Nope," George said. Though he wished he could stand there and make his son remember all the good times the family had shared.

Maybe that might bring him to his senses. "Neil's in the truck, and he's pretty worked up about something."

David turned back around, rested his elbows on the rail, looking out across the river. "You believe me, don't you, Dad?" His voice was low and raw.

The only way George knew to honor David's honesty was by being honest himself. "I want to."

"But you think I did it?" David's eyes narrowed. "Just like everyone else."

"No. Not just like everyone else. You're my son, a son who hasn't come home in fifteen years, a son who hasn't spoken to me in ten." George struggled to not to let anger get the best of him. He didn't come to fight with David; he came to help him. "I'm just having a hard time trusting someone who doesn't seem to have any valid explanation for his sudden appearance."

"I explained it all to Neil."

"Yeah. You told Neil but not the rest of us—your family. We're trying to hold out hope blindly. We're trying to be supportive, all the while walking on eggshells because nothing we do or say seems to be good enough for you." George restrained himself from arguing any further. "I just don't want to lose you again, and I don't know how to stop that from happening. Please, help Neil help you." George made his final plea before he left David standing alone.

Neil met George halfway across the road. "You go ahead and go back. I'll get a ride back with David."

"All right." George nodded.

"It will be okay." He patted George on the shoulder. "I wouldn't have taken the case if I thought he was guilty."

George nodded. He needed to hear that. He needed to hear that someone else believed in David's innocence. He needed reassurance to overcome the doubt that kept nagging him. Inside the cab of his truck, George lowered his head onto the steering wheel. *Please, God. Give me strength.*

*****

Neil found David on the deck gazing out over the water, apparently lost in thought. "You ready to talk?"

"Do I have a choice?" David snapped back.

"Not if you want me to defend you," Neil shot back quickly.

"What's that supposed to mean?" David looked up at Neil.

"It means you've got some explaining to do." Neil's abruptness had worked. It had gotten his attention.

"About what?" David shrugged.

"Like the fact that there is no record of you calling the coach, nor him you." Neil hoped that by exposing David's untruths, it would force him to tell what really happened.

David sank onto the bench and put his head in his hands.

"You want to tell me the truth, like the real reason you went out there?" Neil looked David in the eyes as he said it. He was searching for any clue to let him know if David was telling him the truth this time.

"I was too late." David shook his head.

"Okay, you've got my attention." Neil sank down on the bench beside him.

"I got a call from a friend," David began.

"Was this friend at Coyote Creek Café?" Neil tried to coax the details based on what little he knew in hopes of getting the truth this time. The phone records that the DA's office faxed over identified calls made to David's cell phone from a Sisters, Oregon, number which they tracked down to a pay phone at Coyote Creek Café.

"Yeah, how'd you know?" David looked at him incredulously.

"I'll tell you later. This friend, you think he pulled the trigger?"

"I don't know for certain. We haven't talked since then."

"What makes you think that he did it?"

"Because he knew about the coach's history of abuse." David scrunched his nose in disgust. "And because the coach had started with my friend's younger brother. It hadn't gone very far yet, but he wasn't about to let it happen again. Those were his words."

"Who?"

"No. Not yet." David stood and went over to the railing.

245

"You could go to prison or worse." Neil wasn't trying to threaten. It was a fact, and he wanted to remind David of the consequences he faced for covering up for someone else's crime.

"I thought you said they didn't have a very strong case. Besides, I didn't do it, and that's the honest to God truth."

Neil hated this case. The lawyer in him needed to know who this so-called friend was, although, if he worked hard enough, he could probably piece it together. It would serve justice to hand over the real killer to the authorities like in one of those television crime dramas. Get the guilty man on the stand and deliver the questions that inevitably led to his confession. But the man in him wanted the guy to get away with it. Pedophiles were the lowest form of human scum no matter how they disguised themselves. He had no idea how he would react if his brother, or worse yet, his son, had been a victim of someone like that. He hated to even think it—the coach had deserved to die. Now he needed to decide how to proceed with this case. He could defend David with a clear conscience, knowing he hadn't committed the crime, but could he let a cold-blooded killer walk free? Could he allow David to maintain his silence and protect someone who could be the real killer?

"Okay. For now, we'll leave it alone. But let's head back to town so I can work on some other things I've been working on."

David nodded and began heading toward the stairs. Neil followed close behind. He weighed whether or not he should tell anyone else, including George, about this discovery. For the moment, he would keep it to himself, until he knew for certain what course of action he was prepared to take.

Chapter 39

Barbecue season had officially ended, and George had grown tired of microwaveable boxed dinners. Rachel had given him an open invitation to dinner at their house, but with David staying there, it was too awkward. He wasn't comfortable eating alone in restaurants, especially with David's trouble. People now looked at him with a mix of pity and disgust. Coyote Creek had become a lifesaver. George could order anything off their regular menu, pick it up, and take it back to the office and eat.

He snuck in through the lounge doors. It was easier than facing the sidelong glances and the whispers when he entered the room. He almost did a double take when he spotted David in the lounge at Coyote Creek. He was sitting alone at a table, looking out at the mountains. A drink sat on the table in front of him. George wondered what was in the glass and how many David had consumed.

George wanted to confront him, to let him know he wasn't doing himself any favors by getting drunk—and not just because of his impending trial. He took a step toward the lounge. Then he felt his resolve fading. He didn't want another fight with David, particularly not in public. As Neil had pointed out, David didn't need to draw any more attention to himself. People in town were already watching him with daggers.

"What are you doing here?" David spat indignantly when he saw him standing there.

"I could ask you the same thing."

"So is it your turn to follow me? I thought that was Michael's job," David said with heavy sarcasm.

"No. I'm not following you. I'm picking up some dinner. And I saw you in here, and I thought we could talk."

"Haven't we talked enough?" David looked around nervously.

"No. We haven't really talked."

"Ugh." David rolled his eyes and turned his head away.

"What?" George practically yelled. Several heads turned and looked at them.

"It's not bad enough that you think I'm guilty, but now you think I'm in here getting smashed."

"That's not true, I…" George eyed the half-empty glass not sure what to say.

David held up the glass and shook it from side to side, the ice tinkling against the sides. "Double Pepsi on the rocks." He shook his head in disgust. "Nothing ever changes."

"What's that supposed to mean?" George tried to keep his voice down this time.

"David's in trouble…better go get him and drag him home to give him a good talking to," David said mockingly.

"I didn't come here to lecture you." George became flustered as he tried to explain. He noticed more people eyeing their conversation and probably listening as well.

"Why did you come here?" David asked defiantly.

"Like I said, I came to pick up dinner."

"Well, then don't keep dinner waiting."

George backed away, knowing another fight wouldn't help either of them. After David's confession about the abuse and the moment of reminiscing at the bridge, George thought they might be able to start being civil to one another, start making strides toward a truce. Now he wasn't so certain. He walked down the hall up to the register and picked up his to-go bag.

As George turned to leave, he saw Scott, the bartender, drop a note on David's table. It wasn't obvious to the rest of the room, and if he hadn't been watching, he'd have missed it too. Scott used a tray of glasses to disguise the drop.

Scott Defoe had been David's best friend since the third grade. Scott had tagged along on numerous family vacations. He'd spent so many nights at their house; at one point, George had considered building him his own room. If Scott was involved, would David cover for him? That was a dangerous game. But why would Scott want to kill the coach? It didn't make any more sense than David.

George debated whether he should confront David directly or merely pass what he suspected on to Neil. After the scene minutes ago, it might be best to let Neil handle it.

*****

At the office, George stared at the phone for a long time before picking it up and dialing. Neil was unavailable, so he left a message to meet him at the store in the morning. He wasn't sure if he was overreacting about the note. He had been wrong about David's drinking. Maybe he was jumping to conclusions. Maybe it was a girl's phone number, or maybe he just wanted to catch up on old times. Maybe it was nothing. But then, David had seemed more agitated than normal, although that was hard to judge these days. It seemed no matter what George said or did, David had an argument waiting.

*****

In the darkness of the predawn hours, George sat at the kitchen table sipping a glass of milk. Sleep eluded him once again, and his stomach was tied in knots. Antacids couldn't begin to qualm the turbulence. His indigestion wasn't caused by something he ate but rather the anxiety over David. Seeing him with Scott brought back all the worrisome fears from David's teenage years. Deep down, Scott was a good kid, but he always managed to find trouble and drag David right into the middle of it. This time, it was serious; someone would go to prison for murder.

Through the window, George saw the first hint of light and decided to go to work. At least at the store, he had distractions.

George was in his office by six-thirty and began going over the return lists. It was something he hated to do. It involved a lot of paperwork, hunting down original sales orders and credit orders and making sure they matched. If it was a defective product, then he'd have to locate either the purchase order or the vendor invoice. He hated it, but it kept him busy. Around a quarter to nine, Neil arrived with coffee and pastries from Sisters Bakery.

"What's up, George?" Neil made himself comfortable on the couch.

"I saw David receive a note from Scott Defoe at Coyote Creek yesterday."

"Do you know what was on the note?" Neil held the bag of pastries open to offer one to George.

George refused politely, his stomach still upset from the night before. "No. I didn't see it."

"Scott was David's best friend in high school. Right?"

"Since the third grade." George could remember times the two had practically been inseparable. Scott dragged David into all sorts of trouble in high school, like the time they cut class and took Scott's Dad's truck for a joy ride up to HooDoo or the time that they flushed two M-50s down the toilet in the locker room and burst the pipes.

"Defoe. Hmm." Neil flipped through some of his notes with one hand while he munched on his pastry with the other. He wiped some of the crumbs from his hands before pulling a particular sheet from the file. "Yeah, here it is. David said Tyler Green had been looking for a current victim of the coach, and this year's roster had a Ryan Defoe listed."

"That's Scott's younger brother." All George knew about Ryan was that he had decided to stay in town and live with Scott after their parents died a few years back. The boys had two sisters—one in Washington and one in Southern California. But Ryan wanted to play football for the Outlaws.

"Huh." Neil licked the glaze from his fingers and flipped through some pages on his legal pad. "Yesterday, David told me he got there too late, as if he had known ahead of time that someone meant to kill Coach Fisher. I wasn't sure how to pursue it since David refused to give me a name of this so-called friend. And to be honest, I wasn't 100 percent certain I wanted to pursue it. As long as I know David is innocent…" Neil paused, shaking his head. Then he pulled a sheet of paper from his file. "At any rate, the phone records help substantiate his story. David received a call from a pay phone at Coyote Creek the evening of the murder. He'd also received three other calls from that same number earlier that same week, one just a half hour before he booked his flight here."

"And you think that person might be Scott?" George tried hard to give Scott the benefit of the doubt, but when he saw him drop that note, he immediately presumed that if he wasn't guilty, he was at least in on it.

"Well, David also said that this friend of his suspected the coach had started abusing his younger brother." Neil flipped through his notes on his legal pad. "Didn't Scott have a sister? What was her name?"

"He had two of them, Jennifer and Heather."

"Heather. That's it. Heather Defoe married Chad Green, Tyler Green's brother."

"Tyler Green?" George wasn't at all familiar with the name.

"The reporter. But see, that's how Tyler Green knew so much about the coach's history, through Scott," Neil explained. "Do you happen to know if Scott owned any guns?"

"Yes, he did. He and his father used to hunt around here. He's got a nice trophy elk over at his place. He got it up behind Suttle Lake using an old 30-30."

"That's a rifle. What about handguns?"

"I'm not sure. I know his dad served in Vietnam, so I imagine he might. Why?"

"We know what type of gun was used. And I was thinking if you knew he owned one like it. That, along with what David has told us, it might be enough for Sheriff Bricker to get a warrant. But why is David covering for the guy?"

"Beats me." George could only guess it was because of their friendship. But he couldn't understand why David would risk everything to help Scott.

Neil stood abruptly. "I think it's time to go talk with Sheriff Bricker."

*****

David drove slowly on the gravel road. He'd borrowed Rachel's Explorer in case of snow higher up in the hills. Unpaved roads zigzagged off in various directions—forestry roads used mainly to fight fires or access remote areas to keep them from becoming a fire hazard. The main road was well maintained and as wide as any two-lane road. It led to a wilderness area just below the mountains. Die-hard hikers and climbers used the trail to access the mountain. The South Sister was the easiest to climb, and people ascended it until late November or early December depending on the weather.

The note Scott gave him said to meet him at the Pole Creek Trail Head at ten o'clock. He left early. It had been so long since he'd been up there. He couldn't remember how long it took to get there. When he was in high school, they used to cut class and go hang out up there. Only hikers and woodcutters ever ventured that far off the main road. It was the ideal place to be alone. It was that very spot where Scott had found him and stopped him years ago. No one, except the two of them, knew about that day. He'd almost thrown away his life, all because of Coach Fisher. He would have gone through with it if Scott hadn't saved his life.

In his rearview mirror, he could see a car back a half mile or so. It could've been Scott, but then it turned off at Cow Camp.

Right now, he needed to hear from Scott what happened. That night he called, David could hear the rage in Scott's voice when he talked about the coach and about confronting him. David had tried to calm him down, but Scott had come unhinged over the coach's newfound interest in Ryan. Now he needed to know for certain if Scott had been the one who shot Coach Fisher. He needed to know that protecting him had been the right thing to do.

David pulled into the parking area. Another car was parked at the far end with a little frost on the windshield. It probably belonged to some hikers. He was fifteen minutes early, but Scott would show up, that much he knew.

*****

He followed David up the long winding gravel road, not too close. Not that it would matter—not in the end. He had considered merely planting the gun he'd used to kill the coach in David's car. But there were ways to trace its origin. It could secure a guilty verdict for David, or it could blow up in his face and unravel the entire scheme if they traced the gun.

No, he needed a way to make David look guilty beyond a shadow of doubt. A suicide confession note should do the trick. It really was a shame that David wound up in the middle of all this. Just dumb luck. But there was no turning back now. David's lawyer was still snooping, and it was only a matter of time before all his careful machinations were for nothing. Revenge required planning, and everything had gone according to plan…until David showed up.

The plan had been simple—kill Coach and let the whole world discover what kind of sick and twisted freak he really was. He'd made certain that the reporter got all the information he needed. Then he waited until he knew the body would be discovered right away. He'd snuck in through the trails and snuck in through the back door. Fisher wasn't even repentant for his sins. All the lives he'd destroyed! And he showed no remorse even with a gun pointed at him. He'd only meant to shoot him once, but he kept pulling the trigger until the coach fell to the floor. Afterward, he started to remove any trace of his presence there.

But then David showed up and mucked things up. He hadn't even heard David's car pull up that night. He barely got through the backdoor before David came inside. Now he had to take care of David, or else he might be exposed. He couldn't go to jail; he'd never survive. And if he died, the coach won.

Chapter 40

Friday afternoons, Sheriff Bricker held staff meetings in Sisters. Consequently, he spent most of the day at the Sisters station. That was a lucky break for Neil and George, since the Sisters sheriff office was only six blocks east of Patterson Hardware. Neil and George drove over there quickly.

Neil nodded toward the secretary, and she waved them back toward the office. Neil found the sheriff in a small corner office going over some papers.

"What can I do for you?" Fred seemed agitated by their barging in.

"Hey, Sheriff, I have a new lead you might want to look into," Neil said as they stood up against the wall in the sheriff's office.

"I heard you boys had been snooping around. You think you found something?" Fred shot them a skeptical glance.

"A couple of things actually," Neil clarified.

"Such as?" Fred removed his reading glasses and looked directly at Neil with a scowl of displeasure.

"We found a casing at Chuck Fisher's house," Neil explained.

"And where is the casing now?" Fred appeared disturbed by the news.

"At the OSP lab in Portland," Neil answered flatly.

"Why didn't I know about this before now? You want me to nail you for obstruction, counselor?" Fred bellowed.

"Not really. And I don't think you will. This afternoon, Matt should have the results on the fingerprint they lifted from it. He's actually on his way back from the valley right now."

"They got a print?"

"Yes. A pretty decent one too. And the markings on the casing are consistent with a firing pin from a 1911-1A," Neil detailed the facts he knew thus far.

"Military?" Fred scratched his head. "So who is this lead you've got for me?"

"I think you ought to take a look at Scott Defoe as a possible suspect."

"The bartender at Coyote Creek?" Fred arched one eyebrow.

"Yep." Neil started to explain the story from what they'd pieced together so far when Matt barged in through the front doors, winded.

"Rachel told me you were here. I'm glad I found you. Take a look at this." Matt shoved a sheet of paper into Neil's hands.

"What am I looking at?" He stared at a high school transcript report from Beaverton High School for Richard A. Sanders. "It's the same last name as the guy from the article. What's the tie in?"

"Richard Sanders is Chris Sanders brother," Matt said, still trying to catch his breath.

"Brothers?"

"And here's where it gets interesting." Matt handed Neil another piece of paper.

"That is interesting. How'd you find this?"

"I tracked down the mother of Chris Sanders. She'd remarried, so it was a little more difficult to find her, but I did. And it turns out that her new husband adopted young Richard after his brother's untimely death. Their father died years before—drug overdose." Matt fished around in his file and pulled out another sheet of paper. "But here's the clincher. The print on our casing belongs to Richard A. Sanders, aka Drew Webber."

"Drew Webber?" Fred echoed in surprise.

"Richard Andrew Webber is Chris Sanders younger brother." Neil handed the papers to Fred, who put on his glasses to read for himself.

"Who is Chris Sanders?" Fred asked.

"Chris Sanders was the quarterback before David," George interrupted.

"That's right," Neil answered. "Chris committed suicide during spring break of his freshman year of college."

"What does any of that have to do with Chuck Fisher?"

"His mother said that Chris's suicide note blamed his despair on an incident at the coach's house. She tried to get charges brought against Coach Fisher, but since Chris was deceased and couldn't testify, the note was inadmissible, and no charges were brought against him."

Fred shook his head in disbelief as Matt explained the whole sordid story. Then he walked out toward the dispatcher. "Amy, where's Drew Webber?"

"Not on duty yet. He'll be in around one for the meeting," she answered.

"Locate him. I want to see him now," he barked to her and then turned back to Neil, Matt, and George. "We have GPS in all of our vehicles, so we can find him wherever he is."

"That's odd," Amy called out over her shoulder. They all came out and stood around her desk as she typed on her keyboard. They watched her monitor as she talked. "He's out on Pole Creek Road headed toward Cow Camp."

"What in the world is he doing out there?"

"Beats me." Amy shrugged. "He lives on the other side of town, out near Cloverdale Road."

"Call him and get him in here," Fred ordered.

"I already tried. No response."

Fred walked back the short distance to the office and retrieved his side arm from his desk. "All right I'm going out there. You stay here."

"Not a chance." Neil argued, hot on Fred's heels. Matt and George followed one step behind Neil.

*****

Finally, at ten after ten, Scott's rickety old Dodge pickup rattled up the road and parked next to the Explorer. David felt a sense of relief. For a second or two, David had wondered if Scott would show up. Scott emerged from the cab of his truck with a lit cigarette dangling from his mouth and an open beer can in his hand. He walked to the rear of his truck and dropped the tailgate.

"Hey, man." Scott set his beer down long enough to clasp hands with David.

"Hey, man. I was starting to wonder if you were going to show up."

"Yeah. Well, the old lady wanted to argue about something. I hurried as fast as I could." He pulled a brown bag in the back of the bed closer to them and then hopped up on the tailgate to sit. "You want a beer?" he offered.

"No, thanks, man." David waved him off. He'd been sober now for two years. The last few days, he'd thought about crawling into a bottle of whiskey but had somehow made it through. He wasn't about to start drinking now.

"Look. Sorry about all the cloak-and-dagger routine. But I figured it was the only way we could get a chance to talk. There's no privacy at home or at work." Scott popped the top on another beer. "Besides, with your newfound notoriety, they've probably tapped your phone." He pointed skyward and added. "Big Brother."

David had nearly forgotten about Scott and all of his conspiracy theories. Scott was a full-fledged member of the X-Files fan club. He unequivocally believed in UFOs and Area 51 and that Big Brother was watching us all the time. David appeased him by playing along. "Actually, I think you have to be on the FBI's list to get a bug planted in your phone."

"Cell phones, man. They can monitor everything with satellites."

David just nodded in agreement.

Scott took another swig from his can. "Why'd you do it? Kill Fisher like that?"

"Wait a second. You think I did it? No, it was you." David looked at him, perplexed.

"What have you been smoking? I didn't kill Fisher. You did." Scott gave him an equally perplexed look.

"No. You called, and you were all fired up. You said you were going to kill the—"

"That was all talk. I was just ticked off. I wouldn't actually kill the guy. I'd wind up in prison, and then Ryan would have to go live with one of our shrew sisters. I wouldn't wish that on anyone. Besides, Tyler Green was going to help us out."

"Yeah, some help," David huffed. The article as it was published did in fact expose Coach Fisher's abuse but also painted him as the guilty party responsible for his death.

"So you really didn't do it? It wasn't some plea thing?"

"No. I didn't do it. I thought you did." David reiterated emphatically.

"Then what on earth were you doing out there?"

"You called all upset and said you were going to kill him. So I drove out to Coyote Creek, but your truck was already gone. Then I drove out to Coach's house to try and stop you before you did something stupid."

"Trish took the truck that night. So even if I wanted to kill him, I couldn't. I was stranded." Scott took a long swig from his can. "So you really didn't do it?"

"Nope. But if I didn't do it, and you didn't, then who did?"

The gravity of that revelation suddenly struck him. If Scott hadn't been the real culprit, someone else had shot Chuck Fisher. He could potentially go to jail for a crime he didn't commit. All this time, he thought Scott had done it and knew Scott wouldn't let him go to jail for something he'd done. David assumed that at some point, Scott would come forward, and the whole sordid mess would be dropped. But now he realized that he might not get out of this mess. He might actually go to prison or worse. He could only hope that Neil was some sort of miracle worker.

"You okay, man?"

"I'm not sure. If it wasn't either one of us, and I don't know who did it, then how am I supposed to get out of this mess?"

Chapter 41

The sheriff's Suburban clattered along the gravel road. Dust clouds spewed up behind them as Fred sped up the road. He'd used the lights and sirens to get through traffic in town, but out here, they weren't necessary.

"Amy," Fred talked into the radio, "what's Drew's twenty?"

A brief silence followed before Amy answered over the radio. "By the looks of things, he's about four or five miles ahead of you on fifteen."

"Thanks." He hung up the radio, then pushed harder on the accelerator. George held onto the grip handle mounted above his head as they bounced over washboard in the road and various potholes. Over his shoulder, he could see Neil and Matt enduring the worst of the jarring, nearly getting ejected from their seats.

"All right, you need to turn right in about a hundred yards," Amy's voice announced over the radio, barely audible over the clattering of the truck as it rumbled across the gravel at high speed.

Fred did as she directed. He slowed as they turned onto a smaller older forestry road. They went down a small incline into a cleared area and came upon Drew's patrol car parked off to the side of the road. Fred slammed the Suburban into park with a jolt. He threw open the door and unholstered his side arm as soon as his feet hit the ground.

"Stay here," he barked in hushed tones.

George watched him creep along the road toward the parked patrol car. In the backseat, he heard Matt unsnap something. He turned to see Matt removing his gun from a holster inside his jacket.

They watched as Fred slowly edged around the car, carefully scanning the brush to the left and right of the road. By the looks of things, the car was deserted. Fred made a full circle around the car and then jogged back to the truck at a good clip, still watching the trees alongside the road.

"Car's empty, but the engine is still hot," he said as he climbed back into the truck. In one swift motion, he strapped his seatbelt and slammed the door shut. "Hold on, boys." He threw the truck in reverse and backed up the short road nearly as fast as they had driven down it. "Pole Creek Trail Head is up around the corner. We'll go up there and park and call for backup if we need it."

As they pulled around the bend in the road, George recognized Rachel's Explorer parked next to Scott's old beat-up Dodge. David and Scott were sitting there on the tailgate of the old Dodge. Fred pulled the Suburban to a halt at the other side of the parking lot. Fred hopped out and walked over to talk to the two men. Neil and Matt opened their doors and jumped out close behind him. George fumbled with the seat belt, intending to follow. Fred, Neil, and Matt were almost to Scott and David.

"Either of you two seen Drew Webber around here?" George heard Fred's booming voice across the parking lot.

"Deputy Webber?" Scott asked.

George was still fumbling with the seatbelt, trying to get it to stay inside the cab. He hadn't even got the door closed when he felt something hard poke him in the back. "Hey there, George. Don't make a sound. That is what you think it is."

"Drew?" George tried to look over his shoulder, but the barrel of a gun pressed harder into his back.

"Yeah. It's me. Why is Sheriff Bricker up here looking for me? Your lawyer over there figured things out?" Drew spoke softly, but his tone was sinister.

George wasn't certain how to respond. He'd never had a gun pointed at him before. Terror grabbed ahold of him. Drew had been crazy enough to kill Coach Fisher for revenge. There was nothing standing in his way of killing him. He looked toward the bright-blue sky. *Please, God, don't let it end like this.*

"What…what do you want, Drew?" George stammered.

"If your son's fancy lawyer has really figured things out, then I'm going to need you to help me get out of here," Drew said quietly.

George eyed the men at the other side of the parking lot, wondering how long they would be oblivious to his situation. Drew closed the door to the Suburban quietly and backed up, leading him around to the other side. George wanted to wave or do something to get Fred's attention.

Scott was the first to notice what was going on. He pointed and nodded in George's direction. Fred and Matt quickly drew their guns and crept slowly toward George and Drew.

"Hey there, Drew?" Sheriff Bricker spoke loudly and firmly.

"Hey, Sheriff. You and the lawyer come up here for a social visit?" Drew laughed.

"No, Drew, I think you know why we're here. That's why you've got a gun to poor old George there. Now why don't you let him go, and we can talk about this."

George felt Drew's grip on his shirt tighten, and the gun pressed harder against his back.

"Let's not and say we did. You and I both know how that talk would end." He pushed George up closer to the driver's side door. "I guess you Podunk sheriffs are smarter than I gave you credit for."

With his gun drawn and pointed directly at Drew, Fred inched closer in a crouched position.

"Oh, I wouldn't do that, Sheriff." Drew yelled over the top of George. Drew moved the gun up to George's temple. He felt the cold steel of the barrel brush his skin.

Fred said something quietly to David, who jumped off the tailgate and began following him. Fred whispered something more.

"Hey, Dad," David shouted from across the parking lot.

"What are you doing?" Drew shouted nervously. "Stay where you are."

Fred and David stopped, but David continued talking. "Dad, do you remember the time when we tried to teach Michael to fly fish down by Bowman Dam?" David spoke slowly and loudly as if he were deliberately choosing his words. George nodded the affirmative but felt the gun press harder against him.

"What are you babbling about?" Drew waved the gun in David's direction, then quickly returned it to George.

David seemed to ignore Drew and the fact he was pointing a loaded pistol at George's head because he continued talking. "You remember how Michael got caught up in his line when he tried to cast? Fred wondered if you might show him how you taught Michael to untangle himself."

For a moment, George was baffled why David was telling this story now. But when he saw David's face, as he stressed each word, he understood.

"Look, Sheriff, I'm going to take old George here with me. And we're going to drive out of here without any trouble. And you're not going to call dispatch on me, or George here gets it." Drew started to move forward, pushing George in front of him. He stopped at the driver's side door and fumbled with the handle.

"Dad, could you do it…" David looked at Fred who nodded, and he yelled, "Now."

George understood and quickly leaned over at the waist away from the gun. Simultaneously, Fred fired a shot directly at Drew and struck him in the chest. George fell to the ground. Drew's gun fired into the air as he fell backward.

Fred sprinted over to George and pushed him out of the way in front of the Suburban while he checked on Drew. Drew was wounded but not dead. Fred disarmed him and nodded for Matt to come assist. Fred reached in through the driver's side window and grabbed the radio.

"This is Sheriff Bricker. I need an OSP patrol and AirLife dispatched to the Pole Creek Trail Head. Officer down."

David ran over to where George was in front of the suburban. "Are you okay, Dad?"

"I think so." George stood and wiped the dirt from his pants. "But I won't need any coffee for a month," he joked nervously. He looked around the side of the truck and watched as Fred tended to Drew's wounds while Matt held a gun on him.

Chapter 42

Rachel and Michael were both waiting for them at the house. George was too shaken up to go back to the store, and David had called Rachel once they were halfway back toward town. Rachel brought over groceries and made dinner while they had waited.

"Dad, are you all right?" She fussed over him the second he walked through the door.

"Not a scratch on me." George downplayed the whole incident. He knew the outcome could have been a lot worse. He could have been the one shot—or dead. It would take a while to fully absorb the magnitude of what happened.

"I'm so glad you're okay," Rachel said tearfully.

"Me too," Michael mumbled as he came up and hugged his father.

"Thanks guys." He looked from Rachel to Michael to David. It was the first time in a long time that he'd been able to see all three of his kids at once.

Rachel had turned on the television and tuned to the local news. The blond newscaster broke the story. "And now for some breaking news on the Coach Chuck Fisher murder trial. For details, we go to Stan who is live at the courthouse where the district attorney, Bruce Heywood, is about to give a short press conference."

"Oh, Dad, I can turn that off," Rachel offered with a note of concern.

"No. Turn it up." He sat on the couch in front of the television. Michael and David sat on either side of him. They watched as the camera showed the DA perfectly poised, standing at the top of the steps of the courthouse. An American flag flew behind him—ever the politician. Fred stood off to his left, and Neil stood in the background with Matt.

"Thank you, ladies and gentlemen of the press. Today, we had some late-breaking developments in the ongoing investigation into the murder of Chuck Fisher. New evidence was brought forward which pinpointed the identity of the true culprit for this crime. Unfortunately, it saddens me to announce this was one of our own Deschutes County deputies, Drew Webber. A short standoff occurred involving a hostage when Sheriff Fred Bricker attempted to arrest Drew Webber. Shots were fired, and Deputy Webber is receiving treatment for gunshot wounds. As for the prior arrest of David Patterson, all charges against him have been dropped."

"Yahoo," George and David yelled at the television.

"Our deepest apologies to Mr. Patterson and his family. I can only say that the justice system is a human institution and, therefore, fallible. It's not often that we make mistakes, but when we do, it is our duty to rectify them. Thank you for your time."

"Mr. Heywood," one of the older reporters yelled, "what led you to investigate Drew Webber?"

"I am going to have to defer that question to my esteemed colleague, Neil Cohen." He stepped backward and allowed Neil to come forward and answer the press. Everyone could see Matt literally having to push Neil forward. George suspected Matt might have a new job with the Deschutes County Sheriff's Department come Monday morning.

"Um. As counsel for the defense, it is my obligation and duty to prepare the best defense for my client," Neil began.

George was surprised by how suave and articulate he was in front of the cameras—all of that time back East.

"When my team began investigating, we found certain pieces of evidence. That, coupled with some dumb luck, led us straight to Drew Webber."

George reached for the remote and turned off the set as the press began asking more questions. They'd all seen enough to last a lifetime.

"Rachel, what smells so good?" George had smelled the aroma when he walked in the front door.

"Mom's kielbasa and potatoes." She smiled. It had been a favorite of all of them.

George stood and started toward the dining room.

Michael hung back and stood in David's path. George turned to make sure there wasn't going to be another scuffle.

"David, I owe you an apology. A big one," Michael said, very contrite.

"It's okay. It's all okay." David stuck out his hand. Michael grabbed for a shake but then pulled David in for a manly hug.

Steve arrived with Nikki and all the kids. George led the way into the dining room. They gathered around the table just as they had at Easter and Mother's Day. This time, the chairs were filled, except Kate's. But as he looked around the table at the faces around him, he could see her.

*****

With everyone gathered, he knew it was time to tell the kids about Kate's final wishes for them.

"Before we dig into this wonderful feast, I wanted to clear a few things up about the Odell house and your mother's estate," George began. Then as an afterthought, he stood and went over to the buffet hutch. He kept the papers in the top drawer. He pulled out three envelopes and handed one to Michael, one to David, and the other to Rachel. "Your mother wanted so many things for you, all three of you." He looked directly at David. "She never dealt with her parents' estate, so she passed it on to the three of you."

Rachel and Michael opened their envelopes and read, wide-eyed. Kate had left the house across from Drake Park to Michael and Nikki. The other property in Bend, a small house at Awbry Glen, she left to Rachel. And to David, she left an old cabin in Camp Sherman on the Metolius.

"Oh, Dad," Rachel gasped.

"It's what your mother wanted. And I tried to uphold her wishes, even acting like her—getting the ducks in a row before telling you. I'm sorry if I hurt the two of you by not telling you before I sold the Odell house, but I couldn't hold on to it. And she had other things in mind for you to hold on to."

"So this is for real?" Michael asked.

"Yeah. Probate should be finalized in thirty days, and then you and Nikki can do whatever you want with the house. But I think your mom wanted you to live there."

Michael sat back quietly and nodded in agreement. David didn't say a word but merely locked eyes with George.

"Enough of that. Let's eat." George passed the bowls around.

*****

After dinner, George sat on the bench by the pond, Kate's bench. David came out and sat beside him.

"Do you think Neil was right? It was just dumb luck?"

"No, I don't. A friend of mine told me recently that God has a plan for our lives. I think He had His hand in this one."

"I think so too." David leaned over with his elbows on his knees. "Seeing you with that gun to your head today and knowing I was the reason…" He grew quiet. "I thought you might die for me, and it reminded me of the One who did die for me. All I could do was pray and hope that God was listening. Even though I didn't deserve it, He answered. And I started thinking that maybe now that Coach Fisher is dead, it's time to put the pain and hate behind me."

David leaned back. They sat quietly, watching the sun begin its descent to the west. The mountains glowed in shades of gold, orange, and pink.

"About Mom…" David began.

"David, you don't need to—"

"I do. I'm so sorry. And I'm the one who has to live with it." David plowed his fingers through his hair. George patted him on the back the way a father comforts a son. The last speck of glowing orange slid behind the butte as they sat—not another word spoken.

George finally broke the silence. "What now? Back to Seattle?"

"Actually, I was thinking about staying around here. I have these nephews and a niece that I'd like to get to know. But I'll need a place to stay. Do you know of any place I could stay?"

George nodded, trying to dispel the lump growing in his throat. David was home.

"And I was thinking. You want to go fishing tomorrow?"

"You have to ask?" George looked at him, astonished. "Bull trout are running on the Metolius, or there's always steelhead on the Lower Deschutes."

"Steelhead sounds good." David smiled.

"Next weekend, I'm going on a fishing trip of sorts. Do you want to tag along?"

"Who's going?"

"Just some men from the church," George said casually.

"If there's fishing involved, count me in."

George placed his arm around David's shoulder, and for the first time in years, his son didn't pull away. He lifted his eyes skyward at the heavens, twinkling with lights from afar. His heart had stopped aching.

"Thank you, Lord," he whispered.

Uncharted territory now lie before them. Their relationship had been turbulent for so long, and now they sat here peacefully. If God could find a way to bring peace between them, God could do anything. It was simply a matter of trust.

About the Author

Sunny Anne Aleshire was born in Sandpoint, Idaho, in 1972 to Dan and Jody Aleshire, where her father began his career in the electrical field. The following year, the family moved back to Oregon where she spent her childhood and adult life.

Throughout her career, Sunny was involved in the operational side of health services, eventually becoming the business manager of a drug-and-alcohol treatment facility. Her experiences allowed her to draw many of the ideas for her books. She was a devoted wife to Rob Kaiser, partnering with him in the administrative side of their construction business.

She was a loving and steadfast mother to her children, Robbie, Justine, and stepdaughter, Lacey. They were the joy of her life. She was a caring daughter, sister, and friend and enjoyed spending time with her loved ones. Family was very important to Sunny, and she loved to plan family events and activities, making the holidays and special days treasured memories for all.

Sunny's passion was writing, with a unique and creative way of relating stories as demonstrated in her books and poetry. Loving history, she also delved into her heritage, tracing her family ancestry and enthusiastically sharing her discoveries. Her other interests included cooking, baking, reading, and spending time along the ocean beaches of Oregon.

Sunny lost her battle with ovarian cancer in 2011 and will always be cherished for her passion of life, love of family, and her service to others.

Lightning Source UK Ltd.
Milton Keynes UK
UKHW010621310123
416230UK00001B/87